ISBN: 978-1-667-84042-0 Paperback

ISBN: 978-1-667-84043-7 eBook

THE BROADWAY TRANE

A Novel

CHARLIE GIRARD

CHAPTER 1

The sky grew dark as the evening approached and the color of the buildings changed from pasty silver to ash gray in the night sky, but that's when the lights on Broadway came to life. The stars always shined bright on that stretch of real estate that was known as Broadway between West 40th and West 54th street. This is the place where dreams were made and the place where they were crushed out like a smoldering cigarette in the gutter. Behind the scenes, young actors, and actresses alike, hopeful to get their shot at the bright lights, worked any menial task just to be part of a show that resided on Broadway. There was a pecking order on Broadway that defined the actor's worth in the eyes of the adoring devotees of the theatre. The actors who were at the top of their craft, demanded all the lead parts and the best dressing rooms, they felt that they were intitled since they were the reason people flocked to their shows. The newbies would clean toilet bowls just to get on stage and say a line, just so they could confirm that they hadn't just wasted half of their life on acting lessons or unremarkable community plays. And the old actors, the has bens, those who hadn't seen the stage or screen in years, could often be seen pleading with a director or a producer just for the chance to walk on the stage to connect with an audience one last time.

Making it here was no less than a long shot, but the one man who could make dreams come true, stood in the path of every performer who put on makeup and stood on a stage anywhere on Broadway. His name was Heinrich King. But everyone knew him as "King

Heini." Heini was not much to look at. He was 54 years old with a grey combover. He stood about five feet nine inches tall with pasty white skin and a crooked smile. He weighed in at about 225 pounds. When he stood up and walked, he was a little hunched over, probably because of his large stomach. He liked to smoke cheap cigars and he smoked them wherever he wanted to. He didn't care that the smoke offended mostly everyone within twenty feet of his presence. His wardrobe was what you might call vintage. But that description would be kind. His wardrobe consisted of polyester leisure suits dating from the 1970's and it seemed that he had a closet full of them, all in bright 1970's colors. There was a canary yellow suit, a bright green suit, a flaming red suit, and an orange suite that could best be described as *Burger King* orange. It didn't really make sense why he wore these tacky suits because he was also a very wealthy man. No doubt it spoke volumes about his abrasive personality. Broadway had been very good to him. He had risen through the ranks of small-time promoter to the most influential man on Broadway. A show didn't make it to Broadway without Heini's approval. And that usually meant a little padding to Heini's bankbook or a young starlet on his arm. A star did not become a star on Broadway without "King Heini" benefitting somehow before he gave his approval. The producers didn't hire any actors unless "King Heini" gave them the OK. Maybe, that is why Heini seemed to have an abundance of questionable relationships with so many beautiful budding actresses. They were all looking for their big break in the business and they all had to go through "King Heini." The fact is, that Heini had made a lot of influential friends over the years. He had a friendship with the mayor. The police commissioner was regularly seen at his afterparties. Several sports stars from Yankees, the Rangers and Knicks were all seen with Heini at one time are another. But for every friend he had made, he had also made at least two enemies.

2

Not everyone got the parts that they were promised, and the producers were tired of dealing with "King Heini." It seemed that sooner or later his self-indulgent narcissistic attitude would catch up with him, but he didn't care. He always seemed to get what he wanted. He had the power, the wealth, and the fame that most men dream about, and he wielded them like a sharp sword.

The fact is that most men would not have the stamina to live like "King Heini" even for a week. To live life in Heini's shoes would take a man who was arrogant. It would take a man who thought of himself as a demigod. And it would take a man who cared absolutely nothing for the feelings or concerns of anyone but himself. But if this was the price for success, Heini was willing to sell his grandmother to the highest bidder, and then ask for change. This was Heini's life, and this past week typical of what it was to be "King Heini."

On Monday Heini's selfish and boorish behavior was on full display. Marie Robbin had been Heini's assistant for the past 15 years. She had done everything that Heini had asked her to do, even things that made her skin crawl. She always went above and beyond what Heini demanded. Everything from buying his ties and making his coffee, to lying to clients and setting up pretty little actresses for interviews. She had often worked long hours into the nights, and she even worked most weekends with no extra pay. She did what she had to do. As a result, she did feel a certain security because of her loyalty to Heini and the promises that were made to her. She was dead wrong. On Monday morning Heini called Marie into his office. She was always well dressed, with a short skirt and a tight blouse. She usually wore jewelry around her neck and on her fingers. She represented Heinrich King, the most powerful man on Broadway. But Heini was as superficial as they come. He had noticed that Marie was on the other side of 45 years old and there were little lines forming at the sides of her eyes.

In his mind he could better. He asked Marie to sit down in the chair in front of his desk. Marie thought that Heini was going to give her some dictation or ask her for another favor, so she sat down and crossed her legs. Just then a young and pretty woman about 26 years old entered the office. Her name was Kristen Monree. She had long dark hair and her makeup was impeccable. Her eyelashes were the kind you see in *Maybelline* ads, long and voluminous. She looked like a fashion model. She had no prior experience in the entertainment business, but she was good looking, and her perfume was fresh and sweet. That was good enough for "King Heini." With his nose in the air and a smile on his face, Heini turned to Marie and said, "meet Kristen Monree, she is your replacement." Marie sat expressionless in front of Heini. The color drained from her face. Then her face got beet red. She should have known that eventually this would be coming, down deep she knew who "King Heini" was, but still the shock left her speechless. Marie Robbin stood up and glared at Heinrich King with eyes like daggers. Marie was furious, she said, "After all that I've done for you, this is how you repay me?" Heini took a puff on his cigar and said, "Hey, that' show business, honey." Marie was just too upset to respond, so she muttered under her breath, "you just better watch your back Heini, I'll get you for this." Then she slowly walked out of the office and has not been seen since. Heini sat back in his chair, had a little chuckle and asked Kristen Monree to give him another his cigar. And she did.

On Tuesday, "King Heini" displayed another facet of his personality, lust. He invited a promising young dancer and singer who had auditioned for an upcoming part in a new play "Taking care of Business" up to his office. He told her that he thought that she had talent, she was going places and he wanted to interview her to get to know her better. Her name was Tori Pichettes. She was young and beautiful; her dark hair was pulled back, and she dressed with a particular panache. She was born in France but had been in New York for the past 5 years looking for her big break. She had heard about "King Heini" when she arrived on Broadway, and she was determined not to give into his demands. She came to Heini's office at about 10:00 AM. Kristen Monree showed her into Heini's office and left them alone. "King Heini" looked Tori up and down as only a dirty old man would do, and then he offered her a drink and asked her to come and sit next to him on the couch and get comfortable. Heini did his best to get his arms around Tori, but when she resisted his advances and crushed the cigar in Heini's mouth, Tori Pichettes fate was sealed. Heini made sure that she didn't get the part in the upcoming show. And from that point on, she was as good as blacklisted on Broadway.

Later that day Heini made a phone call to Siobhan Peison. She was a fashion designer and she had been in talks with the producer of one of the current shows on Broadway to provide all the costumes for an upcoming play. Siobhan knew that this would really put her designs on the map and would get her a place in the upcoming show in Paris. Heini asked her to come to his office to discuss the details of her new fashion line. Siobhan came prepared to discuss business. She was wearing a light grey business suit with a white scarf. She had shoulder length black hair and had an unassuming way about her. When she arrived at Heini's office, Kristen Monree showed her in to see "King Heini." Siobhan held her hand out to shake Heini's hand, but instead he took her hand and kissed it. Then he looked up at Siobhan with a crooked smile. He invited her to come sit on the couch and get comfortable. Siobhan agreed and sat down. Siobhan had her fashion business on her mind. Heini had funny business on his. The meeting ended with Siobhan delivering a slap to 'King Heini's" face. As a result, she didn't get the contract to develop the costumes for the show. Her place in the Paris fashion show would also not happen. Siobhan was furious at what had just happened. On her way out of the office, she picked up a glass paperweight from Kristen's desk and hurled it at Heini. It missed hitting him, but the glass smashed all over the side of his desk. Heini lit up a new cigar and sat back in his chair. He called in Kristen Monree to clean up the mess.

On Wednesday Heini remembered that he owed one of his Hollywood associates a favor. In the theatre one hand always washed the other, whether it was stage or screen. There was always enough corruption to go around. One of his associates in Hollywood needed to get a part on Broadway for the son of a very influential politician out in California. Heini was glad to do the favor because he knew that one day, he would ask his Hollywood associate for a favor as well. So, "King Heini" called Peter Boggs, the producer of one of the shows currently running on Broadway and told him that he needed to replace the lead character with a new face. Dean James was currently playing the lead part. He was an up-and-coming actor with a strong young following. He had been playing the part for the past 4 months with rave reviews. But starting next week a new face, Bobby Boyd was going to be playing the role. Peter Boggs protested but to no avail. "King Heini" had all the power. When Dean James learned that he was being fired, replaced by some unknown actor from California, it didn't sit well. Dean had worked hard to get this role and he worked even harder to keep it fresh every night. Dean had an ego as most actors do, but he also had a temper. When he got control of his emotions, he took a taxi over to Heini's office. He walked into the office unannounced and stormed past Kristen Monree's desk and into Heini's office. He pointed his finger in Heini's face and began telling Heini what was on his mind. The conversation was long and loud. There was spitting and cursing. There was paper flying off the top of the desk and paper being crumpled and thrown on the floor. But nothing seemed to phase "King

Heini." When Dean James had said everything that he had to say, he left Heini's office. But as he left, he looked back and screamed at the top of his voice, "I'll get you for this Heini, you're going to pay, I swear you're going to pay for this." Heini sat back in his chair and puffed his cigar with a crooked smile on his face.

On Thursday, Heini visited the set of one of the new shows that was set to open in a couple of weeks. He liked to make his presence felt, he liked to make the little people feel even littler, particularly the directors and the actors. He wanted everyone to know who he was and the power he had. On this day, Heini was wearing a bright yellow leisure suit, He stood out like a walking banana. No one could miss him even if they wanted to. As he was casually strolling backstage, puffing his nasty cigar, suddenly a young stage assistant carrying a tray of coffee bumped into him. Her name was Audrey Linn. She had worked backstage for the past 3 years, and she was involved with everything backstage from helping with the makeup to getting meals for the staff. Everyone liked Audrey, she was positive and always had something encouraging to say to everyone on the staff. She was working her way up the Broadway pecking order. Unfortunately, when she bumped into Heini, the coffee on her tray spilled all over Heini's canary yellow leisure suite. There were deep dark coffee stains from the right sleeve of his suit all the way down his right pants leg. A couple of guys on the stage crew let out a laugh when they saw what had happened and that "King Heini's" yellow suit was covered in coffee. Audrey didn't recognize Heini at first, she just began apologizing and trying to wipe off his suit with the napkins that she had on the coffee tray. Heini was outraged. His face grew red and twisted. He screamed at Audrey. "You little boob, look what you've done to my suit! You're fired! Did you hear me? You're fired!" Audrey apologized again and she started crying.

Heini yelled at her again, "Get Out! Get out of my sight!" Audrey left he theatre in tears and hasn't been seen on Broadway since.

On Friday morning, Heini displayed yet another facet of his personality. He was insensitive and a bully. He was sitting in his office contemplating ways that he could avoid paying some of the legal bills that were mounting because of his detestable conduct. He was also thinking about the huge gambling losses he had incurred this week, and that someone would be coming around to collect soon. He was also heavy in debt to five different banks that were financing current shows. He was not in the best of spirits; in fact, he was starting to sweat where his hair was combed over. He called out to Kristen Monree to bring in a cup of coffee. When Kristen came into Heini's office with his morning coffee, she came in with a smile, but Heini had his head in his hands as if his head was about to explode. He glared at Kristen and yelled, "What are you looking at?" Kristen timidly placed the coffee on the desk in front of Heini and slowly backed away from Heini's desk. His coffee was always black, no sugar, just black. It matched his personality. Kristen watched as Heini sipped his coffee to make sure that it met with his approval. Then she backed up a few steps and sheepishly asked Heini "Mr. King would you mind terribly if I took off this weekend to go and visit my sick grandmother in the hospital? She's been very sick, and we don't know how long she has." Heini squinted at Kristen and growled at her, "What do you think I'm running here? Some kind of country club?" Kristen looked like someone had just slowly rolled over her toes with a bowling ball. She started to back out of the office while facing Heini. He screamed at her "If you take the weekend off, you're fired! We're not here to visit sick people, we're here to make money!" Kristen slowly backed all the way to her desk and sat down. A little teardrop rolled down her cheek.

This was a typical week for "King Heini." He was a ruthless and mean man. Even his friends really didn't like him. They just tolerated him because they had no choice. They say what goes around comes around and often this plays out in real life. That is exactly what happened on one Friday night. On the stage, things are always planned and rehearsed, but in real life things take place sometimes in a random way and are usually unrehearsed. Things had definitely started to close in on Heini. The bankers were looking for their money. There had been several lawsuits filed because of his inappropriate behavior. His two ex-wives were threatening to sue him for more money. And the bookies were coming to collect their money. It was like a noose was tightening around his neck. He needed a way out and he was about to find one. Heini had the stars in his eyes, the real stars. In fact, on this particular Friday night, Heini found himself looking straight up at the stars in the dark night sky. His eyes were wide open, but his pupils did not dilate, and his eyes didn't close, they couldn't close. They were frozen in this position. He was dressed in a lime green leisure suite; it was still pressed with no wrinkles. His shoes were white with no scuff marks. His body was contorted in a strange way. His arms were reaching over his head, and his legs were at odd angles to each other. "King Heini" just laid motionless on top of a pile of trash in a dumpster behind the main stage of the Majestic Theater on Broadway. There were red bruise marks around his neck and a little blood trickled from the back of his head.

What goes around comes around. "King Heini" would never again fire another actor, actress, producer, or stagehand. He would never again invite some pretty little actress up to his office for an interview. Never again would a producer or director need to clear their show through Heinrich King. For "King Heini" the curtain had come down and the show was over. Heinrich King was dead.

CHAPTER 2

It was a bright clear morning in early May. Jack Trane loved the spring. Not because of the flowers, the green grass or the birds chirping in the trees. But because baseball was in full-swing and his beloved Red Sox would be in the city soon to play the Yankees. There was nothing that Jack enjoyed more than a good trouncing of the Yankees at the hands of the Red Sox.

It was about 8:00 AM and the alarm had just gone off. Jack reached over and pushed the button on the top of the digital clock and the ear-piercing buzzing stopped. He sat up in bed and rubbed his eyes. He took a deep breath and coughed a couple of times. He had left his window open last night and there was a chill in the morning air. He got up and walked across the cold wood floor and shut widow. He was rubbing his arms trying to warm up and he made his way to the bathroom. After a nice hot shower and a shave, he was ready for the day. All of Jack's clothes were in his walk-in closet, but the closet has been so full of junk and old broken-down appliances, that Jack hasn't actually been able to walk into his walk-in closet for a couple of years. But he had a system. He would reach into his closet as far as his arm could go and pull out a pair of pants, usually the ones hanging closest to the door. Then he would reach back in and pull out a sport coat and a tie. This morning he reached in and pulled out a pair of dark blue dockers. He reached in again and pulled out a blue stripe tie. Once more he reached in and pulled out a solid blue sport coat. This was the trifecta. He didn't know how, but it seemed that every morning he would pull out three perfectly matched pieces. He draped the pants, coat, and tie over a chair next to his bed and he opened his armoire and lifted out a perfectly pressed white button-down shirt. This was his standard attire for the day.

Jack got dressed and now he was focused on breakfast. His favorite breakfast spot was the Coffee Café. It was a small restaurant within walking distance from his apartment. He had been eating breakfast there for years. He liked the atmosphere there but probably the main reason he went there every morning is because other than chips, beer and TV dinners, there was hardly ever any food in his apartment at all. He picked up his cell phone from the end table next to his bed and grabbed his keys from the dresser and put them in his jacket pocket. He put on his favorite hat, a *Flechet Fedora* and made his way out the door. He placed a matchstick below the bottom hinge in the door jamb as he left. This was a simple security measure that had served him well. If the matchstick was on the ground when he returned, he would know that someone was either in his apartment or had been there.

Jack made his way down the stairs, out the door and onto the street. The traffic was buzzing, and the sidewalk was crowded with average people heading to their average jobs earning their average pay. Jack passed each man and woman with a nod and a smile. He enjoyed the connection with the people of the city. He had never worked an average job in his life. He had been a private investigator for the past 25 years. There had been ups and downs, but he would never call his job average. Unfortunately, he hadn't had a case in over a month, not that he needed the money, but the inactivity made him a little restless. He had a feeling in the pit of his stomach that something was about to break. Or maybe that was just his stomach growling for breakfast. He stopped into the local newsstand to pick up the morning paper. The owner of the newsstand was Nicky, and Jack knew him by name. But

Nicky was not exactly what you would call warm and friendly. He was about 60 years old, heavy set with a large nose and red ears. His face was always half shaved, and he had a permanent scowl on his face. Jack picked up the paper from the counter and dropped down two dollars next to the cash register. Nicky was on the other side of the newsstand arranging the pocket toiletries. Jack yelled to Nicky, "Have a good day, old man." Nicky mumbled something under his breath and made a gesture directed towards Jack. Jack laughed and left the newsstand with his paper under his arm. He thought to himself, "that guy should probably run for mayor" then he laughed out loud.

Jack breathed deeply as he strode down the avenue and continued walking until he arrived at the Coffee Café. This was his routine. Breakfast at the Coffee Café and a little playful banter with his favorite waitress Betty, a few laughs, and a morning Vanilla Latte. This was how he normally started his day. He opened the door to the Cafe and walked in. He saw Betty standing near the cash register. He called out, "Betty, how's my girl this morning?" Betty smiled and said, "Gee, Jack, if I was your girl, how come I didn't see you last night?" Jack laughed, he said, "That's because you're my morning girl, Betty, the night girl is a whole other story." They both laughed and Jack sat down at a table near the window. Betty came over with a towel over her shoulder and a pad in her hand. Betty was a natural blond, and she wore her hair short. She had bright blue eyes and a great smile. She was in her late 30's and she was single and attractive, and she loved to flirt with the customers. It was good for tips. She was wearing her standard uniform, a tight blue shirt with the top two buttons open. And there was white piping around the collar. She also wore a short blue skirt and a white apron. She said to Jack, "What's it going to be today, Jack?" He looked at her and said, "Come on Betty you know what I like." She smiled a wry smile and said "Yeah, but what do you want for breakfast?" Jack smiled back, "How are the pancakes today, Betty?" She was still smiling, "The best Jack, the best!" He was still smiling, he said "That's what I like Betty, you always tell me what I want to hear." She took her towel off of her shoulder and hit Jack with it. She said, "OK Jack, an order of Blueberry pancakes, Vermont maple syrup, a small glass of orange juice and a large Vanilla latte. How did I do?" Jack smiled, "like I said Betty, you know what I like."

She went back to the kitchen to put in his order and Jack opened the paper and read the headlines. He liked to stay on top of the news because he never knew when he might get a case that involved some headline story. But today there was nothing new in the paper. It's as if the headlines were reading "Bla..Bla.Bla..Bla.." Ten minutes later Betty came back with his order. She put a plate with a stack of steaming blueberry pancakes right under Jack's nose. The aroma of the pancakes made his mouth water. She placed his Vanilla Latte down by his right hand. The orange juice was to his left just in front of his plate and she put a fresh bottle of pure Vermont syrup in the middle of the table. Just the way Jack liked it. She patted Jack on the shoulder and said, "Enjoy." Jack looked up and smiled as he grabbed his Vanilla Latte. He said, "You're the best, Betty." She hit him with her wash towel and went back behind the register.

Between the time Jack drizzled the organic Vermont maple syrup on his pancakes and he took his last sip from his Latte, about 5 minutes had passed. He was fully satisfied and ready for the day. There was nothing that Jack liked better than a stack of blueberry pancakes and a Vanilla Latte to start the day. Betty came back over to the table and looked at Jack's empty plate. She opened her eyes wide and said, "Jack, what did you do, inhale it?" Jack laughed, "come on Betty you know what they say; if everything is under control, you're not going fast enough." They both laughed. Jack paid his bill and left his usual $10 tip for Betty. She gave him a wink and he winked back. He left the Coffee Café and headed towards the parking garage where he kept his car.

As he walked up the street, Jack whistled to a song that came into his head, the old *Bachman Turner Overdrive* song, **Taking care of Business.** This was one of Jack's favorite songs and he whistled it often. He entered the garage and gave a wave to Fernando the attendant and Fernando waved back. Jack put his card into the small box on the wall, it looked much like a vending machine, and his car keys came down the chute. He made his way up the ramp to the second level where his car was parked. When he reached the second level, he walked about 12 steps to his left and stood in front of his car. Before he opened the car door, he studied all the lines of the cars exterior to make sure there were no new bumps or scratches. This was his pride and joy. A 1968 Mustang Shelby GT-500. It was Highland Green and as close to mint condition as you could get. There were almost 500 horses under the hood and a black leather interior that fit Jack like a glove. He got in and started the engine. He always loved the sound of the engine turning over then the low growl of the tailpipes as he idled. He put the car in gear and made his way out of the garage. He gave Fernando a wave and Fernando opened the gate. Jack took a left as he exited the garage and made his way to his office. It was approaching 9:30 AM so Jack was imagining all the guff he was going to catch from his assistant Trudy. She loved to give him a hard time. No doubt she had been in the office since 8:00 AM. He thought that Trudy got in early just so she could complain about him coming in late every day. But in Jack's mind Trudy was the best. She kept Jack's office organized and running smoothly. If anyone knew how to take care of business, it was Trudy. She had helped Jack out of more than a few jams in the past and she was as loyal as a bass player in a jazz band. Jack always told her that she was the best, and he meant it.

When Jack arrived at the office, he parked about three spaces from the entrance to the building. It's a rare occurrence in the city that there would be a parking spot at all, but on this day the spot was open, so he laid his claim. He locked the car and started walking towards the building, but then he caught sight of a street vendor and knew that he had to get a cup of coffee, not for himself, but for Trudy. He didn't want to walk in empty-handed. It was part of his morning routine. He walked up to street vendor. It was actually a small trailer with an opening on the side and there was a man selling fresh muffins, hot buns, and coffee. The man inside the trailer looked to be a middle-aged man wearing a Yankee's hat and he seemed to have a permanent smile on his face. He had a little name tag that said "MARIO." Jack approached the trailer and said in a loud voice "Good Morning, Mario!" The smile on Mario's face never left. He said, "What can I get for you friend?" Jack ordered a large coffee with cream and two sugars, just the way that Trudy likes it. He also ordered a fresh blueberry muffin. With a smile on his face, Mario put the muffin in a bag and handed it to Jack with the coffee. The muffin and the coffee came to $6. Jack handed Mario a $10 bill and said, "Keep the change my friend." Mario's smile got even bigger if that was possible. He said, "Thank you my good friend, please come again." Jack smiled; he knew that he probably would come again.

Jack walked into the office building and went up the stairs to the second floor. He opened the door to his office and went in. Trudy was sitting at her desk with her chin resting in her hand and her elbow on the desk. Trudy was an attractive young woman. She was almost 30 years old. She had medium length blond hair and she always wore tight shirts and short skirts. It kind of fit her personality. Her perfume was sweet and subtle and when she spoke, her New York accent gave her away. As Jack entered the office, she had one eyebrow raised and she said, "Glad you could make it, Jack." She looked up at the clock and said sarcastically, "And look it's not even 10 O'clock." Jack just smiled and put the bag with the muffin and the coffee on Trudy's desk right in front of her. This was a scene that repeated itself just about every morning. Trudy's demeanor changed immediately. She let out a little "Oh, for me?" She lifted the muffin out of the bag and took a sip of the coffee, then she put the muffin on a small napkin that was already in place on her desk. She smiled at Jack and gave him a good morning wink. Jack knew how to keep Trudy happy. It usually involved food, clothing, or straight up cash. This time he got away with just the food.

He went into his office and sat down at his desk. This is something that he had done for just about 25 years. The furniture had changed, and room had been re-painted a couple of times, but this is where Jack belonged. This felt more like home than his apartment. He had made a bundle on his last case, but he hadn't had a case in over a month now and he was starting to get a little bit anxious. He drummed his fingers on the desk because he had nothing else to do. Then Trudy came into his office. She was twirling her blond hair between the fingers on her right hand, and she said, "Oh, by the way, I forgot to tell you, your friend Harry Soul down at the precinct called and said that he wanted you to call him back when you get in." Jack looked up and raised one eyebrow. He thought for a minute and said, "Hey Trudy, you paid my outstanding parking tickets, didn't you?" Trudy smiled, "Relax Jack, I put a check in the mail for those a month ago." Jack shook his head back and forth. He said, "I wonder what he wants?" Harry Soul had his eye on Trudy now for a couple of years and had tried every which way to get a date with her without any success. Harry wasn't the most attractive bachelor on the market, but he was persistent. Trudy gave Jack a look and said, "If that creep is looking for a date with me, you better tell him that's not going to happen!" She made a shuddering sound and went back to her office. Jack laughed, "Don't worry Trudy,

I'll tell him that he has a better chance of landing on Mars." Trudy yelled from the next office, "Make it Pluto." Jack laughed and dialed up the phone number for his good friend Harry Soul. He and Harry had gone to the police academy together back in the day. They both had become detectives, just in different places.

Harry answered the phone, "Detective Soul, 23rd precinct." Jack responded, "Harry, it's Jack. Trudy told me that you called me this morning." Harry paused for a minute and said, "Oh, yeah, Trudy, how is Trudy doing? Any chance…." Jack broke in, "forget about it, Harry, no chance, no time no way. She's out of your league." Harry answered back in a dejected voice "Ok, I was just asking. Look Jack, the real reason that I called, is that I thought that you might like to work with the department on a few cases."

It was unusual for Harry to make such an offer. Jack had become a nemesis for a few of the officers of the NYPD, but on his last case he proved to be instrumental in helping to put a mobster behind bars. Jack raised his right eyebrow and said, "Do you mean that you'd like me to work with the department out of the generosity of my heart or for some real hard cash?" Harry let out a sigh, "Of course it would be for money. Look, here's the deal, the cold cases have started to pile up and there are some high-profile cases that have gone unsolved over the past year and the city has given us a budget to hire some consultants to work on some of these unsolved cases. The city wants to bring some of these cold cases to a close." Jack was taking this all in. He stared up at the ceiling and said, "How much money are we talking about here, Harry?" Harry continued, "it's simple Jack, if you solve a case, you get a cool $5,000. If you don't solve it, you get nothing." Jack was nodding his head up and down, "Yeah, I can live with that. What kind of cases are you looking to solve?" Harry told him, "Why don't you come on down to the precinct. Look over the cold cases, pick one out, and we'll do the paperwork to get you started." It seemed too simple. Jack had always wanted to work as a detective for the NYPD, but he just couldn't handle the structure. This seemed like he could have his cake and eat it too. Jack agreed. He said, "I'll be down to the precinct in about half an hour. I'll solve one of your cold cases before you can get and envelope and put $5,000 in it with my name on it." Harry was shaking his head, "Yeah, right, just come on down to the precinct and we'll get you started."

They both hung up the phone and Jack stood up from his desk and stretched. He reached high for the ceiling and the sound of his bones cracking could be heard in Trudy's office and got her attention. She said, "what's going on in there, Jack? It sounds like you're crushing peanuts on the floor." She laughed. Jack put on his hat and walked into Trudy's office. He said, "It looks like we're going to be helping the NYPD solve some of their cold cases. I knew that is was only a matter of time before they came running to us for help." Trudy looked up at Jack and said, "they're going to pay us, right?" Jack said of course. We're going to clean up. We're going to get $5000 per case." Trudy smiled, "That sounds pretty good Jack. $2500 for you and $2500 for me." Jack looked at Trudy with a serious look. "Let's not get ahead of ourselves *Jill Munroe*, we have to actually solve the cases." Trudy rolled her eyes, she said "Piece of cake Jack, piece of cake. He smirked back, "Let's just hope it's not devil's food cake." They both looked at each other for about 4 seconds in silence.

Jack said, "I'm going to go down to the 23rd precinct to meet with Harry Soul. I'm going to grab a cold case that I think we can solve. I'll come back after lunch, and we can put together a strategy." Trudy made her voice real low and gravelly, "OK Boss, whatever you say." Then she took the last bite of her muffin and swallowed the last sip of her coffee. Jack smiled and headed out the door, down the stairs and into his car. He started his car and pulled into traffic. Twenty-five minutes later Jack pulled into the parking lot for the 23rd precinct. He had high hopes for his collaboration with the NYPD. For the past 25 years he had worked around the police department to solve his cases, he had stepped on some toes. Now he was going to have their blessing and cooperation and well as $5000 to do their work. At least that what he thought was going to happen.

CHAPTER 3

Jack walked up the stairs to the 23rd precinct. He had been here countless times over the years. As a suspect, as a person who rubbed the department the wrong way, and for disregarding police orders among other things. But never before was he was invited to come to the 23rd precinct to work with the NYPD. It kind of threw Jack off his game a little. He didn't really know how he should act or respond when he met with the detectives inside. He had history.

He entered the building and walked up to the main desk. The floor had white tiles but because of the heavy foot traffic, they had aged to an ash gray. There were fluorescent lights overhead, but they were flickering on and off every 4 or 5 seconds. For some reason, the dirty floor and flickering lights made Jack comfortable. There was an officer sitting behind a glass window with a little opening at the bottom of the window. He was middle aged with his hair combed back. He wore glasses towards the bottom of his nose, and he had a name tag "Officer McRae". He also had sergeant stripes on his sleeves. He watched as Jack approached the window, then he asked, "Can I help you?" Jack smiled at the officer and said, "Good Morning, Officer McRae, I'm here to see Detective Harry Soul." Officer McRae looked Jack up and down and said, "Have a seat over there." And he pointed to an old bench next to the wall. The bench looked like it had been here since the Eisenhower administration and had names and descriptive words carved in it from top to bottom. The paint was all worn off and the bench listed to one side. Jack took a seat and waited for Harry to come out and bring him in to the precinct building.

While Jack was sitting on the bench waiting, several people came through the door and walked up to the front desk. There was an older woman who was complaining that she was just mugged outside the police station. There was a man in a suit reporting that his car was broken in to and some valuables were stolen. Then there were a couple of young kids selling cookies. Interestingly, they all got the same response. "Please take a seat and someone will be with you in a moment." They could have had a recording at the window, and it would have accomplished the same thing. That's one of the reasons why Jack decided to become a private detective rather than work with the police force. Too much structure and not enough action.

Finally, the door to the inner precinct opened and Harry came through. He looked at Jack and said, "You been waiting long?" Then Harry laughed. He knew that the wheels of justice turned slowly, he was part of the system. Harry was wearing some well-worn blue pants. He had a suitcoat to match but that was draped on the back of the chair in his office. He also had on a white shirt with the top button open and a dirty black tie worn loosely around his neck. Jack looked at Harry and said, "I see that you're still dressing for success." Jack laughed, Harry didn't, and they walked through the door into the police squad room. Most of the detectives were familiar to Jack. He passed by detective Jim Bottoms and raised his chin to say hello. Detective Bottoms returned the gesture. He also passed by the desk of detective Danny Watts. Jack was a true nemesis for Danny. There had been several heated conversations in the past because Jack had crossed over the line on a few cases that Danny was working. Danny was a cocky young punk of a detective. He wore $1,200 imported suits and Italian shoes. His strategy to get an upper hand was to try to intimidate, bully or coerce anyone that disagreed with him. Jack was not one to be intimidated and this had led to some heated conversations in the past. As Jack passed Danny's desk, Danny looked up and saw Jack walking by with Harry. Danny got up out of his chair and glared at Jack with squinted eyes and pointed his finger at Jack as if he had a gun. Jack glared back with squinted eyes and at the same time he smiled. He knew that would irritate Danny in a big way. Danny's face got all red and he sat back down.

Harry led Jack into his office, and then he closed the door. There were a couple of flies buzzing around the trash can that was placed on the side of Harry's desk and the smell of yesterday's lunch was still in the air. Jack sat down in a chair directly in front of Harry's desk. The office was drab. The walls were painted an off white. At least they were off white when they were painted in 1960. The casings around the window and doors were an ugly green. And there was a plate glass window that had a view of the squad room and the detectives under Harry's command. At that moment, Jack was glad that he had chosen to be a private detective rather than a city cop. As basic as Jack's office was, it was still ten times better than this one. Harry sat down in his chair and let out a long sigh as if to release some bottled-up stress. He looked at Jack with a serious look and said, "OK, now as I said over the phone…" Jack broke in, "Hey Harry, what is this? No coffee? No donuts? Isn't this a police station? We can't have an intelligent conversation without coffee and donuts." Harry made a disgusted face. He said, "Look Jack, contrary to popular belief, this is not a donut shop. If you want coffee and donuts, why don't you take a drive down Lexington Avenue. There is a "Dunkin" about every six blocks. But do you think you can focus for a few minutes on why I called you in here?" Jack put his hands up as if to apologize. He said, "Hey, I'm sorry. I didn't think coffee and donuts were such a touchy subject."

Harry looked down at the floor and said, "Sorry Jack, it's just that I'm under a lot of pressure right now to make these cold cases go away and some of the guys in the precinct really don't like the fact that I brought you in here as a consultant. The thing is, if you solve any of these cases, you make them look bad because they couldn't solve the case. If you don't solve any cases, then I look bad because I'm the one who brought you in. So, I'm kind of in a no-win situation here." Jack smiled, "Don't worry, my friend, you can't please everyone, but you can please the ones who count. When I'm finished, you're going to come out of this looking good to the mayor, the captain, and anyone else who cares about these cases. Don't worry about these other guys in the precinct. I think I can handle them.' Jack had an air of confidence. "Now let me take a look at some of these cases that need to be closed."

Harry reached in back of his chair where there was a table with about 10 bursting manilla file folders. He grabbed all the files and put them on his desk in front of Jack. The files were about a foot high. Then he said to Jack, "take your pick." Jack got serious and started fanning through the files. Each file consisted of a heavy manilla envelope with a name on a label which identified the case. He studied the names of the cases, *"76th Street homicide, Steakhouse robbery and homicide, Queensboro Bridge homicide, Broadway...,"* He stopped when he got to the file that just read Broadway. He remembered and old radio show that was called *"Broadway is my beat."* It focused on detective Danny Clover and all the crime that took place on Broadway. He always kind of pictured himself as Danny Clover in real life. The thought of working Broadway truly intrigued Jack. Broadway was close to Jack's heart. He said to Harry, "I'll take this one." Harry looked at Jack with his eyes opened wide and said, "But Jack, you haven't even looked at the case. You don't even know what the crime was!" Jack laughed. "Don't worry Harry, I'll have this case solved in no time."

Harry sat back in his chair and looked up at the ceiling. He said in a slow deliberate manner, "Jack, this is a very complicated case. This is probably the most difficult of all the cold cases we have. Jack broke in, "Then maybe I should get $10,000 for solving it." He sat smiling at Harry. There was silence for about 20 seconds and Harry said, "Let me explain why this case is so different from the others. Do you remember the death of Heinrich King, the Broadway producer?" Jack was nodding his head up and down. "Oh yeah, King Heini, I remember the headlines when he was found in a dumpster. Come on, you guys couldn't solve that? How difficult could it be?" Harry sat back in his chair and took out a bottle of *Jack Daniel's* from the bottom drawer in his desk and placed the bottle on his desk between him and Jack. Then he took two small whiskey glasses from the same drawer, and he poured two drinks and gave one to Jack. Normally Jack didn't drink whiskey and certainly not before noon, but it appeared that in order for Harry to go further into the case history it was going to involve taking a drink. So, Jack took the glass with whiskey and slugged it down. Harry did the same. Harry said to Jack, "this guy Heinrich King had more enemies than a New York mayor. From our investigation, we found that he was a womanizer, a cheat, a fraud, a swindler, an embezzler, a thief, and an all-around bad guy. Pretty much everyone he ever came in contact with had a motive to kill him. We spent a lot of hours on this case investigating every Tom, Dick, and Harry, and came up with nothing. It's all there in the file."

Jack put his hand on his chin and looked Harry in the eye with a determined look. He said, "This is the case, Harry. I'm going to solve this case." Harry put a little more whiskey in his glass and took a sip. He said, "Jack, just a word of caution, Danny Watts was the detective that was handling this case. If he finds out that you're working on his cold case, it's not going to sit well with him. He already doesn't like you very much as it is, but if you solve a case that he couldn't even come up with a solid lead on, it's going to make him look pretty bad. Just a word to the wise, watch your back on this one." Jack laughed, "Danny Watts, that punk. Don't worry about me I can handle him. When I finish with this case, the department can put Danny out on donut patrol, because that's where he belongs." Harry just sat there smiling, he didn't say a word. Jack didn't know if he was agreeing with him, or maybe it was just the whiskey. Jack asked Harry, "Do I get a badge or something since I am working with the NYPD?" Harry laughed, he said, "Sorry Jack, no badge." He reached into his top drawer and pulled out a card and slid it over the table to Jack. It said, "**Consultant NYPD.**" Jack picked it up and looked at it. He said, "That's it? Just a card that says consultant?" Jack thought for a moment and said, "but what if I need to search some-place, don't I need a warrant?" Harry smiled and said, "Jack, you're not a police officer, you don't need a warrant." Jack smiled, "Oh yeah, I see how this might work out to my advantage." They both laughed loud. The laughing was loud enough that the detectives outside in the squad room were looking in to see what was so amusing.

Harry sat back in his chair. Jack said, "Thanks Harry, I won't let you down on this. Trudy and I will have this case solved in no time. But one thing though. If I should get into any tight jams investigating this case, you have my back, right?" Harry shook his head. He said, "Jack, just don't get into any tight jams. I don't think I have enough *Jack Daniels* in my desk drawer to undo your jams" Jack smiled "Right Harry, it's not like I've ever get myself into any trouble." Just then the two flies from the trash can landed on the Broadway file and Jack brushed them away. They both rose from their chairs and Jack gave Harry a wink. He opened the door and left Harry's office. As Jack walked towards the exit, the detectives under Harry's command all watched as he strolled by with the manilla folder under his arm. Danny

Watts stood up and followed Jack to the door. As Jack reached the exit, Danny grabbed Jack by the shoulder and turned him around. Danny was now in Jack's face. He said, "Look Trane, I don't know what you're up to, but if you know what's good for you, you'll stay out of police work, it can be very dangerous, you could get hurt, if you know what I mean." Jack smiled and said, "Hey Danny, you might want to think about using some mouthwash, your breath a little dangerous, if you know what I mean." Danny's face got beet red, and he was clenching his fists and gritting his teeth. Jack smiled as he turned away and walked out the exit door.

Jack got into his car and drove back to his office. He found a parking space about 2 blocks away and he pulled into the space before anyone else could grab it. Parking spaces in the city are extremely hard to come by so he was pretty pleased with himself. He put the file under his arm and got out of the car and headed towards the office. The sun was out, and it was about 60 degrees, a truly beautiful day in May. Jack began whistling again "*Taking care of business...*" As he was walking towards his office, he passed a street vendor selling Mexican food. The aroma from the tacos made him stop whistling and start humming the song "*Tequila*" from "The Champs." There always seemed to be a song that fit his situation. He thought that he might score a few more points with Trudy if he showed up with lunch. He walked up to the taco wagon, and he saw a small man inside the wagon. The man looked to be about 30 years old. He had on a name tag that read "Cedro". He also had short dark hair and a thin mustache and spoke in a Spanish accent. Cedro asked Jack, "What can I get for you, man?" Jack said, "I'll have 4 large tacos with everything on them, a bag of tortilla chips and a large bottle of Cola." Cedro smiled and said, "Coming right up, man." Cedro turned his back to Jack and prepared the tacos. With all the arm movements and hand changes, it looked like Cedro was conducting an orchestra, but 2 minutes later Cedro was facing Jack and there were four tacos on the counter in front of him. Jack was impressed. He said, "You're an artist Cedro, a regular Picasso in a taco wagon." Cedro laughed, he said, "Picasso, he was like an artist, right, man?" Jack shook his head, he said, "Yeah something like that. How much do I owe you for the tacos, chips, and soda?" Cedro seemed to be adding things up in his head, he said, "That comes to $21.75." Jack gave him $30 and said, "Keep the change *Mi amigo*." Cedro said, "Gracias, Gracias, Thank you very much. Please come again." Jack smiled, "Maybe I will Cedro, maybe I will."

Jack made his way up the street towards his office with a bag in one hand and the manilla envelope under his arm. He entered the building and walked up the stairs to the second floor and went into his office. Trudy was sitting at her desk staring at her computer screen. Jack couldn't tell if she was actually working or just buying a new accessory online. As Jack approached her desk, Trudy lifted her head from the screen and looked at Jack and said, "I smell something good. What's in the bag Jack? Do I smell Tacos?" Jack smiled, "I can't fool you Trudy, you always know what's in the bag." Trudy laughed and raised one eyebrow, "Jack, you always bring either tacos or hot dogs, it's not rocket science." Jack reached into the bag and put two tacos on Trudy's desk. He smiled and said, "Maybe not, but these tacos will take you to the moon and back." Trudy said, "Gracias, Jack. You know how to keep a girl happy." Jack shook his head and said, "Now that would be rocket science." They both laughed and he went into his office and sat down at his desk.

After he had consumed the two tacos, the bag of chips and the bottle of cola, he cleared all the crumbs and paper from his desk, and he opened up the manilla envelope for the cold case that had the label BROADWAY. On the very top of all the paperwork in the file were pictures of the crime scene. The pictures were taken from every angle possible. He flipped through the different pictures, but one caught his eye and he pulled it out and placed it on the desk. The picture showed Heinrich King on top of the trash in a dumpster. He was wearing a truly ugly green colored suit and there appeared to be bruises on his neck and some blood on the back of his head. His head was positioned in a way that he was staring straight up at the stars in the sky. What was interesting is that his suite was perfectly clean. It was as if he had just come from the cleaner. Jack continued to sift through the file, and he came across a list of possible witnesses and persons of interest. He scanned the list for clues but after every name on the list, it read "Alibi." And then there was a sentence or two with their story. The list seemed endless as it appeared that "King Heini" had made a lot of enemies.

Jack called Trudy into his office. She came in twirling her blond hair between her fingers and snapping her gum. She said, "What's up Jack? Are you giving me that afternoon off?" Jack made a disgusted face, "Come on Trudy, sit down, we have some work to do." She made her voice low and gravelly and said, "Yes Boss." Jack handed Trudy the pages with the names of all the suspects that had been cleared by the police department. He figured that someone on this list had to know something. He said, "Trudy, I need you to do a background check on all these people along with current addresses and social network activity. And if you can get any bank account balances that would be good too." Trudy stood there looking at Jack with her mouth open, "Jack, there must be more than thirty people on this list! This is going to take a couple of weeks to do backgrounds on everyone. How much money did you say this case was worth?" Jack answered, "The city is going to pay us $5000 for solving the case, but I think we can do it in less than a week." Jack was usually optimistic when he took a case, and his overconfidence had led to some serious problems in the past, but this time he may have bitten off a little more than he could chew. Trudy picked up the list from the desk and said, "OK, Jack, but we split this case 50/50, right? $2500 for me and $2500 for you." Jack gave his look of approval. "That's right Trudy we split this one 50/50. You do all the computer stuff and I do all the leg work. And maybe we'll even take a field trip down to Broadway." Trudy smiled a playful smile and said, "I like the sound of that Jack. I haven't seen *Hamilton* yet." Jack looked at Trudy with one eyebrow raised and a half-smile and said, "Come on Trudy, let's get to work."

CHAPTER 4

Jack unbuttoned the top button on his shirt and loosened his tie. Then he rolled up his shirt sleeves and pulled out a black marking pen from his top drawer. All of his cases started with a good plan, and he was ready to put a good plan in motion. In the back of Jack's office there was a large storage closet. There were items in there that he hadn't seen since flip phones were popular. But deep in the recesses of the closet, there was a very large whiteboard that he had used when he first opened his office as a private investigator. This case seemed to have so many suspects that he thought that it would be a good time to break it out again and set up a strategy that would hopefully lead him straight to the killer. That was wishful thinking. He dragged the whiteboard out of the closet and set it up just to the right side of his desk, opposite the window. There was a trail of dust from the closet to the point where he set up the whiteboard and the dust particles danced in the air all across the room like snowflakes in an open field.

Jack picked up his marking pen and in the middle of the whiteboard, he wrote the name in big dark letters "**Heinrich King**". Then on the left side of the white board he started listing the names of all the persons of interest. On the top of the list, he wrote the name, "Jackie King", Heinrich's current wife. Then he started to list the names of all the individuals that had been interviewed by Danny Watts. He was sure that Danny was so incompetent that he probably missed something that would have led him to an active suspect.

Under Jackie King's name he listed the names, Marie Robbin, Kristen Monree, Tori Pichettes, Siobhan Peison, Audrey Linn, Dean James, and the list went on for about thirty more suspects. He listed them all and as he got to the bottom of the whiteboard, his writing was getting smaller and smaller just so he could fit all the names. When he finished, he sat back down in his chair and just stared at the whiteboard. It was just a bunch of unconnected names. He thought to himself, "Someone on this list either killed Heinrich King, or knows who did." He walked over to the window and opened it about ten inches. The fresh spring air smelled good, and he took a deep breath hoping to stimulate his thinking, then he coughed a couple of times. He went back and sat at his desk and just continued staring at all the names on the whiteboard. He was trying to develop a strategy, but instead, he just kept burping the tacos he had for lunch.

The phone rang and he picked up. "Hi Jack, I was just calling to see what time you're picking me up tonight." It was Debra Thorn. He had started dating her after his last case. She was smart, beautiful and a redhead, probably out of Jack's league but they just seemed to click. She was a New York City detective assigned to the theft and larceny division and she was good at what she did. Jack smiled and said, "Hi babe, look, about tonight, something has come up and I'm probably going to be working late. What if we just meet down at *Big Jim's Sports Bar*" at about 8 o'clock?" There was silence, Jack was biting his lip, hoping that Debra would understand. She was a detective. She knew about long hours and unexpected circumstances. She said, "That's OK Jack, I have another date lined up anyway." There was a pause then she laughed, "I'm just kidding, Jack, yes, no problem, I'll meet you at *Big Jim's* about 8 o'clock." Then she laughed again. Jack was smiling, "You had me going there for a minute, babe. You're the best!" Debra smiled,

"And don't forget that, Jack." He held the phone close to his ear and said, "See you later, babe." They both hung up and Jack got back to work.

Jack called into the next office, "How are you doing with the suspect list, Trudy?' She answered back, "Jack, I've only had the list for like 20 minutes, who do you think I am *Houdini*?" She snapped her gum a couple of times and she said, "Why don't you just go out and interview the first couple of names on the list and I'll continue to gather as much information as I can here." Jack was shaking his head up and down, he said, "You know Trudy, sometimes you come up with some good ideas. You keep this up and you just might make it someday as a private investigator." Trudy tilted her head to one side and raised one eyebrow and said, "Jack, we're splitting the $5,000 for this case 50/50, so as far as I'm concerned, as long as we're on this case, I am a private investigator." Jack looked up at the ceiling looking for some quick comeback, but he had nothing. He said, "Ok Trudy, but for now, I'll do all the leg work and you work behind the scenes." Trudy gave him a glare and said, "Ok, Jack, but at some point, during this investigation, I'm coming out in the field with you. It's not like it's an active murder, how dangerous could it be?" Jack thought for a moment and said very slowly, "Yeah, how dangerous could it be?" He knew that Trudy wanted to get out of the office. She had worked for him for the past 8 years and for the most part the four walls of this office were her work home. She was the best assistant he could ever have and although there were times in the past that he had to protect her; he knew that he owed it to her to let her come out with him on the investigation. He said, "OK, Trudy, why don't you just get as much information as you can on the top 5 people on the list and when you're finished with that, you can come out into the field, and we'll do some serious interviewing." Trudy smiled, she said, "That's what I'm talking about Jack. Should I get a handgun? How about a knife?" Jack had his hand up and shaking his head back and forth. He said, "Trudy, you know I feel about guns. Besides, you're the last person I want to see with a gun. You'd probably shoot me." Trudy laughed, "I'm only kidding Jack. I just like to see that vein stick out in your neck when you get nervous." Jack made a face, "You're a real barrel of laughs Trudy." He put on his jacket and hat and stood in front of Trudy's desk for a minute. He started to speak and said, "Do you have the address for…" Trudy broke in "Jackie King?" and she handed him a slip of paper with Jackie King's address. Jack smiled and said, "It's like you can read my mind." Trudy smiled and said, "Well it's not like discovering plutonium, Jack." Trudy laughed hard and Jack laughed lightly. Trudy always seemed to know what Jack was looking for, that's why they made such a good team. He said, "I'm going to visit Jackie King and then I'm going to take a look at the scene of the crime, that's probably the best place to start. Why don't you just continue here and close up the office when you think the time is right. Trudy continued to stare at her computer screen and punch the keys on the keyboard and said in a low gravelly voice "Yes Boss." Jack said, I'll see you in the morning. Trudy said, "I like the chocolate covered donuts, and a large coffee would be good." Jack gave her a wink and left the office.

He walked up the street and got into his Mustang, put the key in the ignition, and started the engine. He opened his window and listened for a minute as the engine idled. The smell of the rich fuel exhaust mixed with the aroma of whatever was in the gutter was like a shot of adrenalin for Jack. He was ready to go. He looked down at the slip of paper that Trudy had given him, and it read; Jackie King, 600 West 57th Street. It appeared that Jackie King was maintaining a luxury apartment in Midtown West. Jack put the car in gear and headed over to her apartment. It was about 2:00 PM and it was a beautiful day in the city. Jack could hear the birds chirping, but it was drowned out by the sound of the pigeons cooing on the sidewalk. He arrived at Jackie

King's apartment building at about 3:00 PM. He walked up the stairs to the building and went in. This was a high security building and there was a guard sitting at a desk in the middle of the floor. Jack walked up to the guard and noticed that he had a name tag, Joe Bourdon. Jack said, "How are you doing Joe, I'm here to see Mrs. Jackie King. Can you buzz me up?" Joe looked Jack up and down and said, "It doesn't work that way sport. I'll give her a call and see if she wants to see you. What did you say your name was?" Jack smiled, "Oh, I didn't say. My name is Jack Trane, investigator with the NYPD. I have some questions for Mrs. King." Joe looked at Jack with one eye closed and said, "You got a badge?" Jack handed him the card that said on the back **"Consultant NYPD."** Joe took the card and looked at it closely like he was examining a counterfeit $10 bill, and then he let out a sarcastic laugh and said, "What, did you just have this printed up at *Kinko's*?" He gave Jack the card back. Jack knew that nobody was going to take him seriously with the lame card that Harry Soul had given him, so he started to talk tough. He said, "Look buddy, I'm consulting for the NYPD, are you going to make the call or not?" He knew the security guard was just having some fun with him, but he wasn't amused. Joe got serious and said sarcastically, "Yes, inspector Trane, I'll make the call right now." Jack gave him the stink eye and Joe made the call. About 20 seconds later Joe hung up the phone and said to Jack, "take the elevator to the 50th floor, apartment 5001. I told her you were with the NYPD." Jack smiled at Joe and gave him a wink. He said, "I owe you one buddy and dropped $10 dollars on the desk as a gesture of good will. Joe picked up the $10 dollars, put it in his shirt pocket, and winked back. Jack got into the elevator and pushed the button for the 50th floor and the elevator rose like it some kind of turbo lift. It rose so fast Jack's ears were popping, then suddenly it stopped, and the door opened, and he stepped out. Directly in front of him was apartment 5001.

Jack walked across the hall so that he was standing in front of the door, and he rang the bell, he didn't know what to expect, but Jackie King was certainly not what he expected. The door opened and there stood Jackie King. She had long shiny black hair and stood about six feet tall. She had strong features, high cheek bones, a prominent nose and large lips covered in dark red lipstick. The way she wore her eye makeup reminded him of Cleopatra. She wasn't what Jack would call attractive, but he couldn't take his eyes off her. She was wearing a long red evening dress, sleeveless and low cut with silver sequins all down the front of the dress. She had shiny red pumps on her feet. She flipped her hair back with her right hand and said in a low sultry voice, "Come in, please." Jack walked into the apartment. It was a corner unit with white tile extending about twelve feet back from the entrance. Inside he could see the living room carpeted in a deep orange rug with a dark brown rug border. One wall was completely windows with a view of the city the other wall was covered in what looked like raised tan-colored tiles and there were fancy lights hanging from the ceiling. She motioned to the modern gray couch in the middle of the room and Jack went in and sat down. She sat in a gray matching chair opposite the couch, and there was a clear glass accent table to her right.

Jack cleared his throat and said, "I forgot to introduce myself, my name is Jack Trane and I'm working with the NYPD on your late husband's unfortunate demise." Jackie made a sour look and in her low sultry voice said, "Well detective Trane, I went over all this with that other detective, I believe that his name was detective Wasp or something." Jack smiled, "Yes detective Watts. But Mrs. King, I'm here because the department was unable to solve this case. I'm a special consultant, hired to solve cold cases. And Mrs. King, your late husband's case is very cold." Jackie got up and took a bottle of wine from the bottom of a wine cooler at the far end of the room. She sat back down and poured herself a glass of what looked like *Pinot Noir*. She smiled at Jack and said, "I'm sure you don't drink on the job detective, otherwise I would offer you a glass." She smiled and sipped her wine. Jack felt like a character in *Sunset Boulevard*. He didn't know whether to cross his legs, sit back and look casual, or stand up and do some interrogating. He settled for sitting straight up and asking some probing questions.

He sat forward a little and asked her, "Mrs. King, do you know of anyone who would want to hurt your late husband?" Jackie laughed so hard she spilled some of her wine on the glass accent table. In her low sultry voice, she said, "Mr. Trane, my late husband was a vile man. Almost everyone he knew probably wanted to hurt him, and most of them probably wanted to kill him. He hurt people, Mr. Trane. Big people, small people, all because he could. He cheated on me with other women, then he cheated on them with more women. He fired someone every day and never had a good word to say about anyone. He gambled, he smoked, he drank, and he owed people money. I'm not surprised he was murdered, I just surprised it took this long." She raised one eyebrow and stared in Jack's direction. Jack tried to show no emotion, he said, "When was the last time you saw him?" She took another sip of wine and said, "The day he died, I saw him that morning before he left for his office on Broadway. There was nothing special, nothing unusual, nothing different. Just a fat, smelly, bald man leaving for work in the morning. He never came back, and Mr. Trane, no I'm not sorry he's gone." She was cold and exact with her words. Jack figured that she was as good a suspect as anyone else, so he asked her, "Mrs. King, was your late husband insured in the event of his untimely death?" She smiled again and said, "Why yes, darling, He was insured for a cool ten million dollars." She smiled and her eyebrows raised. Jack's eyebrows raised too. Ten million dollars was a pretty good reason to have Heinrich King killed, but there was no evidence. But at least he was clear on a motive. Jack leaned forward just a little bit more and asked, "Mrs. King can you tell me where you were the night your husband was murdered." Jackie smiled, "Of course darling, around 4:00 PM I was getting my nails done." She extended her hands to show Jack her nails. Then she continued, "Then at about 5:00 PM I was having dinner at the *Leopard Room*, then I came home and went to bed." She sat back and took another sip of her wine."

Jack knew this was probably as much information that he was going to get. He stood up from the couch. He said, "Well, Mrs. King, I want to thank you for your time, you've been very helpful. I think I can show myself out." Jackie took the bottle and poured some wine into her glass. In her low sultry voice, she said, "Nice to meet you detective Trane, maybe we'll meet again sometime." Jack was thinking to himself "Count on it lady." But instead, he said, "If I need any more information, we'll be in touch." He walked over the orange carpet onto the white tile floor and let himself out the door. He got into the elevator and pushed the button for the bottom floor. The elevator was much slower on the way down. Jack was thinking that Jackie King had ten million reasons to bump off "King Heini". He put Jackie King on the top of his list. He exited the elevator and gave Joe the security guard a wave and exited the building. His next stop was the crime scene.

Jack hopped into his Mustang, started the engine, and made his way over to 8th Avenue. It was getting late in the day and the tall buildings were now starting to hide the sunlight. He was always suspicious of any car that followed him for too long and maybe it was his imagination, but it looked like a dark blue Subaru WRX, with darkened windows was following him for the past few miles. He turned onto West 44th Street and the Subaru didn't follow, Jack was glad. There was a fire lane just opposite the Majestic Theatre that was supposed to be kept open. Jack parked in the fire lane knowing that his car would be towed if he stayed there. But he also knew that it would take the tow truck at least 15 minutes to get here in the city traffic. He locked his car and went down the alley on the side of the Majestic. There he found the dumpster where Heinrich King's body had been found. The spot that the dumpster was in was well hidden from the street, so there would probably be no one passing by that would have seen anything. He looked around the ally and found no surveillance cameras that could have recorded any activity on the night of the murder. Then he measured the height of the dumpster and found that it was six feet from the ground to the top of the dumpster. Someone would have had to lift Heinrich King's lifeless 225 body over the 6-foot edge of the dumpster and place it on the top of the trash. This looked like it had to be more than a 1-man job. He took out a small pad from his jacket and made some notes. Then he hurried back to his car before the tow truck arrived.

It was now dark. He got into his car and turned on the radio. The song that was playing was "*The nights on Broadway*" an old Bee Gees song from the 1970s. The lyrics were a little haunting. The song seemed to fit. He put the car in gear and headed over to *Big Jim's Sports Bar* to meet up with Debra Thorn. On the drive over to *Big Jim's*, Jack tried to piece together what he had on this case so far. The only thing he could come up with is that he needed to interview more people on his list. He pulled into the parking lot at *Big Jim's*, locked his car and went in.

It was still early, about 7:00 PM so Jack decided to have a quick drink before Debra showed up. He sat down at the bar and within 10 seconds an ice-cold Guinness came sliding down the bar and stopped right in front of him. Jack looked down the bar and yelled, "Teddy K! you still got it." Teddy K came walking over to Jack and said, "come on Jack, I never lost it." They both laughed then Jack held his glass up to

Teddy and took a sip of the rich dark head on top of his beer. Jack and Teddy had been friends for years and Jack loved coming here especially when there was a Red Sox-Yankees game on the TV. Tonight though, there was no game, Jack was just here to meet Debra. Teddy asked Jack, "What can I get for you tonight, Jack?" Jack smiled, "Nothing yet, Teddy, I'm just here to meet up with a very special lady." Teddy laughed and said, "And you're bringing her here? Real classy Jack." Jack was shaking his head, "No, it's not like that Teddy. We're just meeting here because I'm working a case, and this just seemed like the best place to meet." Teddy laughed, "Like I said Jack, real classy." Teddy K put his towel over his shoulder and walked away.

About a beer and a half later, Debra came walking through the door. She had just come from the job too, so she was wearing a pair of tan slacks, a white turtleneck, and a light tan leather jacket. Her short reddish-blond hair was the perfect accent. As she got closer to Jack, he could smell her perfume. It was *Chanel Coco Mademoiselle*. Jack knew because he had bought it for her on a whim. Jack kissed her softly on the cheek. He said, "How are doing, babe?" She gave Jack a hug and they went over and sat at a table. After 2 deluxe burgers and some large fries, and a little small talk, Debra looked at Jack seriously and said, "I heard that you were working a cold case with the 23rd precinct." Jack smiled, he said, "That's right babe. I'm consulting with the NYPD. They know who to call when their cases fall apart." Then he laughed. Debra looked at Jack again with a serious face, "Look, Jack, I heard that you are working the Heinrich King case, the Broadway murder." Jack smiled a half smile and said, "That's right, why is there a problem?" Debra sighed and said, "Jack, that was Danny Watts case. He botched that case pretty badly. If you solve that case, it's going to make him look like the clumsy boob that his is. He's not going to like that, Jack. You had better watch your back." Jack laughed, "Relax Debra,

I can handle Danny Watts, he's like a fruit fly on a banana. Annoying but pretty harmless." They both smirked and Jack laughed a little. Jack said, "With the $5000 I get for solving this case, maybe I'll get Danny a banana and put it on his desk. Debra covered her mouth and laughed, and Jack took a sip of his *Guinness*. A fitting end to a great day.

CHAPTER 5

Jack opened his eyes and looked over at the clock on his nightstand. It said 8:25 AM. The alarm had gone off 25 minutes ago, and the sun was shining through the window into his eyes, but he just couldn't get out of bed. He had stayed out a little longer than he had planned last night with Debra Thorn, but it was worth the early morning lag that he was suffering now. He finally managed to get up and then sat back down on the side of the bed for a moment and he smiled as he reflected on last night. Then something caught his eye. From his bedroom, he could see his front door. And at the bottom of his door, was an eight-by-ten manilla envelope that someone had slid under the door. He got up and walked over and picked it up. It's never usually a good message inside an envelope that's delivered sometime during the night. The envelope was sealed, it had a name on the front of the envelope, his name, Jack Trane. He opened the envelope and inside there was just a plain sheet of paper with words written in black magic marker. It read; "**IF YOU KNOW WHAT'S GOOD FOR YOU, YOU'LL DROP THIS CASE!**" Jack stood there in his shorts and t-shirt for a few minutes trying to figure out who would have sent him this threatening message. Only a few people knew that he was working this case. Danny Watts knew, Jackie King knew. But Debra Thorn knew too. That meant that there must be a lot of other people who knew that Jack was working the Broadway murder case. The grapevine was alive and well in the big city.

Jack thought to himself, this changes everything. Maybe that Subaru WRX was following him yesterday after all. Maybe there was more to this case than meets the eye. Maybe he should jump in the shower and get dressed. Jack folded the paper and put it on the top of his dresser and headed into the bathroom for a quick shower and a shave. About 20 minutes later he came out of the bathroom and headed over to his walk-in closet. He reached in and pulled out a pair of light brown dockers. He reached in again and pulled out a brown paisley tie. He reached in one more time and pulled out a brown tweed sports-jacket. Once again, the trifecta. He walked over to his armoire and took out a pristine white button-down shirt. He got dressed, then he picked up the paper from the top of his dresser and read it again "**IF YOU KNOW WHAT'S GOOD FOR YOU, YOU'LL DROP THIS CASE!**" He stood there thinking for a moment and then he made sure that he put on his custom-made shoes. The ones with the 2-inch knife blades concealed in each heel. He also took a pair of brass knuckles out of his dresser drawer and put them in his jacket pocket. This case had just gotten a little more interesting and he was hoping that he wouldn't have to use any of his accessories, but he was ready if things started to go sideways.

Jack left his apartment and put the matchstick in the bottom of the door. In the back of his mind, he was contemplating the threatening note he had just received, but in the front of his mind he was thinking about breakfast, and he was headed down to the *Coffee Café*. As he left the building, he became aware of his surroundings. The two men standing on the street corner, the three men just standing on opposite sides of the street, the two men following him from about twenty feet behind, all became very suspicious in Jack's mind. It was like everyone who cast a shadow was a threat. A blue car passed by, and Jack turned and stared at the car. Even the cars were starting to look suspicious. Jack thought to himself, "I've been in tougher situations than this one, relax and just go with the flow." He smiled to himself and started whistling the Cat Stevens tune "*Moon Shadow*" as he watched his own shadow on the pavement. He picked up his pace and he was at the *Coffee Café* within 5 minutes.

Jack walked into the *Café* and looked over and saw his favorite waitress. He yelled out, "How is my favorite Senorita today?" Betty smiled and said, "Hola, Jack, I didn't know you were so world-class." Jack smiled and said, "There's a lot of things you don't know about me Betty, I'm just a man of mystery." He sat down at a table and Betty came over and hit him with her towel and said, "Real mysterious Jack, blueberry pancakes, a side of orange juice, a vanilla latte and organic Vermont maple syrup." Jack just sat there smiling, he said, "And how about a side of bacon with that?" Betty let out a little scream, "Oooohhh Jack, you're just full of surprises, aren't you?" They both laughed and Betty went back to get his order. He forgot to stop at the newsstand this morning, but he saw a newspaper on the table next to him. He reached over for the paper, but another hand got there first. A tall man with a dark complexion and a black shirt and a garnet ring on his little finger grabbed the paper and looked at Jack as he lifted it from the table. The man said, "Sorry buddy, you can have it when I'm done." Jack looked at him with one eyebrow raised and just nodded his head up and down. Soon Betty was back with his order, and she put the pancakes, juice, syrup, bacon, and coffee in front of Jack and said, "Enjoy." He smiled and said, "Just seeing your face this morning brings me joy, Betty." She laughed a little and hit Jack again with her towel and went back behind the counter. They both loved this morning banter.

About 10 minutes later pancakes and bacon were gone and Jack was sipping his last sip of the Latte. He looked over to where the man in the black shirt was and all he saw was the newspaper on the table. The man with the black shirt and garnet pinkie ring was gone. He made a mental note in case he ran into "Mr. garnet pinkie ring" again.

Betty came over to the table and asked, "how was it, Jack?" Jack had a big smile, "Unbelievable Betty, unbelievable." Betty smiled and said, "I meant the meal, Jack," They both laughed and Jack paid the bill and left his customary $10 tip for Betty. She said, "See you soon, Jack." He winked at her and said, "Count on it."

He left the *Café* and walked up to the garage to get his car. He gave Fernando a wave as he entered the garage. He quickly got into his car and left the garage. It was about 9:45 AM and he knew that Trudy would be waiting in the office for the donuts. Fortunately, there is a *Dunkin* on just about every corner in Manhattan. He was close to 1st Avenue, so he stopped into the *Dunkin,* and got a half dozen donuts. He got three chocolate-covered and 3 Bavarian cream and a large coffee for Trudy. He had just had a big breakfast, but he knew that by 10:30 AM he would be ready for a little snack. As he left the *Dunkin,* he turned and started walking up the street towards his car and immediately someone bumped into him, and all the donuts spilled into the street. Jack looked up. To his surprise, it was the man in the dark shirt with the garnet pinkie ring. The man said, "Oh, I'm sorry, I probably should look where I'm going and not got be going places where I shouldn't be." The man just smiled at Jack and walked away. Jack stood there with the empty box in his hands, and he knew that this was no coincidence. The man with the garnet pinkie ring was sending a message, but for who? Jack went back into the *Dunkin* and got more donuts, then he got into his car and headed over to his office.

Jack walked into his office and before he got two feet in, he could hear Trudy's high pitched New York voice, "Jack, it's after 10 O'clock. I'm starving. Where are the donuts?" He dropped the box on her desk and gently placed the coffee in front of her and stood there smiling. She opened the box and said, "You did good, Jack. Chocolate covered and a large coffee. You're going to make someone a good hubby someday."

44

Then she let out a little laugh. Jack made a face at her and said, "Keep it up Trudy, I'll set you up on a date with my friend Harry Soul." Trudy made a disgusted face and held her nose. "OK Jack, you win. I'll go easy on you this morning." Jack looked at Trudy the way a father looks at a daughter. Trudy had a quick wit and a strong attitude. She kept him on his toes, but he still felt the need to protect her at times. He went into his office and came back with a bottle of pepper spray. He placed it on Trudy's desk and said, "I got a message last night advising me do drop the Broadway case. Then, just about 15 minutes ago I had a little altercation with a man outside the donut shop. I think to be safe you should carry this pepper spray in your purse." Trudy had a mouthful of donut and she had just taken a sip of her coffee. She opened her eyes wide and swallowed. She said, "I don't know if I like this, Jack. I think I'd rather have a gun." Jack pursed his lips and said, "Trudy, you know how I feel about guns." He patted her on her shoulder and said, "Don't worry, you probably won't have to use the pepper spray and besides, you know that I won't let anything happen to you. You're the straw that stirs the drink, the spark that starts the fire, the mouse that finds the cheese. And besides you're the only one of the two us that can use a computer." Trudy took another bite of her donut and a sip of her coffee and said, "Yeah and you're the guy who drinks the drink, the straw that's in the fire, and the mouse that gave away the cheese." Jack smiled and said, "You see, that's why I keep you around Trudy. You keep me on my toes."

Jack didn't want to alarm Trudy, but between the envelope with the warning and his run in with "Mr. garnet pinkie ring" he was very concerned about what might happen next. He went back into his office and took the marker from his desk drawer and began to write on the whiteboard next to the name "Jackie King". He wrote, **prime suspect-has motive and opportunity.** He put the marker back in his desk drawer and called out to Trudy, "How are you doing on that list, Trudy?" She was just finishing her donut and still working on her coffee. She yelled back to Jack's office, "I've completed about six people from the top of the list down. Take your pick." Jack sat down in his chair, and he rubbed his chin with his right hand. He said, "How about Marie Robbin, I'll bet she's got a tale or two to tell." Jack could hear the printer working in Trudy's office. Before he could get up from his desk, Trudy came in Jack's office with as many facts about Marie Robbin that would fit on two pieces of paper. Jack sat there with his mouth open, he said, "Trudy you're amazing, one of these day's you're going to make someone a good assistant." Trudy answered back, "Ha, Ha, very funny Jack, just remember, I get to go out in the field on this case, right?" Jack rolled eyes and said, "Yeah, just keep the pepper spray handy." Trudy went back to her desk and took out another donut in one hand and was working the computer keys with the other.

Jack studied the papers with the information on Marie Robbin. It appeared that at one time she was a performer, but sometime around the age of twenty-nine she stopped performing and began working for "King Heini." He figured that there would be a story behind that. He got up from his desk and put on his jacket and his hat and walked into Trudy's office. He said, "I'm going to pay Marie Robbin a visit and see what her story is. If I'm not back by 3:00 PM just close the office when you feel the time is right." Trudy swallowed her last piece of donut and her last sip of coffee. In her low gravelly voice she said, "Yes Boss." Jack grabbed a Bavarian cream donut from the box and gave Trudy a wink and left the office.

Jack's car was about 2 blocks up the street, but before he reached his car his donut was gone and there was a little piece of chocolate on his chin that he was not aware of. He wiped his hands on his jacket and opened the door to his car and got in. He checked his paper for Marie

Robbin's address, and it read: 1900 Murray Street, Queens NY. Jack put the address into his GPS. It was just off of 20th Road. He figured that he would take the Queensboro Bridge to 36th Street, then let the GPS do the rest. He started his car and opened the windows about a third of the way down and let the engine idle for a minute. The low growl of the engine gave Jack confidence that he could outrun anyone on the road and get where he was going without a hitch. And usually that was the case. However, there are exceptions to every rule. He put the car in gear and pulled into traffic heading down FDR drive. Within about 20 seconds, he noticed a blue Subaru WRX directly behind him. When he changed lanes the WRX changed lanes. This was the same blue WRX he had seen yesterday. Now he was being followed for sure. He tightened his seat belt as he approached a traffic light. He stopped at the light and the WRX was right behind him. Jack waited, he revved the engine a couple of times, then the light changed. Jack popped the clutch and his tires spun on the dry pavement. Blue smoke rose from his tires for about 3 seconds and his Mustang took off like a bullet out of a gun. The WRX reacted to Jack's move, but it was about three car lengths behind. Jack made a hard right onto East 78th Street and the WRX followed. It was a narrow street with cars parked on both sides of the street. It was a one-way street and Jack accelerated quickly up to seventy miles per hour. The WRX followed. As they approached Cherokee Lane, Jack saw a mom and two small children on bicycles on his right. He swerved left quickly to avoid them and the WRX did the same. As they approached York Street the traffic got much heavier. Jack narrowly missed a motorcycle parked on the side of the road. The WRX clipped the motorcycle but kept on following Jack. They approached a traffic light and Jack could see that it was green, so he gunned the engine and went through the intersection at about eighty miles per hour. As he entered East 78th Street again, it was still a one-way street, but Jack was now going the wrong way. There were two yellow taxis approaching the intersection. Jack swerved left and went up on the sidewalk to avoid them. The WRX tried to slam on their brakes as they entered East 78th Street but it was too late. The WRX skidded sideways, and its rear end met with the front of one of the taxis. Jack could see all the dust and smoke in his rearview mirror. He immediately slowed down and pulled into a vacant parking lot and turned around. He drove back towards the WRX and tried to see who was behind the wheel as he passed the wreck. But as he passed the wreck, he noticed that the driver's door was open, and no one was behind the wheel. The driver was gone. He had a sneaking suspicion that the man with the garnet pinkie ring might somehow be involved. He was pretty sure he would be seeing him again at some point in this investigation. Sirens were blaring, traffic had slowed down, and Jack continued on to his destination in Queens. Once again, his Mustang did not let him down.

About 45 minutes later, He parked his car on the street outside Marie Robbin's house on Murray Street in Queens. The apartment building looked to be a brick duplex and she lived on the left side. He walked up and knocked on the door. He waited for about 10 seconds and the door opened. She was an attractive woman. She looked to be about forty, but sometimes looks are deceiving. She had short dark hair styled nicely in somewhat of a rounded bob. She had hazel-colored eyes that seemed to stare right through Jack. She was light on the make-up but that didn't seem to take away from her natural beauty. She was wearing a tight white pullover shirt and a pair of black slacks. She said, "Can I help you?" Jack smiled and said, "Are you Marie Robbin?" She seemed a little annoyed and said, "Yes, what do you want?" Jack showed her his card that said he was a consultant with the NYPD. She didn't seem very impressed. He said, "Ms. Robbin, my name is Jack

Trane, and I'm working on the murder of Heinrich King, I think you're familiar with Mr. King." Marie curled one lip like Elvis, and said, "Yeah, I knew that piece of crud all right." Jack raised one eyebrow and said, "can I come in and ask you a few questions?" She hesitated, but then said, "All right, you can come in, but you're probably not going to like what I have to say." Jack smiled politely and went into the house.

Marie looked Jack up and down as if he had just taken the last chocolate chip from the cookie jar. Then she led him into a living room where there was a couch and two matching chairs. The room had somewhat of an Irish look. The couch was a 3-seater, it was a cream-colored tufted fabric, and there were little Irish trinkets throughout the room. She said, "Sit down." She pointed to the couch, and she sat in one of the matching chairs. Jack started his questioning. He said, "Ms. Robbin, what was your relationship with Heinrich King?" Marie made a disgusted face and said, "All right, first of all, it's Marie. And secondly, I did not have a relationship with Heinrich King. He was my boss, period." Jack smiled, "Well, Marie, I understand that you worked for Mr. King for some 16 years. During all those years, you must have gotten to know him quite well. In fact, I would…" Marie broke in before Jack finished his sentence, "Stop right there. I worked for Heinrich King for 16 years, but I could have been somebody. I was a performer; I was going places. I had talent, but Heinrich King took all that away. I was twenty-nine and very impressionable, and he promised to give me part in a big show on Broadway. He took advantage of me in more ways than one and he kept promising that soon my part would come around. He had me work in his office to keep me close. One year led to another and soon my time had come and gone. There would be no part for me on Broadway. There was never a part for me. Heinrich King just used me for his own selfish impulses, and in the end, he discarded me like an old piece of chewing gum. And by the way did you know you have a smudge of chocolate on your chin?"

Jack sat up in the couch, looking a little embarrassed and he wiped the chocolate off of his chin with a tissue he had in his jacket pocket. Then he said, "I'm really sorry to hear that, Marie. But since you worked for him for so long, do you know of anyone who would like to have killed him?" She let out a big laugh, as she spoke, her voice continued to get louder and louder, "You've got to be kidding. You mean besides me? Look, Mr. Trane, Heinrich King hurt or offended everyone he came into contact with. He was a sleaze. He was a cheat. He was a thief. He took advantage of countless women. He fired everyone from directors down to the actors. He ruined careers. He gambled and he lost big. The man had no friends. He had associates who were just as loathsome as he was. And no, I'm not sorry he dead, I only wish that I could have been the one to do it!" Jack could feel the anger in Marie's voice. He half-smiled at her and in a delicate way said, "Well Marie, you've been very helpful, but I do have one more question, "Where were you on the night that he was murdered?" Marie sat back in her chair looking all comfortable and said, "I happened to be out with a few friends that night from about 7:00 PM until about 1:00 AM. Just as I said to that other policeman, detective Wisk or something." Jack smiled, "You mean detective Watts. Can you tell me who your friends were, so they can corroborate your alibi?" Marie smiled a wry smile at Jack and said, "Really, Mr. Trane, do you think I'm big and strong enough to strangle and throw a big, fat, smelly man like "Heini King" into a dumpster?" She laughed out loud and said, "My friends are, Audrey Linn, Victoria Pichettes, and Siobhan Peison. I'm sure they will corroborate my whereabouts that night." There was silence in the room for about 10 seconds and then she said, "Is that all? Because I really need to get back to my TV show. I was in the middle of a *Law-and-Order* episode.

Did you know that there are so many ways to get away with murder?" She laughed a little and showed Jack to the door. He said, "Thank you, Marie, I'm glad we had this conversation. You've been very helpful."

Jack walked back to his car and sat there for a few minutes. Jackie King seemed like a prime suspect, but after talking with Marie Robbin, she had just as much of a motive and the opportunity to kill Heinrich King. Jack figured that her alibi for the night of "King Heini's murder would be backed up by her three friends. His next move would be to interview the three friends. Jack thought that the easiest way to do this would be alphabetically, so Audrey Linn would be next on his list. He called Trudy on his cellphone, and she answered on the first ring. "Hello Jack, do you need something, or did you just butt dial me?" Jack rolled his eyes. He said, "Trudy I need the info on Audrey Linn. I want to interview her next. Send what you have to my phone." Jack looked down at his phone and the text had already been sent. Jack said, "You're the best Trudy." Trudy was snapping her gum. She said, "Don't forget, I get to come out into the field tomorrow." Jack rolled his eyes again and said, "We'll talk in the morning, Trudy." Trudy answered back, "Yes we will, Jack," They both hung up the phone. He looked down at the text. It looked like Audrey Linn lived on Bellemeade Avenue in Fort Lee, New Jersey, which was just across the Hudson River. According to her profile she was an honor student. She had graduated from Columbia University with a degree in performing arts and had listed that one of her goals was to work her way up the ladder and eventually produce or direct a Broadway show. She took menial jobs in the theatre just to get her foot in the door, but she had high hopes. Jack had enough information to get to his next interview. He started his car and began driving back to the city. He put on the radio to the oldies station and old Eddie Rabbit song came on "*I get these Suspicions*" He had only interviewed two persons of interest, but they both remained high on the list of suspects. He could only imagine how this case would unfold as he interviewed Marie's 3 friends. Or maybe he couldn't.

CHAPTER 6

Jack crossed over the Queensboro bridge back into Manhattan. It was just after 1:00 PM and the sun was high in the sky. He put on his *Ray-Bans* to shield his eyes from the sun, but mostly because he thought they made him look cool.

Fort Lee was on the other side of the Hudson River so Jack expected that with all the traffic he would be on the road for at least an hour before he got to Audrey Linn's house. So, he started to look for a street vendor where he might find a bite to eat before he went over to Fort Lee. Almost immediately on 2nd Avenue, he spotted a small silver cart with a bright yellow umbrella covering it. Jack didn't know what kind of food they served, but he was willing to take a chance. He quickly pulled over and found a place to park. He walked up to the food cart and noticed a small rectangular name on the front of the cart. It said *"Odgens Ethiopian Delight."* Jack had never had Ethiopian food before, especially not on the street from a silver cart with a yellow umbrella. But from where he was standing, it smelled good.

There was a young girl who looked to be in her mid-20's behind the counter and her name tag read *"Jahzara,"* She was about average height with a very dark complexion. Her eyes were dark brown with a sparkle, and she had very smooth skin. Her hair was black and pulled back into a ponytail. She smiled at Jack as he approached. Jack read her name tag and said, "Well Jahzara, what is your special today?" She had a distinct accent, Jack figured it was probably Ethiopian. She said,

"Well sir, we don't usually have a special, but please pick something from the menu, I will make it special for you." Jack smiled; he had no idea what any of the items on the menu were. He looked about halfway down the menu and picked an item that he couldn't even pronounce. Jahzara took an aluminum tray with three divided spaces and filled each one with something different. One of the spaces was filled with some squishy injera, like sourdough with veggies on top, and another space had what looked like a lentil stew and collard greens, and the largest space was filled with yellow rice, beef, and some kind of sauce. Jack truly enjoyed the variety of different ethnic foods in the city, and he was about to experience one that he had not tried before. Jahzara put the tray along with a plastic fork and knife in a napkin in front of Jack and said that will be $9. He pulled out a $20 bill and gave it to her and said, "Keep the change, Jahzara." She smiled a big smile. Her teeth were white as ivory, and she said, "Thank you, sir, please come again," He smiled and said, "Maybe I will Jahzara, maybe I will."

The food seemed very spicy, and he didn't want to smell up his car, so he found an empty bench on the sidewalk and sat down and ate his meal. This food was a treat for his senses. He took in the aroma and his mouth began watering before the first bite. Every bite seemed more delicious than the one before and the three courses seemed to complement each other. Jack loved to support the street vendors and he made a mental note to come back soon.

He got back into his Mustang and put Audrey Linn's address into his GPS, and he followed the directions that the woman with the English accent gave from the GPS unit. About an hour later he was in Fort Lee on Bellemeade Avenue, directly in front of Audrey Linn's house. It was a quaint neighborhood, and the house was a small yellow and white brick house with a very small yard in front, and a small walkway up to the front door. Jack got out of his car and walked up to the front door and knocked three or four times and then he stood back and waited. About 15 seconds later the door opened and a young woman said, "Can I help you?" It was Audrey Linn. She was thirty something and very attractive even without makeup. She had shoulder-length brown wavy hair and hazel eyes with little specks of yellow. She stood about five foot 6 inches tall and had a very athletic build. Jack said, "Hi, my name is Jack Trane, and I'm working with the NYPD on a homicide case, and I'd like to ask you a few questions if you don't mind." Audrey looked a bit shocked, she said, "Homicide! Did someone get murdered? Why do you want to talk to me?" Jack smiled and said, "Now relax, Audrey, this is regarding the murder of Heinrich King. I just thought that you might have some insight that would be useful on this case." Audrey raised one suspicious eyebrow and said, "Do you have a badge?" Jack handed her the card that said, "NYPD consultant." She said, "What's this? This is not a badge." Jack was irritated. He knew that this flimsy card would get him no respect. He said, "Look Audrey, I'm a special consultant with the NYPD and I've been hired to close this case. Can I come in and ask you a few questions?" She slowly opened the door while she was squinting at Jack and said, "OK, you can come in."

Jack entered the house and immediately he found himself in the living room. There was a maroon-colored couch against one wall and an easy chair at the far end of the room and some artsy pictures decorating the walls. There was also a TV on one wall and a gray tabby cat on the windowsill staring Jack down like he was about to be his next meal. Jack sat on the couch and immediately the cat sprang from the window and sat next to Jack on the couch. Audrey smiled and said, "Don't mind him, he doesn't usually take to people. You must be a cat person." Jack smiled and said, "Well that would be up to the cat. What's his name?" Audrey smiled and said, "It's Lenny." Lenny's ears perked up when he heard his name, then he put his face back down on Jack's lap. Jack awkwardly petted the cat as he tried to interrogate Audrey. He said, Audrey, I understand that you worked in the theater for a few years. She looked at the wall but appeared to be looking in a distance, and she said in a low, sorrowful voice, "Yes, I worked on Broadway for 3 years and about 6 months ago, I was fired." Her voice got louder. "I was fired for spilling coffee on Heinrich King. It was an accident. It's not like anyone got killed. I spilled a little coffee on the ugliest suit ever made, and Heinrich King tossed me out like a day-old tuna fish sandwich." Jack raised one eyebrow, he said, "I'll bet that made you pretty mad." Audrey regained her composure. She said, "Mr. Trane, what Heinrich King did to me was unfair, undeserved, and just plain mean. I'm sorry, but the man deserved what he got. I know a lot of other people in the theatre that he fired too for no good reason. I'm sure they all feel the same way I do." Jack was grimacing a little. The cat was now sitting on Jack's lap and his claws were working Jack's legs as he was purring loudly. Jack forced a smile and said, "Well, that leads me to my last question, "Where were you on the night that he was murdered?" Audrey had been standing in front of Jack through-out his questioning, but now backed up as she looked at Jack, and sat down. She looked calm and comfortable in the easy chair. With almost no expression she said, "I was out with a few friends that night from 7:00 PM to about 1:00 AM." Jack tried to remove the cat from his lap, but its claws were attached to his pants, so he let him stay and petted him a little more. He thought to himself, "Her alibi is almost the same exact story as what Marie Robbin had given him. What are the odds of these two birds having the same story on the tip of their tongues?" He wasn't surprised, he suspected that there was some sort of conspiracy at play. But he just didn't know how many suspects that the conspiracy would include.

Audrey stood up and lifted the cat from Jack's lap. She put Lenny back on the windowsill and came back to speak with Jack. She said, "Look, Mr. Trane, I didn't kill Heinrich King. I went over all this with that other detective, I think his name was Wisp" Jack smiled, and the cat made his way back onto his lap. He said, "Yes, you mean detective Watts. Audrey agreed, "Yes, Detective Watts." Jack smiled, "OK, Audrey, I'm just trying to tie up a few loose ends here, and you've been very helpful. If I need anything else, we'll be in touch." Jack tried to remove Lenny again from his lap but once again his claws were clinging to his pants. Audrey removed Lenny and held him close. Both she and the cat looked at Jack with squinted eyes. Jack got up from the couch and brushed off the cat hair from his pants and made his way over to the door. He could tell that Audrey was just as suspicious of him as he was of her. He said, "Goodbye Lenny." Then he waved to Audrey and left the house. He was sure there was more here than meets the eye, but he still had to interview Victoria Pichettes and Siobhan Peison to get the whole story.

Jack got back into his car and started driving back to the city. He pulled out his cellphone and dialed Trudy's number. The phone rang three or four times and then Trudy answered, "Hello, Jack, did you solve the case? Are you on your way to the office with my $2500?" Jack rolled his eyes, "Come on Trudy, I'm going to need all the information for the next person on the list, Victoria Pichettes. If you can text it to my phone, that would be great." Just then his cellphone dinged, he looked down and all the information for Victoria Pichettes had already been sent by Trudy. Jack shook his head, "Trudy, your amazing!" Trudy was a little smug, "I know Jack, it's a gift. What can I say?" She was giggling a little. Jack was still a little concerned because of his run-in with the blue Subaru WRX earlier in the day and his little altercation with the man in the dark shirt who wore the garnet pinkie ring. So, he asked

Trudy, "Have you noticed anything suspicious around the office today? He was hoping to hear no. But that's not what he heard. Trudy sat up in her chair, she said. "Now that you mention it, Jack, there was something a little weird this afternoon. That detective Danny Watts came by looking for you. He said that he had something that he wanted to talk to you about and he wanted to know when you would be in. I told him that I didn't know, but I would let you know that he was looking for you." Jack broke in, "That punk. I wonder what he wants?" Trudy continued, "Then about a half an hour later, about 2 o'clock, I was just sitting at my desk, doing my background checks, and I saw a small manilla envelope come sliding under the door. But I didn't open it, Jack. It has your name on it. I just put it on your desk. I figured that if it was important, they would have come in and handed it to me. So, it's on your desk, you can check it in the morning."

Jack pulled the car over to the side of the road. He had a serious look on his face and had a sober tone, he said, "Trudy, I want you to open the envelope and tell me what's inside." Trudy made a face like she was in pain. She got up and went into Jack's office and brought the small manilla envelope back to her desk and opened it. She read the words to herself, and her mouth just hung open. On the other end of the line Jack was speaking, "Trudy, what does it say?" It was just a plain piece of white paper and there were words written in *black sharpie*. Trudy spoke slowly into the phone, "It says, **DROP THIS CASE, NO MORE WARNINGS!**" Trudy's hands were shaking a little. She had been in tight spots before because of Jack's taking on sensitive cases and she wasn't looking forward to being shot at, abducted, or threatened. On the other end of the line, Jack was now sweating a little under the brim of his hat. He wondered to himself, "Could Danny Watts be trying to scare him off this case? Of could it be the man in the dark shirt with the garnet pinkie ring?" There were more suspects to this case than he could keep track of.

He was concerned that Trudy would possibly be in danger since she was alone in the office. He said, "Trudy, remember that pepper spray that I gave you this morning?" Trudy pulled it out of her bag. She said, "Yeah, what about it, Jack?" He said, "I want you to keep it next to you on your desk. Lock the office door and don't let anyone in. I'll be there in about 40 minutes and I'm going to take you home, just to be safe." Trudy rolled her eyes, "Yeah, Jack, I've heard that before, you're going to pick me up in 20 minutes. You never show up and I get kidnapped." Jack put his car in gear and pulled into traffic. He said, "No, I mean it, Trudy. Just lock the door and wait for me. I'll be there in 35 minutes." Trudy was snapping her gum. She said, "OK Jack, but I don't know if $2500 is enough for this case, you might have to throw in a Weekend in the Hamptons." Jack was shaking his head, "Very funny, Trudy. Just sit tight and I'll be there in 30 minutes." They both hung up the phone and Jack concentrated on his driving.

Thirty minutes later Jack ran up the stairs to his office. He put in the key and unlocked the door. As he walked into the office, he saw Trudy standing behind the door with the pepper spray pointed at his face. He screamed, "Trudy, It's me! Don't spray!" Trudy lowered the pepper spray and said, "I've been freaking out here, Jack. What's going on?" Jack shook his head and said, "I'm not certain, but I just want to make sure that you're out of harm's way. There is this guy I keep running into with a dark shirt and he wears a garnet ring on his pinky. I'm not sure what his angle is. Then there was a blue Subaru WRX chasing me today. The Subaru crashed, but when I passed the wreck, the driver was gone. And then this note is pretty much the same message that I received yesterday at my apartment. One thing is for sure Trudy, someone wants us off this case. I'm just not sure who it is or how far they are willing to go to make that happen."

Trudy looked concerned, but she gave Jack a little smile, "I guess it's about time to close the office for today, right?" Jack smiled, "I want you to drive home in your car and I'm going to follow you just to make you that you get there safely. When you get home, lock your door, and don't let anyone in, and keep the pepper spray handy. If anything looks suspicious, just call me, and I'll be over." Trudy rolled her eyes, she said, "Jack, who do you think is after us, The Boston Strangler?" He looked at her with one eyebrow raised. She said, "Come on Jack, someone is probably just trying to scare us. Why don't we just quit for the day? I have like ten people on the list checked out. We can get a fresh start in the morning. You can pick me up and we can do some investigating together. What do you say, Jack?" He shook his head, "I don't know if that's such a good idea, Trudy." She pointed her finger at Jack and said, "Look, Jack, you said that I could come out into the field on this case, and I'm coming." Jack pursed his lips and said, "Ok, Trudy, Ok. I'll pick you up in the morning and we'll interrogate one suspect, and then I'm bringing you back home. You can work from there." Trudy was smiling from ear to ear. "Yeah Jack, that's what I'm talking about. I've been watching *Columbo*. I think I have the technique down. *Just one more thing*." Jack shook his head and said, "Let's go, *Columbo*, we're going to get you home so you can watch another episode or two before I pick you up tomorrow morning." They left the office and they each got into their cars and Jack followed Trudy home and made sure she was safe. He had another piece of business to take care of. He needed to clear up a few things. He was on a mission to see detective Danny Watts

As Jack drove through the streets of New York City, he could feel his blood pressure rising like a storm inside a volcano. There was no way to tell if Danny was behind these threatening notes, but Jack was going to get his feeling across anyway. He pulled into the police station parking lot and parked his car in the visitor spot. He pulled out his cellphone and dialed up the number for the precinct. When the operator answered he asked for Danny Watts. The connection went through, and Danny answered, "Detective Watts." Jack spoke with clenched teeth, he said, "Danny, this is Jack Trane. You wanted to see me today, well I'm outside the precinct and now I want to see you. I think it's best that you come out rather than me going in." Danny spoke loudly into the phone, "I'll be right out." That was Danny Watts, impulsive and cocky. Jack got out of his car and waited near the steps to the precinct. Danny Watts came through the door and walked towards Jack. Jack let Danny reach the bottom of the stairs and then got close so that he was in Dany's face. Jack's temper was rising, his face was red, and his teeth were clenched. He said, "Look Danny, I don't know if you're behind those threatening notes that I've been getting, but I'm warning you right now, you stay out of my way, and I don't want to see you again until this case is solved. You got that Watts?" Danny backed up. He looked at Jack with a puzzled look and said, "What are you talking about Trane? I went down to your office today to offer you a little help. But it sounds like you've been catching a little heat from someone else. You know what they say Trane; If you can't take the heat, get out of the kitchen." Danny let out a laugh. Jack was not laughing. He had a serious look on his face, he said, "You'd like me to drop this case, wouldn't you Danny? Because when I solve this case, it's going to make you look like the incompetent fool that you are." Danny's face was getting red, he said, "You got a lot of nerve talking to me like that you 2-bit half-rate gumshoe. I ought to take you apart right here and feed you to the pigeons." Jack laughed, "I love to see you try Danny. I'd love to see you try."

Danny made a gesture at Jack and Jack just glared back at Danny with squinted eyes. Danny yelled at Jack as he returned up the stairs to the precinct, "You're in over your head Trane. You'll never solve this case!" Jack smiled, "When I do, you'll be the first to know, Danny." Jack laughed to himself and got back into his car. He still didn't know if Danny was behind the threatening messages, but at least Danny now knew that Jack wasn't playing any games and that he was determined to solve this cold case.

It was getting late, and Jack was getting hungry. He started his Mustang and headed over to *Big Jim's Sports Bar* for a bite to eat and maybe a little light conversation. And one out of two wouldn't be bad.

CHAPTER 7

Jack rolled over in bed and let out a silent groan. He looked over at the clock and it read 8:30 AM. Usually, he set the alarm for 8:00 AM but he had stayed out a little longer than he planned at *Big Jim's* last night and had a couple more *Guinness* than he should have and now he was paying the price. His head was groggy, and his body ached. The night before always seems like a good idea until the day after. Jack wasn't getting any younger and each year it always seemed to take a little longer to recover than the year before. While he was lying there on his back looking up at the ceiling, he started thinking about the man with the garnet pinkie ring. He wondered if he was the one behind all the threatening notes. He also wondered if he was behind the wheel in the WRX that had chased him the day before. Whoever was behind these things seemed to have escalated their efforts and Jack didn't expect them to give up without a fight. And that's what Jack was preparing for, the fight. He wondered when he was going to run into the man with the garnet pinkie ring again. He was pretty sure that he was going to find out soon enough.

He got out of bed and made his way to the bathroom for his morning ritual. The bones in his feet made a creaking sound as he walked and the muscles in his back alternated between twitching and a stabbing pain, but Jack accepted this as part of his job. After all the hits, falls, poundings, and battles he had been in over the past 25 years, this was just par for the course. When he had finished showering and shaving, he walked over to his walk-in closet to find something to wear.

He reached into the closet and stretched in as far as he could, but he just couldn't seem to reach any pants. He squeezed his way into the closet, and he could see a pair of brown dockers hanging there just out of his reach. He forced his way in just a little further, reached up, and grabbed the dockers. He also found a yellow paisley tie on the floor, and he picked it up. Behind the door there was a brown jacket hanging, he grabbed that too. He got out of the closet and walked over and dropped his clothes on the bed. He walked over to his armoire, and took out a pristine white button-down collar shirt, and he dropped that on the bed too. He put on the pants, but they were about a size too big for him, and the back pockets were a bit oversized. It was late so Jack just put them on and figured that he could just tighten his belt to keep them up. He put on his shirt and tie. Then he put on his custom shoes, the ones with the knife blades in the heels. He grabbed his jacket and put his brass knuckles in the jacket pocket. He picked up his cellphone and wallet from his end table. He put his cellphone in the inside jacket pocket, and he put his wallet in the right front pocket of his pants, then he left his apartment.

Jack came down the stairs and opened the door to the street outside. It was a nice bright sunny day in the city. The first breath of fresh air was enough to let him know that if he was going to drink more than 2 *Guinness* after a meal, there was going to be a price to be paid. He shook the cobwebs out of his head and continued walking towards the *Coffee Café*. He figured that today was a good day to eat light, no blueberry pancakes this morning. He stopped in at the newsstand for the morning paper. Nicky was behind the counter and gave Jack the customary grunt and Jack dropped the usual $2 on the counter and left. As he walked down the street, he continued to scan the people on both sides of the street. He was expecting to see the man with the garnet pinkie ring appear anytime. He made his way to the *Coffee Café*, opened the door, and saw Betty standing by the cash register. He yelled out, "Good Morning, Sunshine." Betty smiled and said, "Sounds like the rooster is out of the pen." Betty enjoyed Jack's compliments and looked forward to their morning banter. Every blond hair on Betty's head was in place and her makeup was flawless. Jack laughed as he made his way to a table. He looked Betty's way and said, "I think this rooster needs a Vanilla Latte to start his day." Betty walked over to the table and looked closely at Jack. She bent over and peered into his face and said, "Tough night Jack? You don't look so good this morning." Jack rubbed his eyes, he said, "That's OK, Betty, you're still looking good." She hit him with her towel and said, "What else can I get you, Jack?" He said, "How about just an English muffin with some strawberry jam on the side?" Betty's eyes opened wide. She said, "I guess it was a tough night. Would you like an extra shot of espresso in your Latte?" Jack smiled and said, "Betty you read my mind." She hit him again with her towel and went in the back to place his order.

Jack opened his paper and started to read the headlines. He began reading the top story on page 1, but out of the corner of his eye, he saw a dark figure pass by the window that overlooks the street. To Jack, it appeared that it was the man with the dark shirt and garnet pinkie ring. The dark figure passed by the window very quickly, but Jack was sure that it was him. He quickly jumped up from his chair, the chair fell over, and Jack ran towards the door. He opened the door and looked down the street, but the man with the garnet pinkie ring was nowhere in sight. There was no one on the street at all. It was empty. Either he disappeared down an alley or went into a building, or it wasn't him at all. Jack thought to himself, "I must be getting paranoid." He shook his head and went back into the *Café*. Betty looked at Jack with a puzzled face and asked, "Jack did you need some fresh air, or was it something I said? You ran out of here like you were on fire!"

Jack composed himself. He said, "No, I just thought that I saw some-one that I knew." Betty smiled, "You're such a man of mystery, Jack." He was nodding his head up and down with a half-smile and said, "What can I say, Betty, I guess I'm just a puzzle waiting to be solved." Betty smiled, "I like jigsaw puzzles, Jack." They both laughed. Betty brought his English muffins to the table along with a small cup of strawberry jam and put them in front of Jack. The aroma from the muffins and jam filled the air. He looked at the muffins and said, "Smells really good." Betty smiled and said, "Thanks Jack, they call it *Beautiful, by Estee Lauder*, you like it?" Jack laughed, then he smiled and said, "It fits you, Betty. It brings out the subtle you." They both laughed and Betty went back behind the counter.

About 10 minutes later Jack had finished his muffins and took the last sip of his Latte. He put the cup down on the table and let out a long exhale. Betty came over with the bill and put it on the table in front of Jack. His order came to $10. He took a $20 out of his pocket and handed it to Betty. He said, "Have a good day, Sunshine." She smiled and hit him with her washcloth and said, "Thanks, Jack. You're the best." Jack gave Betty a wink and said, "That's what I keep telling everyone." They both laughed and Jack left the *Café*. It was about 10:00 AM and Jack knew that he was late. He was supposed to pick up Trudy at 9:00 AM and they were going to interview Victoria Pichettes this morning. Trudy always gave Jack a hard time for being late and today was not going to be any different. He pulled out his cellphone and dialed up Trudy's number. The phone rang about three times and Trudy picked up. "Jack, where are you? I've been waiting for over an hour. You didn't skip out on me and do the interview by yourself did you?" Jack spoke in a calm voice, "Relax Trudy, I'm just running a little late. Just sit tight and I'll be there in about 20 minutes." Jack could picture her rolling her eyes, and she said, "Yeah, right, 20 minutes. I might as well put on a movie and make some popcorn. I know what your 20 minutes are like!" Jack reassured her, "Really Trudy, I'll be there in 20 minutes. Why don't you time me?" He could hear her snapping her gum. She said, "Starting right now." And she hung up the phone.

He picked up his pace and walked towards the garage that his car was parked in. He was almost jogging but he got to the garage in 10 minutes. He entered the garage and gave Fernando, the attendant, a quick wave, and Fernando waved back. He went over to the vending machine on the far wall, put in his card and his car keys came down a chute. He put the keys in his pocket and walked briskly up the ramp to his car in the dimly lit garage. As he got close to his car, he thought that he heard footsteps behind him. Like the scuffing of shoes on the pavement. Before he could turn around, he saw a bright light, there was a sudden pain in the back of his head, and then he hit the floor.

When Jack opened his eyes, he didn't recognize his surroundings. He was on his back staring straight up at a ceiling. It was a very dimly lit area with small lightbulbs dotted across the ceiling. His head was resting on what seemed to be a hard metal bar and his feet too were resting on something that was hard metal. Then he realized that his hands and his feet were both bound with zip ties and the metal bar under his head and underneath his feet were giving off vibrations. Then it all came into focus. He was tied up on the train tracks in the subway and vibrating tracks meant that a train was coming his way. Jack was usually a pretty cool customer but picturing himself cut into three pieces brought an overwhelming feeling of panic. He couldn't really use his hands or feet, so he sat up and rolled himself off of the tracks. He was face down on the ground and the smell of rail oil filled his nose. He could see that there was not much room between the train tracks and the wall. If the train was to come by, he would surely be crushed between the train and the wall. He looked up and he could see the train coming around the bend about two hundred feet away. The bright light on the front of the train was blinding. He managed to get to his feet and began hopping along the tracks in the opposite direction of the train. As he was hopping, he noticed a little opening in the wall where the maintenance men enter the tracks to make repairs and do inspections. The train was approaching fast. The sound of the train echoing off the walls was all Jack could hear. He continued hopping and he made it to the door opening just before the train approached, and he stuffed himself into the opening as far as he could. It got very dark, and Jack could feel the stiff breeze on his back as the train passed by. It lasted for about 15 seconds and then the train was gone and now there was just silence. Jack felt an overwhelming sense of relief. He sat there for a minute trying to process everything that had just happened. And now his mind began to focus on getting out of the subway and finding out who was behind this.

As he sat there in the small opening, he kicked his heel against the sidewall and one of the knife blades came out of his heel and rested on the ground. He picked it up with his two hands and cut through the zip tie on his feet. He stood up and wedged the knife blade in the door jam. Then he cut the zip ties off of his hands and put the blade back into his shoe. He opened the door and went through and found himself in the backroom of the subway station. It was just an empty room with a few lockers on one wall. There was no one else there, but there was a door on the far side of the room. Jack went out the door and found himself on a deserted section of East 51st Street. Whoever had hit Jack, must have dragged him here and put him on the tracks in an attempt to get rid of him and make this Broadway cold case go away once and for all. Jack was perplexed, he didn't know for sure who was behind this, but he was 99.9% sure that the man with the garnet pinkie ring was somehow involved.

Jack got his head together and walked a couple of blocks until he saw a taxi and he hailed it down. His hat was gone, and he had a painful bump on the back of his head, but his clothes were no worse for the wear. That was one of the reasons that he never updated his wardrobe. His clothes took a beating, and he still had a nice crease in the front of his pants. He would never win any awards for his attire, but he took pride in his clothes being as tough as he was. A taxi pulled over and Jack got in. The driver looked to be of Spanish descent, in his early 30's with a thin mustache. There was a name tag over his head that read, "Chico Mendez." He had on a denim shirt and a black leather cap. Chico said to Jack, "Where to man?" Jack gave him the address for his parking garage. Chico said, "No problem, man. You want the scenic route, man?" Jack smiled; he knew how the cab drivers made money by driving tourists all over the city. He said, "No Chico, I live in the city. The last thing I need is the scenic route. Do you think you can get me to the parking garage in 10 minutes or less?" Chico looked straight ahead, and he pulled down the lever for the meter. He said, "I'm on it, man, it's go time." Chico stepped on the gas, Jack's head snapped back, and they swerved into the middle traffic lane. Chico was stopping, starting, and weaving so fast, Jack felt like he was on a speed boat in a riptide. But he didn't complain because he needed to get back as fast as possible. In fact, he didn't even know what time it was. He remembered telling Trudy at 10 o'clock that he would be there in 20 minutes. He looked down at his watch and it was now 1:30 PM. Jack had lost 3 hours in his latest ordeal. He pulled out his cellphone and noticed about ten text messages from Trudy. They all said the same thing "**Where are you, Jack!**" He knew that Trudy was going to give him a hard time, but at least this time he had a good excuse.

As Chico was negotiating the streets of the city like a rat in a maze, Jack took out his cellphone and dialed Trudy's number. The phone rang twice, and Trudy answered. "Jack, where have you been? I've been waiting for like 3 hours. I texted you a bunch of times! What's your excuse this time?" Jack hesitated for a minute and said, "I was tied up and almost run over by a train." In the front seat, Chico's head turned back to look at Jack when he heard what Jack was saying to Trudy. The look on Chico's face was one of total disbelief. He smiled and went back to driving the cab. Trudy's eyes opened wide when Jack said that he was almost run over by the train. She said, "Are you OK, Jack? You're not just making that up because you're so late, are you?" Jack spoke in a calm voice. "No, Trudy, I got hit on the head in the parking garage, I think by the man with the garnet pinkie ring, and he tied me up and put me on the train tracks in the subway. I'm pretty sure that he was trying to rub me out." Trudy was concerned. She said, "Oh my, Jack. Do you think this case is worth the $5000?" Jack's voice got louder. He said, "I don't care if it was only $5 bucks. I'm going to solve this case and I'm going to take care of the scum that trying to stop us." Trudy sounded nervous, "Ok, Jack. If you say so. Are you still coming to pick me up?" Jack calmed down, he said, "I'll be at your apartment in about 30 minutes. Be ready because we're going to get to the bottom of this or else!" Trudy hesitated a little. She said, "Ok, Jack. I'll be ready." She was not so sure that the $2500 coming her way was worth being tied up to any train tracks. They both hung up the phones and Jack relaxed in the back seat of the cab.

Chico was driving with one hand on the wheel, and he turned back and looked at Jack with a smile and one eye closed. He said, "Hey man, you really had your lady going." Jack smiled and said, "Well, she not really my lady" Chico turned back towards the steering wheel. He said, "Yeah, whatever, man. But that was really smooth. I'm going to try that on my lady. Tied up in a subway, almost hit by a train. That's dope, man. Your lady must be pretty sweet." Jack was shaking his head,

"Look, Chico, she's not my lady, and I really was tied up in the subway this morning." Chico was laughing, "Yeah, of course, you were man. And I was dangling from the Empire State building." Jack was shaking his head in the back seat. Chico drove on through the city, shifting lanes, slamming on the brakes, stepping on the gas. Jack could hear Chico singing in a really low voice the words to *La Bamba,* "Para bailar la bamba se necesita una poca de gracia." It actually sounded pretty good. In about 10 minutes they arrived at the parking garage and Chico turned off the meter. He turned to Jack and said, "That will be $18.75, man." Jack pulled out his wallet and took out $30 and gave it to Chico. He said, "Thanks' for the pull Chico." Chico gave Jack a big smile and said, "Stay out of the subway, man." Then he laughed and pulled back into traffic.

Jack went into the parking garage and walked over to Fernando. He wondered if Fernando had seen anything from earlier this morning when he was knocked out and taken from the garage. Jack looked at Fernando with one eye half-closed and said, "Fernando, did you see me come into the garage earlier this morning?" Fernando wouldn't make eye contact with Jack. He was looking down at the floor. He said, "Mr. Trane, many people come into the garage every day. I can't keep track of everyone. I don't think I remember." Jack squinted at Fernando, and said, "Come on Fernando, I waved to you, you waved back." Fernando smiled sheepishly and said, "Mr. Trane, I wave at everybody, I'm a friendly guy." Jack was thinking to himself, "The man with the garnet pinkie ring must have gotten to Fernando and either threatened him or paid him off." Jack raised one eyebrow and asked Fernando, "What about your security camera? Can I take a look at your security camera data from this morning?" Fernando shook his head, "Oh, Mr. Trane, I'm sorry. The camera stopped working at about 9 o'clock this morning. We have a repairman coming in to look at it." Jack smiled, "That's pretty convenient Fernando. If I didn't know better, I would say that you're trying to hide something or someone from me." Fernando looked surprised, "I don't know what you're talking about, Mr. Trane. I'm just doing my job." Jack knew what was happening. Whoever was trying to squash this case, had gotten to Fernando too." Jack wasn't surprised.

Jack walked up the ramp to his car and saw his hat lying next to the front tire. He picked it up, dusted it off, and put it on. He opened the car door and got in. He sat in the car for a minute trying to piece things together. It was like trying to make a jigsaw puzzle in the dark. The pieces were all there, but he just couldn't see how they fit. He started the car and drove down the ramp. He looked at Fernando as he passed the attendant station and Fernando waved at Jack and opened the gate. Jack drove out of the garage and took a left onto the street. There was a pothole in the middle of the road and he couldn't avoid it. His right tire hit the pothole and then he heard a rattling coming from the front end of the car. It really bothered Jack when his car was not in tip-top shape. His car was an extension of himself. When the car was off, so was he. He continued driving, but every time he hit a bump, he could hear the rattle and he would shake his head. There was nothing he could do about it now, but it was first on his list of things to fix after this case was solved.

He pulled up in front of Trudy's apartment, it was just after 2 o'clock. He pulled out his cellphone to call Trudy, but she was already out the door on walking towards the car. She opened the door and got in. She looked at Jack and said, "Are you sure about this Jack? That thing in the subway kind of sends a pretty clear message, don't you think?" Jack was silently staring straight ahead, he said, "This is getting personal, Trudy. I'm not going to get scared off by a couple of threatening letters and a lame attempt to cut me into pieces on the train tracks. We must be getting close, otherwise, someone wouldn't be trying so hard to stop us." Trudy was just snapping her gum while she listened to Jack trying to convince himself that he was still in control. Trudy wasn't convinced.

CHAPTER 8

As Jack drove through the streets of New York City, there was a new sense of focus and determination in his voice. He stared straight ahead as if he was driving into a tunnel and he said to Trudy, "Victoria Pichettes, put her address into your GPS, and give me the directions." Trudy was a native New Yorker, and she didn't have any tolerance for rude speech, even though that's what New Yorkers are known for. She looked at Jack with one eye squinted and said, "Jack, I know you're upset, but would you care to rephrase that last demand into a friendly request?" Jack looked down at the steering wheel and then back up again, he didn't want to take out his frustration on Trudy. He said, "Look, I'm sorry Trudy. I didn't mean anything by it, I'm just really angry about what happened this morning and now my car is rattling. I didn't mean to take it out on you." Trudy smiled, she said, "That's OK Jack, no big deal, I know you didn't mean anything. I was just ragging on you." She had already put Victoria Pichettes' address into the GPS. She said Victoria Pichettes lives at 731 Coster Street in the Bronx." Jack smiled, "That's the Hunts Point section of South Bronx. I think I know where there's a Chinese Fried Chicken restaurant over there. Maybe after we see Victoria, we can stop in for something to eat. I totally missed lunch." Trudy was shaking her head and snapping her gum. She said, "Well Jack, I've never heard of Chinese Fried Chicken, but if you're buying, I'm flying." Jack gave Trudy a wink and he drove up First Avenue north until he got to the Willis Avenue Bridge. He crossed over the Harlem River and entered the South Bronx. He arrived at Victoria Pichettes address by 3:00 PM.

Jack found an open parking spot on the street and quickly pulled in. As he was parking the car, Trudy said, "OK, now Jack, you said that I could do the interview, so this one is mine, right?" Jack smirked as he pushed in the car's emergency brake. In a deep gravelly voice, he said, "Yes Boss, whatever you say." Trudy made a disgusted face. She said, "Come on Jack, I'm serious. I get to do the interrogation on this one. You said so." Jack smiled. "Ok Trudy, you get to ask all the questions on this one. But If I have something I need to say, I'm going to jump in, OK?" Trudy smiled with one eye squinted, she said, "Of course Jack, we're a team, right?" Jack smiled and nodded his head up and down. And they both got out of the car and started walking towards Victoria Pichettes' apartment.

The apartment was a 2-story brick building with three steps leading up to the front door. There was a bright yellow awning hanging over the door. They walked up the steps and Trudy looked at Jack, then she knocked on the door, four times with firm loud knocks. They waited for about 20 seconds, but no one came to the door. But Trudy was determined. She knocked again firmly, four times. They waited again for about 20 seconds, but this time the door opened about six inches and Jack and Trudy could see the nose, mouth, and one eye of the person behind the door. The voice came from the mouth behind the door, "Can I help you?" It was definitely a French accent. No doubt It was Victoria Pichettes. Trudy spoke up, she said, "Are you Victoria Pichettes?" The one eye behind the door squinted and the mouth opened and said, "That's right. Who are you and what do you want?" Trudy was very deadpan in her response, almost like Jack Webb in *Dragnet*. She said very bluntly, "We'd like to talk to you about the murder of Heinrich King." Jack thought to himself, "Real smooth Trudy. Why not just tell her where here to arrest her?" The voice behind the door spoke in a French accent, "Who are you? Do you have any identification?" Trudy looked at Jack and he pulled out the card that Harry had given him from the precinct. The door opened a little more and Jack handed the card to Victoria Pichettes. She took it and looked it at it with suspicion, the way a woman examines a bad head of lettuce in the produce aisle at the supermarket. It appeared that she had been cleaning her apartment. She was wearing a pair of well-worn denim jeans. Her hair was tied back into a ponytail, she had on a loose-fitting grey sweatshirt and a pair of old sneakers on her feet. She was still very attractive, and she had that look of a star in her soft blue eyes. After a couple of minutes of looking at the front and back of the card over and over again, she handed the card back to Jack with a suspicious look on her face. She hesitated and said, "OK, come in, but please wipe your feet, I just finished cleaning my apartment, I don't want you tracking in any dirt from this filthy city." Jack smiled and said, "Don't worry, the only dirt on us is yesterday's gossip." Jack smiled and he and Trudy went in.

They both wiped their feet on the welcome carpet just inside the door. Jack said, "Let me introduce myself, I'm Jack Trane of *Trane Investigations*, and this is Trudy, my associate. As my card said, we're consulting with the NYPD on some open cold cases, and we're investigating the death of Heinrich King." Victoria Pichettes handed Jack back his card and said, "Well I already told that other detective Whip or something, everything I know. That was about 5 months ago, and I don't much care about the death of Heinrich King. What do you think about that?" Jack smiled, he said, "Oh yes, you mean detective Watts. Well, you see, we're just..." Trudy broke in. "Victoria, we have reason to believe that all the facts of this case have still not been uncovered, so we just wanted to ask you a few questions to tie up some loose ends. This shouldn't take very long." Victoria made a disgusted face and said in her French accent, "I suppose I can give you some of my time, but

76

I'd like to pin a medal on the person who killed Heinrich King." Jack looked at Victoria with one eyebrow raised and said, "I take it, he wasn't your *Meilleur ami*? Victoria looked at Jack with almost no expression and said, "He was no one's friend." Trudy looked at Jack with a stink eye. This was her interrogation and Jack was stepping all over it. Jack looked back at Trudy and shrugged his shoulders. Trudy looked at Victoria and said, "Perhaps we could all sit down for a few minutes and relax. Victoria said, "Of course, follow me."

Victoria led them down a small hallway into what appeared to be her living room. It was very tastefully decorated with a Tessa Sapphire Blue tufted French sofa at one end of the room with matching armchairs positioned close to each side of the sofa. In the middle of the floor, there was an unusual oriental rug with floral patterns. There was also a coffee table in front of the sofa with some type of elephant figurine covered with what looked like precious gems. Victoria pointed to the sofa and said, "Please sit down." Jack and Trudy sat on the sofa and Victoria sat on the chair to their left. Trudy pulled out a small black pad from her purse and Jack started to make small talk, "This is a nice place you have here, Victoria…" Then Trudy broke in with her *Dragnet* voice. "Ahem…Well Victoria, maybe you can tell us, just what was your relationship with Heinrich King?" Victoria sat there for a minute in silence just staring back at Trudy with very little expression on her face. She said, "Relationship? There was no relationship! That good-for-nothing piece of theatre trash got me blacklisted from Broadway. He was a vile man; I doubt that he could have a relationship with anyone but himself." Jack sat there with his legs crossed as his focus went from Victoria back to Trudy. Trudy wrote down a few notes on her pad and then she looked up at Victoria and said, "Victoria, how is it that Heinrich King got you blacklisted from Broadway?" Victoria made a disgusted face, then she responded, "You want to know how he blacklisted me? You want to know? I'll tell you how." Then Victoria got up from her chair and walked over to a small refrigerator tucked into a corner of the room. She opened the door and pulled out a bottle of wine. It was a *Chateau Rouget Pomerol* 2014. She took a glass out of the rack on the side of the refrigerator and poured herself a glass. She came back and sat down on the chair to the left of Trudy. She took a long sip and said, "My dear, I had paid my dues working long hours in the theatre in France. I sharpened my craft until I knew that I was ready for the American theater. I worked for 5 years in small productions outside of Broadway and finally, I was offered a chance to perform a leading role on the Broadway stage in the new play, *"Taking Care of Business."* Jack chimed in, "Yeah, I've heard of that play, it's supposed to be really good." Both Trudy and Victoria looked at Jack with squinted eyes and he shrunk back into his seat on the couch. Victoria took a sip of her wine and said, "May I continue?" Trudy looked at Jack again, then turned back to Victoria and said, "Please do." Victoria continued to relate her story. She said, "I was invited up to Heinrich King's office to sign a contract for my employment. At least that's what I thought was going to happen, but when I got there, Mr. King had other things on his mind. From the minute that I walked into his office, he made me feel dirty. He had his hands all over me. I kicked him and hit him, and I told him that he had no right to treat me this way. Then I crushed his smelly old cigar right on his ugly face. I walked out of his office and then I was notified by my agent that the part in the show went to someone else. I have not received any calls from Broadway since."

There was an awkward silence in the room, but not for long as Jack broke it. He leaned forward and said, "It sounds like you really have some good reasons to dislike "King Heini" since he got you blacklisted from Broadway and all, but I can't help but notice, that it looks like you've done pretty well for yourself anyway. You must

78

have gotten some very good Off-Broadway roles to keep this place furnished." Victoria stood up and looked at Jack with contempt and said, "I beg your pardon, Mr. Trane. Just what are you suggesting?" Trudy kicked Jack's leg and said, "Relax Victoria, Jack didn't mean anything by that. I'm sure he was just complimenting you on your taste." Trudy looked at Jack with squinted eyes. Victoria sat back down and took a sip of her wine. Trudy cleared her throat and in her dead-pan delivery said, "Victoria, would you know of anyone who would have reason to kill Heinrich King?" Victoria broke out in a long hard laugh. She composed herself and looked at Trudy in the eyes and said in a slow deliberate delivery, "My dear, everyone I know had reason to kill Heinrich King." Then she sat back and laughed again. Jack now kicked Trudy in the leg. She knew what he wanted her to ask next. She leaned forward and asked, "Victoria, where were you on the night he was found murdered?" Victoria didn't move; she said, "I was out with some friends from 7:00 PM to 1:00 AM just like I said to that other detective. I'm sure my friends will back me up on this." Jack chimed in, "I'm sure they will Tori. I'm sure they will." Trudy raised one eyebrow and asked, "Victoria, is there anything else about that day that you can remember that might lead us to a clue as to who killed Heinrich King? Victoria took another sip of her wine and said, "I'm really sorry my dear, but there is nothing else I can tell you. Heinrich King is dead, and the world is a better place." She just stared at Trudy and Jack with no expression on her face.

After another awkward silence, Jack stood up and said, "Well thank you for your time, Victoria, I'm sure that all this has been very helpful. I guess we'll be leaving now." Trudy said, "If you think of anything else that might be helpful in bringing this case to a close, please give us a call." Trudy handed Victoria a business card for Trane Investigations. Victoria said, "Yes, dear, you'll be the first one I call."

Victoria chuckled a little and led Jack and Trudy to the door. Trudy shook Victoria's hand, and they left the apartment and walked to the car. Jack and Trudy got into the car and as both doors closed, Trudy said to Jack, "How did I do? I think I had her reeling when I asked where she was on the night of the murder. I see why you like this stuff Jack, that was quite a rush." Jack was smiling and shaking his head. He said, "Relax Trudy. You did great. But we're really no closer to solving this case than we were before we went in. Victoria Pichettes is as good a suspect as all the other ones so far. In fact, this is starting to look more like a conspiracy all the time. I'll bet that there was a tidy little sum of money deposited to her bank account shortly after Heini King's murder." Trudy's eyes opened wide, she said, "Do you think so Jack? When we get back to the office, I'm going to check into that with my friend at the bank. Let's interview someone else. I really think I'm getting the hang of this now." Jack smiled and laughed and said, "Why don't we just get some Chinese Fried Chicken and think about our next move." Trudy looked at Jack and licked her lips, "Sounds good to me Jack, let's get us some Chinese Fried Chicken."

As Jack put the car in gear and drove off into traffic, he hit a small bump and he heard the rattle in his front end again. He turned to Trudy and said, "Did you hear that? This city should pay for all the damage caused by these potholes!" Trudy laughed, "Yeah sure Jack. When we get back to the office, I'll fill out a form for your engine rattle and all my broken heels and I'll send it to the mayor's office." Jack shook his head, "I'm serious Trudy. The streets in this city are a mess." Trudy patted Jack's arm, she said, "Relax Jack, after some Chinese Fried Chicken, you'll feel much better." She squinted her eyes and said, "Old Chinse proverb says, *A gem is not polished without rubbing, nor is a man perfect without trials.*" Then she laughed. Jack smiled, "Very funny Trudy, now I know why I don't take you out in the field that much." He drove towards Bruckner Boulevard, but he noticed out of the corner of his eye a Chinese Fried Chicken place, it was called the *Happy Terrace*. He quickly pulled over and parked the car. It was a small storefront with a couple of tables and chairs on the street. Jack said to Trudy, "Why don't you stay out here, and I'll go in and order the food?" Trudy nodded and went to sit down at one of the tables. It was a nice sunny day and birds were chirping in the tree that was coming up through the sidewalk. Trudy brushed off one of the chairs and sat down and Jack went into the *Happy Terrace* to place their order.

Jack walked up to the counter and a young girl was waiting for his order. She had on a small white name tag that read, "Alix." She spoke very good English, but she was obviously of Chinese heritage. Jack smiled and said, "Well, Alix, I hear that you have some pretty spicy Fried Chicken here. I'd like two orders to go." Alix smiled a polite smile. She was small with jet black hair, which was pulled back into a ponytail. She said, "Coming right up." Jack waited at the counter for about 2 minutes and Alix placed a bag in front of him and said, "That will be $20.55. Jack pulled $30 out of his wallet and gave it to Alix and said, "Keep the change, my friend." Alix had a big smile on her face, she said, "Please come again." Jack smiled back and said, "Maybe I will Alix, maybe I will."

Jack brought the food outside and placed it on the table next to Trudy. Trudy opened the bag and her eyes got big and she had her mouth open. She could smell the aroma of the Chinese Spicy Fried Chicken and it filled her senses. She said, "Jack this smells incredible!" There were strips of chicken that looked like they were fried in teriyaki sauce and little cartons of fried rice with vegetables. They both had little Styrofoam boxes with their order in them. Trudy put a piece of chicken in her mouth and looked over at Jack. He had just put a piece of chicken in his mouth and they both had the same expression on their faces.

The chicken was spicy hot. Like Kung Pao on steroids. By the time they finished the chicken and the rice, they were both sweating from the spices in the chicken and the mixed rice. Trudy shook her head and said, "That was really awesome Jack, as long as it doesn't kill us." Jack laughed, "Come on Trudy, you're a minor leaguer. That wasn't even that hot. The next time we'll try some Thai food." Jack wiped the sweat off of his forehead and put on his hat. Jack stuffed all the trash into the bag that Alix had given him, and he placed the bag in the trash can next to the door. They both got back into the car and sat there for a few minutes digesting all the spicy chicken and rice. When Jack was ready, he started the car and pulled back into traffic. It was about 4:30 PM.

As Jack cruised down Bruckner Boulevard at about sixty miles per hour, he hit a small pothole and the rattle sound came from the front end again. He shook his head in disgust. He turned to Trudy and said, "Did you hear that?" Trudy smiled she said, "Jack, when I hit a bump, it sounds like there's a bucket of bolts in my trunk, just relax." Jack shook his head and focused on the road. He said, "OK, Trudy, our next stop is Siobhan Peison. Why don't you plug her address into your GPS?" Trudy clicked a few buttons and said, "She lives at 210 Dean Street in Brooklyn. The GPS says that we'll be there in 40 minutes with this traffic." Jack smiled, he said, "I'll bet I can make it in 30 minutes." Jack stepped on the gas and Trudy's head snapped back on the seat. Jack was weaving in and out of traffic and making good time. Trudy looked at Jack with a disgusted face and said, "Jack, if we're going to interrogate Siobhan Peison, I think we should do something about our breath. I feel like my mouth is on fire." Jack smirked, "Trudy, it's not like we're taking her out on a date, we're just going to ask her a few questions. What's the big deal? I never worry about my breath." Trudy looked at Jack with one eyebrow raised, "No kidding Jack, I hadn't noticed. That's probably why we can't grow any plants in the office."

Trudy laughed and Jack didn't. He said, "All right Trudy, I'll stop for some gum down on 135th Street, I know a place." Trudy smiled and said, "You will make a lot of people happy, Jack." Jack smiled a phony smile and took a right onto E 135th Street.

There was a small variety store on the first corner on E 135th Street, the *Millbury Deli, and Grocery*. There was a parking spot just across from the store, so Jack pulled in. He was about to get out of the car when he remembered that he had put a pack of gum in his glove box. He said to Trudy, "Check the glove box, I think that I put a pack of gum in there." Trudy pushed the button for the glove box to open and it made a double click. Jack thought to himself, "That's odd, I don't remember the sound of that click before." Trudy fished through the glove box and then looked over at Jack and said, "No gum Jack. Why don't you just run in and buy a pack of *Dentyne*?" Jack pursed his lips and said, "OK, I'll be right back." He opened the door and got out and started towards the *Millbury Deli and Grocery*. When he got about six steps away, he felt a warm sensation on the back of his head that ran all the way down his body. Suddenly he heard a loud blast, and a strong force threw him forward about 10 feet so that he found himself face down on the street. His ears were ringing from the explosion. All around him, there were shards of sharp metal pieces and strips of rubber, seemingly raining down from the sky. There were little bits of fabric floating in the air like snow. The air was filled with the scent of burning rubber and gasoline. He lifted his head, and he could see men and women on the opposite side of the street running and putting their hands over their heads for protection. Because of the blast he was dazed and little disoriented, but as almost by reflex he turned around and looked at where his car was parked. What he saw was a huge ball of fire with twisted metal all over the road. The flames seemed to engulf everything in his view. As the inferno grew higher, the yellow flames reflected from the store windows and cast shadows on the tall buildings. Thick black smoke rose into the air like a blast furnace. It all seemed like a dream like this wasn't really happening. Shock and panic overtook his mind. He felt helpless and he started to shake. He didn't know if he had suffered any severe injuries but in that moment his heart sank. He could only think of one thing. He screamed at the top of his voice "TRUDY, TRUDY!"

CHAPTER 9

As the thick smoke dissipated into the air Jack could see more clearly to the left of where the car had exploded. He saw what looked like a body lying next to the sidewalk curb. He took a deep breath and gathered himself and limped over to where the body was. On one hand, he was afraid to see who might be laying on the ground, but he had to know. He bent over and went down on one knee. He took a deep breath and looked down very carefully at the still body resting on the curb. He couldn't believe his eyes. It was Trudy and she appeared to be breathing. There was a scrape on one side of her face and a little blood coming from her nose and her eyes were closed, but Jack could see that her chest was moving up and down. She was breathing. He yelled, "Trudy! Can you hear me?" He reached down and stroked her head and said, "Trudy, are you OK?" Trudy opened one eye and said in a low weak voice, "Did you get the gum, Jack?" A tear came to Jack's eye. He said, "Trudy, I thought that I lost you, I'm so sorry this happened. Don't move, I'm going to call 911 and get an ambulance." Trudy gave Jack a weak smile. He didn't know how badly she was hurt, but he knew enough not to move her or try to make her sit up. Before he could dial 911, he could already hear the sounds of sirens coming in his direction. That's one thing about the city, the police, fire, and rescue are usually close, and they are always ready to roll.

Jack held Trudy's hand as the rescue vehicles arrived. He noticed his wallet on the ground next to Trudy's hand. He figured the blast must have dislodged it from his pocket and it must have landed next to Trudy. He picked it up and put it back in his front pocket. An EMT jumped out of an ambulance and ran towards Jack and Trudy. He was wearing a plain blue uniform with a white patch that said "PARA-MEDIC." He bent down and started to evaluate Trudy's injuries. Jack stood up and backed away. Another paramedic came over and asked Jack to come over to the rescue vehicle to be evaluated. He didn't want to leave Trudy alone, but he knew that he had no choice, the paramedic was just doing his job. Everything had happened so fast; Jack wasn't sure if he was injured or not, but he did have a loud ringing in his head. When Jack got to the rescue vehicle, the paramedic made him sit down on the runner on the side of the truck. Then he shined a light in Jack's eyes and moved the light from side to side. Then he asked Jack his name. Jack said, "Jack Trane." He asked Jack to stand up and balance on one leg. Jack stood up and balanced on his right leg and then quickly sat back down. The paramedic said, "it appears that you might have suffered a mild concussion. The paramedic asked him, "Are you experiencing any ringing in your head?" Jack half-smiled and said, "I'm hearing bells but no whistles, so I guess it's not that bad." Jack let out a little laugh, the paramedic didn't laugh. There were small cuts on the backs of his legs from some of the metal shards that exploded from the car and there was a small cut on his forehead from when he hit the pavement. The paramedic stitched up his forehead right there on the scene and put some bandages on the cuts on the back of his legs. Jack could tell that his back was out of alignment since he was feeling a little pain especially when he walked, but he didn't mention anything about that to the paramedic. Jack was trying to downplay his injuries so he could take care of more important things. He was still worried about Trudy. The paramedic said to Jack, "Looks like you were pretty fortunate buddy, this could have been much worse. I think that you should get to the hospital for a full evaluation." Jack nodded his head, he said, "Yeah, that sounds like a good idea." Jack had no plans of getting evaluated at the hospital. He said to the paramedic, "How is my assistant, Trudy? Is she going to be, OK? The paramedic just raised his eyebrows and shrugged. Jack looked over and he could see Trudy being loaded into an ambulance. He asked the paramedic, "What hospital are they taking her to?" The paramedic looked at Jack and said, "Mount Sinai down on Madison Avenue." Jack was ignoring his own pain; his concern was not for himself. He was consumed with guilt and concern over Trudy. His main focus right now was to get to the hospital to be with Trudy. He asked the paramedic, "Hey buddy, can you give me a ride to Mount Sinai? Since my car was just blown up, I have no way to get there." Just then a police officer in a blue uniform tapped Jack on the shoulder. He said, "Sir if that was your car that was just blown up, I'm going to need to ask you some questions." Jack did not want to answer any questions right now. His shoulders sagged as he walked over with the police officer and got into the front seat of the police cruiser.

Jack wanted to be at the hospital, the last thing he wanted to be doing, is wasting time, answering questions that he had no answers to. The police officer was standing outside the car and Jack's door was open. Jack could see the officer's name tag, it read "*Officer McGann.*" He was a middle-aged man in his early 50's, he had thick black hair and he was about thirty pounds overweight. Jack looked up and said, "Officer McGann, I'll answer all your questions, but do you think you could give me a ride over to Mount Sinai Hospital, that's where they took my assistant Trudy. She was hurt in the blast." Officer McGann looked closely at Jack and said, "First of all, what's your name?" Jack answered quickly, "My name is Jack Trane of Trane Investigations and I'm working with the NYPD on cold cases." Officer McGann nodded his head up and down. He said, "Oh, working with the NYPD. I'll tell you what. I'll give you a ride over to Mount Sinai, but along the way, you're going to tell me what happened here." Jack was nodding his head up and down. "Yeah, that's fine. Let's just get going towards Mount Sinai." Officer McGann got into the cruiser, started it up, and began driving in the direction of Mount Sinai Hospital with lights flashing but no siren.

As they were driving through the city streets, passing buildings, streetlights, and pedestrians, Jack was not taking in his surroundings. It was like traveling from one point to another without knowing how you got there. Maybe it was the concussion or maybe it was the fact that he was concerned about Trudy's condition, but he wasn't feeling like himself. He was in a bit of a fog, a little paranoid and he still had some ringing in his head. Jack was trying to piece everything together from the time he stopped and parked his car until the explosion. The blast had completely destroyed his car. He couldn't figure out how Trudy could still be alive. Officer McGann began asking questions. "So, tell me Mr. Trane who are you working with, in the department?" Jack shook his head to clear the cobwebs and looked over at the officer and said, "Harry Soul, a detective down at the 23rd precinct." Jack felt like he was being interrogated. Officer McGann continued, "What case are you working on?" Jack looked out the passenger window like he was staring into space and said, "The Broadway Murder." Officer McGann nodded his head, he said, "I remember that case. Made a lot of head-lines, but no one was ever arrested." Jack sneered and said sarcastically, "That's kind of why I'm working the case." Officer McGann raised one eyebrow and looked at Jack, he said, "So what are you doing in the Bronx? That's nowhere near Broadway?" Jack explained, "I was inter-rogating a suspect. I was on my way back to the city when we stopped for a pack of gum. I got out of the car and the next thing I know I'm face down on the ground, the car is in pieces, and the street looks like a war zone." Officer McGann said, "Hm..Hm..It appears like a pretty serious explosive was used to blow up your car. What do you know about that?" Jack rolled his eyes; he was getting frustrated with Officer McGann's questions. He said, "What do I know about that? I'll tell you what I know about that! I know that somebody is trying to kill me!" Officer McGann looked at Jack and said, "Relax Mr. Trane, I'm just trying to get all the facts. Now, who do you think is trying to kill you?" Jack looked over at Officer McGann with both eyebrows raised and said, "It's obvious that someone doesn't want me to solve this case. There was an attempt on my life this morning and I believe the same person tried to rub me out this afternoon. I'm being followed by a tall thin man who usually dresses in black, and he wears a garnet ring on his right pinkie finger." Officer McGann looked surprised, he said, "Someone tried to kill you this morning? Are you sure?" Jack rolled his eyes again, he said, "Officer McGann, if someone knocked you out, tied you up, and left you on the subway tracks, wouldn't you say that they were trying to kill you?" Officer McGann looked confused, he said, "Mr. Trane, did you report this incident to the police?" Jack looked exhausted. He said, "Officer McGann, I'm working with the police. Why don't you just call Harry Soul down at the 23rd precinct and he'll fill you in on all the details." They were now approaching Mount Sinai Hospital. Jack reached over and shook Officer McGann's hand. He said, "Thanks for the ride, officer." Then he handed the officer his business card and said, "If you need me for anything else just give me a call and we can set something up." He handed Officer McGann $10 and said, "Get a couple of donuts on me." Officer McGann did not look amused, but he took the $10.

Jack limped up the stairs to the hospital. He went through the doors and quickly walked to the information desk which was in the middle of the entrance to the hallway. A woman was sitting behind a desk and there was a glass barrier between her and the visitors. She was about 40 years old, with dark hair and she looked very professional, not too much make-up but she had on dark red lipstick. She was wearing an earphone in one ear and there was a microphone in front of her on the desk. Jack got her attention by tapping on the glass with his index finger, something that most people who work behind glass don't appreciate, and he asked, "Could you tell me if Trudy Fields has been admitted within the last 15 minutes?" The woman looked up at Jack with a look of disbelief. She said, "Sir, I wouldn't have that information. If she arrived by ambulance, you might want to check with the Emergency desk, on the other side of the hospital." She pointed to the wall and said, "Just follow the red lines on the wall and it will lead you right to the Emergency department." She looked back down at a pad on her desk and jotted down something on the pad. Under his breath, he said, "Thanks for nothing." And he limped towards the hallway on the right and followed the red lines on the wall. It seemed like he was a rat in a maze. He went up one hallway, turned a corner, and went down another hallway. At one point, he got into an elevator and went down a floor, then continued following the red line on the hallway wall. Eventually, he arrived at the Emergency Room. There was a frenzy of activity. Doctors and nurses in green scrubs were passing him on each side, moving quickly like someone's life depended on it. Hopefully, it wasn't Trudy's life.

He walked up to the information desk and a woman was sitting down behind the desk, and she very much resembled the woman from the desk upstairs. She had dark hair, in her mid-40s with red lipstick. She looked up at Jack and said, "Can I help you?" Jack was still huffing and puffing from the long walk through the hospital corridors. He said, "Yes, I'm looking for a patient that would have arrived by ambulance over that past 30 minutes. Her name is Trudy Fields." The woman put her pen against her lips and said, "Just a minute please, I'll check the computer." She clicked a few keys on the keyboard and then she looked up at Jack and said, "Excuse me, what is your relationship to the patient? Are you family?" Jack cleared his throat and said, "Yes, that's right we're family. She's, my sister." The woman behind the desk looked at Jack with one eyebrow raised, she said, "And your name is?" Jack smiled, "It's Jack Trane." The woman looked at Jack a little more seriously and one eyebrow raised and said, "Mr. Trane, your sister is being treated right now. Please take a seat and I'll have the doctor speak with you as soon as she is stabilized." Jack backed away from the desk slowly. He thought to himself, "What does she mean stabilized? Was Trudy in worse shape than he thought?"

Jack sat down in a chair next to the vending machine. Jack hated hospitals. He hated the smell. He hated the lights. He hated the sounds. The chair he sat in was cold, hard, and made of an ugly orange plastic, but he didn't care. He was just hoping that Trudy was going to be OK. While he was sitting there his mind began to wander. He kept thinking about the events surrounding the explosion that blew up his car and put Trudy in the hospital. Things were starting to make sense. The rattle that he had been hearing in the front end of his car all day, was no doubt the bomb rattling under the hood of his car. When Trudy pushed the button on the glove box, that probably set the timer for the bomb to go off. He still couldn't figure out how Trudy survived the blast. There was nothing left of the car. How could Trudy still be in one piece? Jack had no doubt that the thin man with the garnet pinkie ring was responsible for placing the bomb in his car. That would make the second time today that he had tried to kill Jack and failed. The wheels in Jack's head started to turn. It was time to set a trap for the man with the garnet pinkie ring. Jack wanted to meet him up close and personal to find out who he was working for. Then he wanted to repay him for all the trouble he had caused, most of all for the explosion that led to Trudy ending up in the hospital. Jack gritted his teeth as he thought about what he was going to do to the thin man with the garnet pinkie ring.

Jack stood up and put a dollar into the vending machine. He made a selection and pushed the button. The machine rumbled and then a fresh pack of *Dentyne* gum dropped down to the bottom tray in the machine. Jack reached in and picked it up and put it into his pocket. He sat back down in the orange plastic chair and closed his eyes and tried to relax. Almost immediately he heard a man's voice, "Excuse me, are you here for Trudy Fields?" Jack opened his eyes. It was a doctor in green scrubs, and he had a stethoscope around his neck. Jack said, "Yes, how is she? Can I see her?" The doctor put his hand on Jack's shoulder and said, "Now relax, she's going to be just fine. She seems to have suffered a concussion, some scrapes, and a few bruises, so we're going to keep her overnight just for observation, but you can go in and see her as soon as she is assigned to a room." Jack was relieved, he smiled from ear to ear. He said, "Thanks Doc, that's good news!" He reached down for his wallet and then he realized that he didn't need to tip the doctor. He shook the doctor's hand and the doctor smiled and walked away. Jack was thrilled, he didn't know what to expect when the receptionist told him that Trudy needed to be stabilized, but he was relieved that Trudy was going to be OK. Now he could begin to refocus his thoughts on the case. The first thing he needed to do is set a trap for the man with the garnet pinkie ring. He figured it wouldn't be too hard. Maybe he'd just let the man come to him.

On the wall, there was a bright green line that led back to the admissions desk, where Jack came from. So, Jack followed the line on the wall up and down the corridors, up the elevator, and down another corridor until he ended up at the admission desk. The same woman in her 40's with the dark hair, from when Jack originally entered the hospital, was still working the desk. Jack walked up to the desk, much calmer than the first time he was here, and he tapped lightly on the glass that separated the visitors from the desk. She looked up and Jack smiled a friendly smile and said, "Sweetheart, could you please tell me what room Trudy Fields is in?" The woman recognized Jack and said, "You again? I thought that I told you that there was no Trudy Fields admitted today." Jack smiled and pointed his finger at the computer. He said, "Could you please try again, I think that you'll find her in a room now." The woman made a disgusted face and shook her head. She pushed a few keys on the keyboard and looked up at Jack again and said, "Room 212, take the elevator to your right." Jack winked at her and said, "You've been very helpful, we really have to stop meeting like this." Jack chuckled and walked away. The woman behind the desk had a pained look on her face.

Jack got into the elevator and pushed the button for the second floor. The elevator reached the second floor in about 5 seconds. Jack got out and followed the signs towards room 212. After passing rooms with beeping sounds and shuffling of feet, He found room 212. He entered the room and he saw Trudy in the hospital bed, and she was hooked up to an "IV." It pained Jack to see Trudy in this condition. She was always so well put together always full of life with a quick comeback. She was just lying there in the bed looking helpless. Jack pulled the pack of *Dentyne* out of his pocket and showed Trudy. He said, "At least this wasn't a total loss, I still got the gum." He was hoping to lighten Trudy's mood with a little levity. Trudy laughed, she said, "Give me a piece Jack. There is a really cute doctor in here and I don't want to scare him away with my fire breath from that chicken." Jack laughed, he said, "Here Trudy, you can have the whole pack." Trudy took the gum and put a piece in her mouth and started chewing. Jack said, "Look Trudy, I'm sorry this happened. I should have known better than to take you out on a dangerous case like this." Jack was looking down at the floor. Trudy opened her eyes wide and said, "What are you talking about, Jack? I wanted to come on this case. And up until the explosion, I think I was doing pretty good." Jack laughed, "Yeah Trudy, until the explosion you were doing pretty good." Jack looked at Trudy with serious eyes and said, "How are you doing? Do you feel OK?" Trudy smiled, she said, "I scared you, didn't I? Now you know how I feel every time you call in from the field after being shot at, beat up, or abducted." Jack was nodding his head. Trudy said, "I'm fine Jack. I'll be out of here tomorrow. I got a little bump on the back of my head and a few scrapes but that's all. It could have been a lot worse." Jack was still nodding his head. He said, "Trudy I still can't figure out how you survived. The car is in about five hundred pieces." Trudy smiled, she looked up at the ceiling and started to recall the events that took place just before the explosion. She said, "This is what I remember, Jack. You got out of the car to get the gum. But when you got up, your wallet fell out of your pocket onto the seat. When I noticed it, you were already out of the car, so I grabbed it and got out of the car to bring it to you and then saw a bright light and that's pretty much all I remember." Jack was nodding his head, he said, "Huh, how do you like that? These oversized pants actually saved your life." Trudy laughed and said, "Yeah, make sure that you put those pants in the front of your closet from now on." Jack laughed.

He knew that Trudy was all right now, so it was time to get a little more serious. He said, "Trudy when you get out of here tomorrow, I want you to go directly home and get some rest. I think I'm going to finish this case by myself." Trudy said, "No way Jack, $2500 is coming my way and I'm going to earn it." Jack smiled and said, "Trudy, I think you've done enough to earn the $2500. I don't want to put you in any more dangerous situations. Remember what I always say Trudy; You're the best! And I want to keep you that way."

Trudy had a determined look on her face, she said, "We'll talk about this when I get out. Right now, I think I have a doctor to see." She put another stick of gum in her mouth. Jack kissed her on the forehead and said, "We'll talk tomorrow. Right now, I have a thin man with a garnet pinkie ring to catch." Trudy smiled and said, "Be careful, Jack. This guy sounds like a psycho." She smiled and waved, and Jack left the hospital. When he walked down the stairs to the outside of the hospital, he realized that he didn't have a car anymore. His precious Mustang was gone. The car that he had pampered and coddled for over 10 years was gone. Reality started to sink in. Jack sat on the steps with his face in his hands as he mourned his priceless 1968 Mustang GT-500.

CHAPTER 10

Jack pulled out his cellphone and dialed the number for Debra Thorn. The phone rang a couple of times and Debra picked up. She said, "Hello Jack, what's the deal? I haven't heard from you all day?" There was a pause and Jack said, "Well, so far today, I've been knocked out, tied up and left on the subway tracks, and almost blown up. But other than that, it's been pretty boring." Debra sounded shocked, "Jack are you serious? Are you OK?" Jack laughed a little into the phone, he was trying to downplay the experience and hide his pain. He said, "Oh, and my car was destroyed in the explosion. Can you come and pick me up?" Debra was still shocked at Jack's daily rundown. She said, "Of course babe, where are you?" Jack hesitated again and said, "I'm at the hospital, Mount Sinai down on Madison Avenue." Debra's eyes opened wide, she said, "Jack, are you OK?" Jack half-smiled and said, "Yeah, I'm OK, but Trudy has a concussion and is going to be in the hospital at least overnight." Debra answered quickly, she said, "I'll be right there, Jack, I'm about 10 minutes away." Jack smiled, "Thanks babe, you're the best." They hung up the phones and Jack stood up and waited for Debra to arrive.

Debra pulled up in front of the hospital and Jack got into the car. He sat back in the passenger seat and just stared out the front window. There was an awkward silence. Debra looked at him with squinted eyes and said, "Hey Jack, you don't look so good." Jack smiled a weak smile and said, "Yeah, I'm more of a morning person." They both laughed and that broke the tension. Jack said, "It's been a tough day, I'm sure glad to see you." Debra smiled and said, "And if it wasn't a tough day, would you be glad to see me?" Debra was dressed in dark maroon slacks and a pink top, with a necklace that had green stones, which all complimented her reddish-blond hair. She had on Jack's favorite perfume, *Chanel Coco Mademoiselle,* and her eyes caught the light from the early evening sunset and sparkled like fresh dew on the green grass. Jack smiled and said, "Babe, I'd be glad to see you every which way but loose." Debra smiled and put the car in gear and drove into traffic. She said to Jack, "Are you hungry?" Jack nodded his head and said, "And thirsty too." She looked at Jack and smiled and said, "I know where we can get some good fish and chips." Jack sat back in his seat and said, "Babe, you read my mind." Debra drove off in the direction of *Big Jim's Sports Bar.*

Debra parked the car outside of *Big Jim's* and they both got out of the car and started walking towards the entrance. Debra now noticed the stitches on the right side of Jack's head and also that he was limping. She said in a serious tone, "Jack, you're limping, and that cut on your head, have you been checked out at the hospital?" Jack gave a wry smile and said, "Yeah, I've been to the hospital." Debra knew that he was just evading the question, she said, "No, Jack, you really should be checked out. You might have suffered a concussion or done something to your back." She looked concerned. Jack smiled and said, "Nothing that a good plate of fish and chips and a *Guinness* won't fix." He put his arm around Debra, and they entered *Big Jim's.* They didn't get a table, instead, they walked up to bar, and sat down. About five seconds later an ice-cold *Guinness* came sliding down the bar and stopped right in front of Jack. Jack yelled out, "Teddy K, you're the man!" Teddy K came walking down and put a glass of *Sauvignon Blanc* on the bar in front of Debra. He had a knack for remembering what his customers drank. Teddy had a bar rag over his shoulder, he said, "Let me guess.

Two orders of fish and chips, bring extra ketchup for the chips." Jack looked at Debra and said, "Now you see why I spend so much time here? If they had a shower and a bed in the back, I'd move in." Teddy K smiled and said, "There is not enough *Guinness* in the world to make that happen." Debra smiled and said to Teddy K, "Teddy, did you know that he was house trained?" Teddy laughed and walked away. As he was walking, he said under his breath, "Trained for what?" Teddy K went into the back room and placed their order.

Jack and Debra made small talk while they were waiting for their fish and chips and then Jack noticed that there was a game on the TV over the bar. It was the Yankees, and they were playing the Red Sox. With everything that had been going on, he had completely forgotten about the Red Sox game. Jack kept one eye on the game, but he started to share his plan to trap the man with the garnet pinkie ring with Debra. Jack looked at Debra with one eyebrow raised and said, "Debra, I have a foolproof plan to trap the man with the garnet pinkie ring. I'm going to lead him right to my apartment and leave the door open." Debra made a cynical face and said, "Oh yeah Jack, that sounds like a great plan. Why don't you just invite him in and cook him a nice meal too?" Jack laughed, he said, "No, you don't understand. I'm going to let him think that he's breaking into my apartment. Then when he gets in, I'm going to hit him with a taser, tie him up and get some answers." Debra was shaking her head, she said, "Jack, I think that's a crazy idea. Why don't you just go down to the precinct tomorrow and tell Harry Soul what's going on? Or maybe you should just drop this case and pick up one that's not so dangerous." Jack was shaking his head, he said, "Debra, someone doesn't want me to solve this case. I must be getting close, otherwise, the thin man with the garnet pinkie ring wouldn't be trying to bump me off. There is no way I'm dropping this case. Since they hurt Trudy and blew up my car, this has gotten very personal. Somebody is going down for this." Just then the Yankees scored a run on the TV and the crowd around them let out a big cheer. Debra raised one eyebrow and just stared at Jack.

Teddy K came back with the fish and chips and put a plate down in front of Jack and Debra. Jack breathed in deep to take in the aroma. He looked at Teddy and said, "The best fish and chips in the city. How about another *Guinness*?"

Teddy gave Jack a wink and said, "I'll be right back." He walked back to the beer tap and poured Jack another beer. He came over and put it on the bar in front of Jack. Jack gave Teddy a wink and said, "The best beer in the city too." Teddy came closer and leaned over to talk to Jack in a low voice. He said, "Jack, did you know that there has been a guy in here asking for you?" Jack looked at Teddy with one eyebrow raised and said, "What does he look like?" Teddy stood back and said, "He's kind of a thin man with dark hair and he was wearing black pants and a black shirt, no distinguishing marks." Jack nodded his head, he said, "Was he wearing a pinkie ring?" Teddy rubbed his chin and said, "Now that you mention it, yes he was wearing a garnet pinkie ring." Debra grabbed Jack's arm and said, "That's it, Jack, you need to go the precinct and tell Harry Soul what's going on. This case is way too dangerous for you to be fooling around with it on your own." Jack looked up at the TV screen and the Red Sox had just scored three runs and the crowd around them was making crude noises. Jack turned to Debra and said, "This is good, the man with the garnet pinkie ring is playing right into my hands." Jack took the ketchup and poured a big blob on his French fries. He said, "I just love to smother my fries in ketchup, don't you Debra? Please pass the salt." Debra shook her head, "Jack, this is not good. The man with the garnet pinkie ring wants to smother you like fries under ketchup." Jack laughed, "Let's get it straight Debra, he's the fries and I'm the ketchup." There was nothing Debra could do to change Jack's mind. He was going to go through with his plan. He said, "Talk to me tomorrow, Babe. The man with the garnet pinkie ring is going to lead me right to his boss and I'm going to solve the *Broadway Murder* case." Debra shook her head, and said, "Whatever you say, Jack." She took a bite of her fish and said, "You're right Jack, the best in town." The crowd cheered as the Yankees had just scored two runs. Jack looked at the TV in disgust.

Jack and Debra finished their meal and Jack took $50 out of his wallet and dropped it on the bar, then he waved at Teddy K. Teddy saw the cash on the bar and gave Jack a wink. Jack and Debra got up from their bar stools and walked out of *Big Jim's*. As they walked out the exit doors and entered the parking lot, they saw a bright flash coming from the entrance to the lot, and then they heard the sound of bullets entering the fender of the car to their left. Out of reflex, Debra pulled out her service weapon and aimed it toward the point where they saw the bright flash coming from. She didn't have a chance to return fire, a black car at the entrance of the lot pulled away quickly. Debra said, "Jack, quick, get into the car." They both got into the car and Debra immediately put the car in gear and began to chase down the car that had fired the shots in their direction. Debra's car was a *Ford Fusion*. It was great on gas, but it couldn't get out of its own way. Debra stepped on the gas and flew out of the parking lot in chase of the black car. Jack looked at Debra and said, "Don't you have one of those little flashing red lights that we can paste to the top of the car, you know, like *Starsky and Hutch*?" Debra looked at Jack with a look of disbelief and said, "Jack, this isn't TV, this is real life." Within about 20 seconds the chase was over. Debra's *Ford Fusion* was no match for the other car. The man with the garnet pinkie ring had lost them. Jack thought to himself, "If I had my Mustang, he never would have gotten away." He was still lamenting the loss of his precious Mustang. Jack was sure that the car they were chasing was the man with the garnet pinkie ring. Debra slammed her fist on the steering wheel. Jack said, "Don't worry Debra, that's the third time today this guy's tried to kill me. Debra looked at Jack and said with a forced smile, "Either he's not that good or he's just not trying that hard." Jack smiled back and said, "Tomorrow it's my turn. I have a plan." Debra looked at Jack with wide-open eyes and said, "Jack, are you crazy? You need to go to the precinct and fill the department in on what's going on. At least get some back-up." Jack shook his head, he said, "Debra, you know that I work alone, besides, the department already washed their hands of this case. Don't worry I got this." Debra was shaking her head. Jack said, "Why don't you just drop me off at my apartment and I'll put my plan in place." She looked at Jack with a surprised look, she said, "Jack, you can't go back to your apartment tonight, it's not safe. You'll stay at my place until we can sort this out. You can sleep on the couch; it turns into a sleeper." Jack laughed, "Thanks' anyway Debra, but I already have this sorted out. Just remember I'm the ketchup and he's the fries." Debra shook her head and said, "That's what I'm worried about Jack, there is only so much ketchup in the bottle." Jack smiled and said, "Relax babe, this is what I do. Like taking candy from a baby." Debra put her hand on her head and drove towards Jack's apartment.

They arrived at Jack's apartment at about 9:30 PM. Debra looked at Jack with a serious look and said, "Be careful, call me tomorrow." Jack kissed her tenderly and went into the apartment building. He walked up the stairs and made his way down the hallway to his door. He was limping a lot less now, he figured it was the *Guinness* kicking in. He looked down and the matchstick was still in the door jamb. He opened the door and went in. Jack's focus now was to set a trap for the man with the garnet pinkie ring. He turned on the TV and put on the Red Sox game. The game had just ended. The Red Sox had won 4-3, this was a good sign. Jack felt that things had started to turn around in his direction, he could feel some momentum on his side. He had recently purchased a surveillance camera but had not taken the time to install it. It was still in the Amazon box that it came in. The box was in the corner to the left of his couch. It had gathered enough dust to track the movements of the flies that had landed on it. He took the camera out of the box and quickly looked through the instructions with one eye. Normally he wouldn't take the time to read the instructions at all, but this was a smart camera. Anything that was considered "smart" was somewhat intimidating to Jack. Technology had not always been his friend. But he had learned to live with it. He figured out the instructions and took out a small power drill and installed the camera just outside of his door. The camera was small and white and very inconspicuous. Then he downloaded an app to his phone that was connected to the camera. This would alert him anytime anyone touched or came within six feet of his door. He also had a taser that he had used in previous jobs that he kept in the bottom drawer of his desk. He took his taser out from the desk drawer and placed it on the floor just inside the door. He had some industrial zip ties in the kitchen. He took four or five large zip ties and placed them next to the taser on the floor. He locked the door, but he did not hook the latch. He wanted it to be a little bit easy for someone to break in. He was expecting the man with the garnet pinkie ring to show up anytime, and everything was now in place. The trap was set. Jack pulled a chair from his kitchen table and placed it behind the door. He turned out the lights and sat down in the chair and waited. Jack liked a good stake-out. It had been a while since he had been involved in one.

Time goes by slowly in the dark. You can hear sounds that are barely audible in the daylight. Sounds like the ticking of a kitchen clock on the wall, or the floor settling and giving out a crack or a creek. The sounds of the traffic outside are amplified and Jack could hear his stomach making the common noises it makes at night. He waited in the dark for three hours. He was fighting to keep his eyelids from closing and letting him get the sleep that his body told him that he needed. Then at about 12:30 AM, Jack's phone lit up bright. He opened the app on his phone for the camera and he got a clear view of the thin man with the garnet pinkie ring resting on the outside of his door. Jack closed the app and put the cell phone down on the floor and grabbed the taser. He moved his chair to the side and stood directly behind the door in the dark. Jack could hear sounds, the shuffling of feet, metal rubbing against metal, and then the sound of the lock releasing. He lifted the taser up and pointed it like a gun. The door opened slightly and the light from the hallway created a small beam of light into his living room. Jack watched closely and kept perfectly still as he could see a hand coming in through the opening of the door. The hand had a garnet pinkie ring. The thin man entered Jack's apartment and closed the door. It was pitch black in the room but based on the last view Jack had when the thin man entered, he had a pretty good idea of where the thin man was standing. Jack raised the taser, pulled the trigger and it fired. The tasers electrodes entered the thin man in the back and Jack heard a loud groaning and then a thump. Jack turned to his right and flipped the switch for the lights. He saw the thin man on the floor rolling around like a wounded animal in pain. Jack pulled out the electrodes and placed the taser on the thin man's neck. He pulled the trigger again and directly tased the man's neck. About 80,000 volts entered the thin man's neck and he passed out. Jack knew that he would be out for about 15 minutes, so he had to work fast. He reached into the thin man's jacket and pulled out the thin man's gun. It was a Glock 19 with a full clip and silencer. The man with the garnet pinkie ring had certainly planned to finish the job tonight. Jack put the gun in his bottom desk drawer. He took the wallet out of the thin man's pocket and found his driver's license. The man with the garnet pinkie ring had a name, it was Mike Mercury. His address was on the lower east side, down on East 6th Street. Jack hoped that this information would come in handy. He put the wallet back in Mike's pocket. Mike was a thin man with a dark complexion, he had a long nose and thin lips. Jack took the cell phone out of Mike's jacket pocket and held it up to his phone. He had an app that would track the location of any phone that was paired with his. Jack paired Mike's phone with his. He would now be able to track Mike Mercury wherever he went, and hopefully, that would lead to whoever was behind the Broadway murder. Jack took the garnet pinkie ring off of Mike's finger just for the fun of it and put it in the top drawer of his desk. Jack was going to use the pinkie ring for leverage, he knew that Mike Mercury would be looking for it and Jack could use it as a bargaining chip. Jack was enjoying this. Jack put the zip ties on Mike's feet and tied them tight. Then he put the zip ties on Mike's hands and left them loose. He wanted Mike Mercury to get away so he could track him. Then Jack dragged Mike out of his apartment and down the stairs and out the front door. He dragged him into an alley on the side of his building and left him lying next to a dumpster. Jack looked at the thin man lying next to the dumpster and let out a laugh. His plan was in place. He knew that Mike Mercury would go back to the hole that he came from, regroup, and come back again tomorrow. Jack now had the upper hand, and he would be ready for the man without the garnet pinkie ring. Jack smiled a satisfied smile and limped back up the stairs to his apartment to get some long-overdue sleep. He got ready for bed and set his alarm for 8:00 AM. He had a lot planned for tomorrow, but he didn't plan for everything tomorrow might bring.

CHAPTER 11

The alarm went off at 8:00 AM and Jack reached over and groaned while he fumbled to shut off the buzzer. He sat up and rubbed his eyes a couple of times to clear the fog. The events from the last couple of days were slowly catching up with him. His back was killing him and the side of his head where the stitches were was sore, but the sun was shining through his window and left a stream of light across the floor leading right up to his bed, and this gave him some positive vibes for his day. He sat on the side of the bed for a moment contemplating all the moves he was going to make today. One thing was for sure, he needed a car. His precious Mustang had been blown up and he knew that a taxi wouldn't get him where he needed to be. One thing in his favor, was that his Mustang was a truly classic car, and his insurance settlement was going to be about six figures, so he decided to get a new car that would hopefully make him feel the way that his old car did, unbeatable and confident. He also needed to interrogate Siobhan Peison today. He suspected a conspiracy and hopefully, by questioning Siobhan, it would confirm that. Jack knew her address was 210 Dean Street in Brooklyn. He made a mental note to make sure his new car had GPS capabilities. He also needed to get Trudy out of the hospital today and make sure that she was in a safe place until she fully recovered from her injuries. He needed Trudy to do some background and finance checking, but that would have to wait. Then there was the matter of Mike Mercury, the thin man who no longer has a garnet pinkie ring. Jack thought that he should contact the precinct and see what information they might have on him. He knew that his friend Harry Soul would help him out.

Then he would be able to track Mike Mercury down and uncover the person behind the Broadway Murder and the attempts on his life. It was a full day, so Jack hopped out of bed and into the shower.

After a quick shower and a shave, he went through his morning ritual of getting dressed. He pulled three matching pieces out of his walk-in closet, got a white shirt from his armoire, and put them all on. He grabbed his wallet and his cellphone and put them in his jacket pockets. Then he put on his hat and walked out the door. He remembered to put the matchstick above the bottom hinge in the door jamb for security. Jack stopped in at the newsstand and picked up the morning paper. Nicky gave him the usual morning grumble and Jack left the usual $2 on the counter. Jack had a big day planned, but the first thing on his list was breakfast down at the *Coffee Café*. He walked into the *Café* and he saw Betty standing next to the counter, he yelled out, "Good morning beautiful." Betty smiled and rubbed her hand across her chest. She said, "Thanks Jack." Jack smiled and said, "Betty, how did you know that I was talking to you?" Betty said, "Come on Jack, six other customers just told me the same thing, I'm starting to believe it." They both laughed and Betty hit Jack with her washcloth. Betty was very attractive, so Jack wasn't stretching the truth. Her short blond hair and her bright blue eyes would brighten anyone's morning. She got closer to Jack and saw the bandage on the side of his head, she said, "Jack what happened to your head? Did it have another situation? Did it have anything to do with that thin man that was in here the other day? I think he was looking for you." Jack smiled and said, "That's funny, now I'm looking for him." Betty smiled, she said, "Jack you're such a man of mystery." He sat back in his chair and said, "I'd argue if I could." Betty hit him again with her washcloth. Jack said, "So how are the pancakes today, my friend?" Betty took out her pad and gave Jack a wink, she said, "Just how you like them Jack, a stack of three with plenty of blueberries." Jack was nodding his head. She said, "I'll bring over a large Vanilla Latte and the pancakes will be up in a minute." Jack smiled, he said, "Now that's what I'm talking about." She went back to the counter, and he opened his newspaper.

Jack needed a car. He scanned the newspaper for new car ads. He found a dealership in Brooklyn, Prime Ford. There was a phone number under the ad. Jack pulled out his cellphone and dialed the dealership. Betty brought over Jack's Latte and put it down on the table in front of him. Jack gave her a wink and she patted him on the shoulder and went back to the counter. For the next ten minutes, Jack went back and forth with the salesman at Prime Ford. In the end, he had made a deal to test drive a brand-new Shelby Mustang GT-500 this morning. He hung up the phone and Betty arrived with his pancakes. She smiled and said, "Enjoy, Jack. I had the cook put in extra blueberries just for you." He smiled and said, "You're the best Betty. What more could a man ask for?" She smiled at Jack with one eye closed and said, "Well Jack, I could think of a few things." She winked at Jack and walked back to the counter. Jack poured the organic maple syrup over the pancakes and took a bite. They were delicious, cooked just right. Fluffy in the middle and a little crispy on the edges. Within about ten minutes the pancakes were gone, and Jack was taking the last sip of his Latte. Betty came back over and asked, "How was it, Jack?" He smiled and said, "Everything I thought it would be." Betty smiled and said, "We're talking about the pancakes, right?" They both laughed and Betty put the check on the table in front of Jack. The bill was fifteen dollars. Jack pulled thirty dollars out of his wallet and put it down on the table. Betty picked it up and said, "Thanks Jack you're the best. What more could a girl ask for?" Jack smiled and said, "I can think of a few things." They both laughed and Jack got up from the table and walked out of the *Coffee Café*.

Jack needed to get to Prime Ford in Brooklyn, so he started look-ing for a taxi. He could see one coming towards him, so he raised his hand and the taxi pulled over and Jack got in. The driver turned around to look at Jack and said, "Where to?" Jack looked at his name tag on the sun visor over the driver's seat and it read "Emad Gamaled." He had a heavy accent, Jack couldn't figure out where it was from, he sounded Middle Eastern, but regardless, Emad was very hard to understand. Jack said, "Prime Ford over in Brooklyn." The driver said, "Yes, very well, the Ford of Brooklyn." Jack smiled and nodded and said, "Right, Prime Ford in Brooklyn." Emad started the meter and pulled out into traffic. Emad drove like he was a steel ball in a pinball machine. He changed lanes at every block and went 0 to 40 in about 3 seconds. Emad crossed over the Brooklyn Bridge and headed east into Brook-lyn towards East Flatbush. Emad turned back and said to Jack, "Nice day, we have today." Jack smiled as his head bobbed from one side to the other because of Emad changing lanes, and said, "Yes, it is a nice day." Under his breath, Jack said, "It will be a nice day if we make it to Prime Ford in one piece." After Emad had cut off about a dozen drivers and exchanged gestures with a dozen more, they pulled up outside the Ford dealership. It was about 9:30 AM. Emad turned off the meter and looked at Jack and said, "Twenty-two, fifty-five." Jack took out $30 and gave it to Emad and said, "Keep the change, my friend." Emad smiled and said, "Thank you very much." And he drove off in the direction of Manhattan.

Jack walked into the dealership and asked for the salesman that he had spoken to on the phone. His name was Steve Swindell. Steve came up to Jack and shook his hand. He was dressed in a cheesy plaid suit and a green plaid tie. He had dirty blond hair which was slicked back with some kind of grease and his aftershave smelled like some-thing from the 1970s. Steve said, "Mr. Trane, so nice to meet you. What do we have to do to get you in that Mustang today?" Jack pulled his hand away and put on his serious voice. He said, "Look, Mr. Swindell, I'll tell you how this is going to go down. I'm going to take the Mustang for a test drive and when we get back, if I like it, you're going to take $2,000 off the sticker price, and then I drive off the lot with a new car. No discussions, no managers, that's the deal. Got it?" Steve backed up and said, "Well Mr. Trane, the customer is always right. Let's see what we can do." The Mustang was parked right out in the front of the dealership. The car was a *Shelby-500GT* and its color was Highland Green. The car had about five hundred horsepower and was turbocharged. Jack couldn't wait to get behind the wheel. Steve handed Jack the key and said, "Let's go, cowboy!" Jack got in the car and sat behind the wheel just looking at all the instruments. The new car smell overwhelmed Jack's senses. There was a cobra on the steering wheel. Jack liked it already. Steve said, "Mr. Trane, let me explain some of these instruments on the dashboard." Jack started the car and said, "Hold that thought, Stevie." Jack had no intention of listening to a long-drawn-out description of the dashboard instruments. He would figure that out for himself. The engine sounded rich, and the exhaust sounded deep with the kind of low growl that Jack had become accustomed to. The car had an automatic shift, which was different from Jack's last car, but he was willing to give it a chance. He put the car in gear and pulled out of the parking lot. There was an open space of road right outside of the dealership, so Jack gave the car some gas. Immediately the car responded and went from 0 to 60 in about 4 seconds. The power felt good. Jack smiled at Steve Swindell and said, "Not bad, Stevie, Not, bad." He drove around for about 10 minutes checking how it handled around corners. Then he turned up the radio to make sure it delivered enough decibels to make sure it met his listening standards. When Jack was satisfied, he drove back to the dealership. Steve looked at Jack and said, "Well Mr. Trane, what do you think?" Jack smiled and said, "If you want to get me in the car today, Stevie, take $2,000 off the sticker price, and I will drive it off the lot, no questions asked." Steve started to speak, but Jack broke in, "Remember what I said Stevie, no discussion. No manager, it's just you and me. Make the deal or I walk." Steve was sweating. Little drips were coming down the sides of his face. He looked towards the office then he looked back at Jack, then he looked towards the office again, then back at Jack. Then he said, "Alright, Mr. Trane, we have a deal." Jack didn't care much for any car salesman, and he loved it when he had the upper hand.

Jack drove off the lot in his brand-new Mustang Shelby GT-500. To Jack, the new car smell was like tulips in an open field. He turned on the radio and the song that was playing was an old Willie Nelson song, "*On the Road Again.*" Jack was back and he had the swagger and confidence he needed to solve this case. He pulled over to the side of the road and pulled out his cellphone and opened the app to track Mike Mercury. He could see from the app that Mike was still at his apartment on East 6th Street. No doubt the thin man was planning his next move. Jack opened his windows pulled into traffic and enjoyed the fresh morning air. This new Mustang was everything that his 1968 Mustang was, with some serious upgrades. He paired the Bluetooth on his phone with the phone app on his dashboard. His first call would be to Trudy. He was hoping that she was being released from the hospital this morning. He wanted to drive over to pick her up. There was a little button on the dashboard with the picture of a phone, so Jack pushed it and said Trudy's phone number in the direction of the steering wheel. He could hear the phone dialing through the stereo speakers. Trudy picked up, she said, "Jack, where have you been? They told me that I could be released at 9:00 AM." Jack smiled, "What? No good morning?" Trudy breathed deeply, she said, "Come on Jack, you got to get me out of here, the food is terrible and there are no cute doctors on the morning shift." Jack laughed, "I'll be there in about 15 minutes, I'm crossing the Brooklyn Bridge right now." Trudy paused and said, "The Brooklyn Bridge? Why are you in Brooklyn Jack? You're not interrogating Siobhan Peison without me, are you?" Jack spoke softly, "Now, Trudy, I thought we agreed that you were going to relax until you recovered." Trudy was snapping her gum, she said, "No, Jack, that's what you agreed to. Just come and pick me up." Jack shook his head, he said, "I'll be there in about 12 minutes." They both hung up the phone and Jack sat back in the driver's seat and enjoyed his trip back to Manhattan.

Jack pulled up outside of Mount Sinai Hospital at about 11:00 AM. Trudy was standing just inside the door. She didn't recognize Jack's new Mustang, so Jack got out and waved to her from his car. Trudy's mouth fell open and she came out the door. She looked fine, even the scratch on the side of her face seemed to be gone. She said, "Jack, you got a new car, this looks awesome! Can I drive?" Jack was shaking his head, he said, "Trudy, sit down, we need to talk." Trudy sat down in the passenger seat. Jack said, "Now Trudy, you've been through a traumatic experience, you were almost killed yesterday. I really want you to go home and get some rest, and if you feel better tomorrow, you can come back to work. I think I'm going to have some background work for you to do after I interrogate Siobhan Peison this…." Trudy broke in, "What? No way Jack. You got blown up too and you're not taking the day off. You said that I get to come out in the field on this case and I get to interrogate Siobhan Peison." She sat there looking at Jack. He was rubbing his forehead with his right hand. He really didn't want to put Trudy in any more danger, but he knew that he wasn't going to win this battle. He looked at Trudy with a serious look and said, "OK, Trudy, but after we interrogate Siobhan Peison, you go back to the office and do some background stuff." Trudy smiled, she said, "Of course Jack, you're the boss." Jack thought to himself, "Sometimes I wonder."

Trudy was fiddling around with all the buttons on the dashboard. She pushed the button for the air conditioning, and she felt a cool breeze under her seat. She said, "Oooh, this is wonderful! Your old car didn't do this." Jack was shaking his head, he said, "Come on Trudy, stop playing with all the buttons. Let's focus for a minute here, I need to call Harry Soul down at the precinct." Trudy made a disgusted face. She said, "That guy gives me the creeps, Jack." Jack smiled, he said, "He's not so bad Trudy, he's like Blue cheese, an acquired taste." He laughed. Trudy made a face and said, "More like moldy cheese." Jack dialed up the number for the precinct and the voice came back over the speakers in the car, "Hello 23rd precinct, how can I direct your call?" Jack looked at Trudy and said, "Pretty cool huh?" Then he responded to the call, "I'd like to speak with Detective Harry Soul," The voice came back, "One moment please." About five seconds later a voice came from the dashboard, "Harry Soul." Jack smiled, "Harry, how are you doing?" Harry answered back quickly, "Jack, I heard about the explosion! How is Trudy?" Harry had been trying to get a date with Trudy forever. Trudy curled one lip like Elvis and squinted her eyes. Jack said, "Trudy is fine. The reason that I called is that I need some information." Harry replied, "Look, Jack, this case that you're on might be a little too dangerous for you to be working on right now. I didn't realize that this may still be an active case." Jack pursed his lips and said, "Harry, this is my case, and I'm going to solve it. I have a plan." Harry's voice was coming through the dashboard, "I don't know Jack." Jack came to a traffic light, and he stopped. He could see the person in the car on the side of him admiring his new Mustang. Jack put on his sunglasses and gave them a wave. He turned his attention back to Harry. He said, "Harry I need some information on a guy named Michael Mercury.

Did he have any priors? What's he ever in prison? Any known connections? That kind of stuff." Harry paused for a moment and said, "Why do you want information on Michael Mercury, Jack?" Jack raised his voice, "Because, I believe that he is responsible for blowing up my car, and I also think that he is the key to solving this case." Harry was shaking his head, he said, "Jack, this Mike Mercury is a very dangerous customer. He's well known to the department for things like larceny and petty theft, but he was also arrested on a murder charge, but he got off because the witness disappeared. He runs with a small gang down in the Bowery section, a small pool room and bar on Wooster Street." Jack was taking this all in, he said, "Thanks Harry this is very helpful." Harry chimed in, "Jack, I don't think you should be going after this guy by yourself, this man is unpredictable. This was Danny Watts case originally, let me assign him as your back-up." Jack was shaking his head, "Absolutely not Harry! I don't want to see that incompetent fool anywhere around this case. He's the reason that it's a cold case in the first place." Harry said, "OK, Jack, but be careful. Don't take any chances and please, keep Trudy out of this." Trudy was making a face and making gestures with her hand like it was mimicking Harry's voice. Jack said, "Don't worry, Harry. We got this under control." Jack pushed the button on the dash and ended the call.

Trudy sat up in her seat, she looked at Jack with big eyes and said, "So, Jack, are we heading down to the Bowery to flush out Mike Mercury and his gang." Jack looked at Trudy with a serious look and said, "What do you mean, we? I'm not taking you down to the Bowery, that's way too dangerous. And besides, I'm tracking the thin man on my phone app and he's still in his apartment down on E 6th Street." Trudy blew a bubble with her gum. She said, "OK, Jack, then where to?" Jack shook his head and said, "Well, I think this might be a good time to travel over to Dean Street over in Brooklyn and have a little talk with

Siobhan Peison. She's kind of the next piece of this puzzle that I need to put in place." Trudy was nodding her head, she said, "Good idea, Jack. I'm going to do the interrogation, right? After Victoria Pichettes, I really think that I'm getting the hang of this." Jack was shaking his head, he said, "OK, Trudy, you can do the interrogation, but the same rules apply. If I need to say something, I'm stepping in." Trudy smiled, she said, "Don't worry Jack, there will be no need for you to step in, I got this." Trudy plugged Siobhan Peison's address into the GPS and Jack turned his car onto the Manhattan Bridge in the direction of Brooklyn. He turned towards Trudy and said, "Let's try not to get my car blown up this time." Trudy waved her hand at Jack and put her head out the window and breathed in some fresh air. Jack put on the satellite radio station and as they passed over the Manhattan bridge, the old Bee Gees song was playing "*Staying Alive.*" Jack was hoping that was a good sign.

CHAPTER 12

Jack parked his car outside of Siobhan Peison's house at 210 Dean Street in Brooklyn. It was a one-way street and cars were parked on both sides. There was a green dumpster on one side of the street taking up about three parking spaces. Either someone was moving out or one of these high-priced apartments was having some work done. The brick buildings lined the street, but so did the trees along the sidewalk. There was an iron gate and about seven steps that led up to the apartment door. Jack and Trudy walked up the stairs and rang the buzzer. As they were standing there Trudy said to Jack, "I hear that there is a cool restaurant just up the street from here called the "*Broad in the Beam*." What do you say you take us out to lunch after this interview?" Jack opened his mouth to answer, and a voice came through the buzzer, "Who is it?" Jack answered, "Hello, my name is Jack Trane and I'm investigating the case of Heinrich King." The voice on the buzzer answered, "Come in." The door buzzed open, and Trudy and Jack went in. Trudy said to Jack, "Remember Jack, this is my interrogation." Jack put his hands up and in a low gravelly voice said, "Whatever you say, Boss." Trudy rolled her eyes and they walked up to the second floor to Siobhan Peison's apartment. The building was very well kept. The carpet on the stairs looked new. It was not the industrial type, but there was a fancy flower pattern on each side of the carpet and the carpet was a deep pink color. The walls were freshly painted an off-yellow and the lights looked to be small Wallingford chandeliers. One thing was for sure, these apartments were way out of Jack's price range. They stood in front of Siobhan's door and Trudy knocked firmly four times. As she took her hand away from the fourth knock the door opened and a strong-looking woman with jet-black hair appeared. She said, "Is there something I can do for you?" Trudy smiled and said, "Yes, we're from Trane Investigations, my name is Trudy." Then she pointed to Jack and said, "This is my associate, Jack. And we're here investigating the murder of Heinrich King." Jack was rolling his eyes. First of all, he wasn't an associate, and secondly, you never mention the word murder in the first sentence of a greeting. Siobhan Peison looked Trudy up and down and said, "Do you have some identification?" Jack took the card that Harry Soul had given him out of his shirt pocket and handed it to Siobhan Peison. She looked at it and curled her lip with a puzzled face and said, "What's this? A card that you got in a Cracker Jacks box?" She looked at Jack with disdain as she handed back the card. Trudy started to speak, but Jack broke in, "Look, Siobhan, we've been hired to work with the NYPD on the Heinrich King murder. We just want to ask you a few questions to tie up some loose ends, that's all." Trudy was looking at Jack with squinted eyes. Siobhan looked at Jack, then at Trudy, and said, "Well I thought I covered all that with that other detective Wapps or something." Jack smiled and said, "Oh yes, detective Watts. I guess…" Trudy broke in, "There are some details that detective Watts left out of his report. We just need to clear up a few things. Do you think we can come in?" Siobhan made a disgusted face and said, "Well, if you have to. But please don't touch anything. I'm in the middle of some very important and delicate work." Trudy smiled and said, "Of course, we're detectives. We don't touch anything without wearing gloves." Jack was rolling his eyes.

They walked into Siobhan's apartment and as they entered the main living room, there were fabrics draped over chairs and pieces laid out on the floor. There were manikin's half-dressed in colorful dresses and tops. There was a sewing machine in the corner of the room next to a window and there were small pieces of cut fabric all over the room. On the couch, there were three or four completed dresses draped from the top of the couch all the way to the floor. It looked like Siobhan was prepping for a new production or fashion show. Jack took in the surroundings and realized that there was nowhere to sit down. He raised his eyebrows and looked at Siobhan and said, "Well, maybe we can all just go sit down in the kitchen and we won't disturb anything in here." Siobhan raised one eyebrow and nodded. Trudy was looking at all the dresses created by Siobhan. She was almost in a daze. Trudy loved fashion and Siobhan's creations were unique and beautiful. Jack snapped his fingers and Trudy snapped out of it and her gaze transitioned from the dresses to Jack. She half-smiled at Jack and raised her shoulders and hands. Jack looked at her with one eyebrow raised and Siobhan led them into the kitchen. There was a small round table in the kitchen with four sturdy chairs. The table was covered with a plain yellow tablecloth and there was a single pink rose in a vase on the table. Siobhan was very creative, and she had an artsy taste. Her apartment certainly reflected that. Jack and Trudy sat next to each other, and Siobhan sat on the other side of the table. Siobhan got up from the table and took a coffee pod out of her cupboard and placed it into the coffee brewer and she made herself a cup of coffee. Jack and Trudy looked at each other through the awkward silence, then Siobhan came back and sat down at the table and placed the coffee cup in front of her. The rich aroma of the freshly brewed coffee filled the air and Jack looked at Trudy again and raised his eyebrows. Siobhan said in an apologetic tone, "Oh, by the way, would either of you like a cup of coffee?" Trudy wanted to say yes but Jack broke in and said, "Thanks anyway Siobhan, we really shouldn't. We'll just ask our questions and we'll be on our way." Trudy looked at Jack with squinted eyes and a serious expression. She really wanted a cup of coffee. Siobhan laughed and said, "Whatever floats your boat, honey."

Trudy broke into her Dragnet voice as she began her interrogation. She looked Siobhan in the face and said, "Siobhan, we heard that you had some kind of trouble with Heinrich King the week before he died. Can you tell us about that?" Siobhan took a sip of her coffee and put the cup back down on the table and said, "You want to hear about the trouble? I'll tell you about the trouble. That good-for-nothing scumbag cost me a chance to show my fashion line in Paris. In Paris! Did you hear that? I came up to his office to sign a deal, but he had other things in mind and when I wouldn't play along, he pulled my costumes from an upcoming production and my line never made it to Paris. Now I'm back where I started, just trying to get noticed in this dog-eat-dog fashion business." Siobhan's voice got louder as she explained her experience. Trudy put on a fake surprised look and said, "It sounds like that made you pretty angry, correct?" Siobhan gritted her teeth and said, "Honey, I could have killed him, I should have killed him, but I didn't. But that doesn't mean that I'm sorry that he's dead. I'd like to congratulate whoever did it with a million dollars." Siobhan took another sip of her coffee. Trudy was about to say something, but Jack broke in, he said, "Siobhan, do you know of anyone else who might have wanted to see King Heini dead?" Siobhan laughed loud and long. She said, "Are you kidding? I can't think of anyone I know who didn't want him dead. He was a cheat, a womanizer, a gambler, a liar, a thief, a bully, and a plain butt ugly man. He got what he deserved." She had a satisfied look on her face, and she sat back and crossed her legs. Trudy looked at Jack and then back to Siobhan, then in her Dragnet voice, she said, "Siobhan, where you on the night that he was murdered?" Siobhan calmy and quickly responded, "I was out with a few friends from 7:00 PM to 1:00 AM. You can check with them. I'm sure they will confirm my alibi." Jack smiled and crossed his legs and said, "I'm sure they will Siobhan, I'm sure they will." Siobhan was getting impatient. She said, "Look, detectives, I really need to get back to work, so if you don't mind, now would be a good time to leave." Trudy looked at Jack then said, "Siobhan, do you know Jackie King?" Siobhan answered, "Of course, honey, she was married to that despicable Heinrich King." Trudy continued, "Did you have any contact with her since the murder?" Siobhan now sounded agitated, "Absolutely not! Why would I have any contact with Jackie King? What kind of question is that? Siobhan stood up from the table and said, "That's it! I've had enough. I've answered all your questions. It's time for you both to go." Siobhan pointed to the door. Jack stood up and said, "Well, it's certainly been a pleasure talking with you this afternoon, and I think you've cleared up a few things for us. We'll just show ourselves out." Trudy got up from the table and she and Jack walked out of the apartment and closed the door behind them.

As they walked down the stairs to the street, Trudy looked at Jack and said, "How did I do, Jack? I think she was starting to come unglued at the end." Jack put his arm around Trudy and said, "Trudy, you did great! Those questions that you asked at the end really struck a chord. What this tells me is that she did have contact with Jackie King after the murder and that all the other girls we interviewed probably did too." Trudy smiled and said, "Jack, now I know why you eat so much, that interview really made me hungry. I could go for a double burger down at the *Broad in the Beam* restaurant. What do you say?" Jack smiled, "After that performance, Trudy, I think we can even throw in some fries." They both laughed and got into the car.

Jack started his new Mustang and sat for a minute just listening to the engine idle. To him, it was like listening to a cat purr on the back of the couch. After about 15 seconds Trudy said, "Well, Jack, the car is not going to move by itself. You need to put in gear." Jack looked at Trudy with a smile and put the car in gear and drove off heading east on Dean Street. When he got to Vanderbilt Street, he took a sharp left, and two blocks later they were at *Broad in the Beam.* Jack parked the car on the street and Trudy jumped out. She said, "I've been looking forward to a double burger at *Broad in the Beam* for a long time." Jack got out of the car and asked her, "Trudy, why do they call it the *Broad in the Beam?* I don't get it." Trudy thought for a minute and said, "Probably to make guys like you ask questions." Trudy had an air of confidence as she entered the restaurant. Jack felt good that Trudy was out of the hospital and working the case with him. Jack looked at Trudy and said, "Well, I guess it's better than the *Wooden Nickel.*"

A maître de came over to greet them. He was in his late 20s with dark hair and he had a thin mustache above his lip. He was wearing the standard white shirt and black pants and he also had a black scarf around his neck. He looked at Jack and said, "Would you like indoor seating or outdoor? We have seating on the roof deck." Jack thought for about half a second and said, "Indoor please." The maître de had a lisp and said, "Excellent, please follow me." He led them into the middle of the restaurant and seated them at an intimate table for two. He said, "The waitress will be with you in a moment. Please enjoy your meal." Then the maître de walked away. Trudy looked at Jack and said, "Gee, Jack, why didn't you want to eat outside? Where is your sense of adventure?" Jack smiled and said, "I guess I left it on the tracks in the subway." Trudy made a face and picked up the fork and examined the pattern. Jack said, "And besides, I don't like sharing my food with the flies, I can do that back at the office." Trudy made a disgusted face and shook her head. The waitress came over and put water on the table. She said, "My name is Melodie, can I take your order?" She was a young girl, she barely looked to be twenty. She had blond hair pulled back into a ponytail. She had on a black skirt and a white shirt with the top two buttons undone. She worked on tips. Trudy spoke up first. She said, "I'll have the double burger with everything and a large side of fries with that." Jack said, "Make that two." Melodie was writing on her pad. She said, "Would you like something to drink?" Jack normally got a *Guinness* with his meal, but he wanted to change it up. He said, "I'll have a *Smithwick's* draught." Melodie turned to Trudy, she said, "I'll have water with a lemon." Melodie smiled and said, "I'll be right back with your drinks." The waitress was gone for about 30 seconds and came back with the drinks. Jack sipped the head off the *Smithwick's* and let out and "Ahhh." The waitress smiled and went back to serving other customers.

While they were sitting in the restaurant waiting for their order, Jack checked his cellphone to see if Mike Mercury had left his apartment. He could see from the movement on the phone that Mike Mercury "A.K.A. the thin man" was on his way towards Wooster Street in the Bowery. He thought that after he finished his burger and fries, it might be a good time to pay the thin man a visit and get some answers and a little payback. He said to Trudy, "I have one more stop after we finish our meal, but I'm going to want you to wait in the car." Trudy was shaking her head, she said, "I don't know Jack. The last time I was supposed to wait in the car, it didn't end up so good." Jack smiled and said, "Don't worry Trudy, this time I'm going after the guy responsible for blowing up the car." Trudy shook her head and said, "I don't know Jack, I kind of get a bad feeling about this." Melody came over and put their burgers and fries on the table and said, "Enjoy." The burgers indeed had everything on them. There was bacon, cheddar cheese, onions, tomatoes, lettuce, a couple of different sauces, a pickle, some mushrooms, and perfectly grilled Angus beef. Trudy took a bite of the burger and her eyes opened wide. She said, "Now I think I know why they call it *Broad in the Beam*. If you eat enough of these burgers, you get broad in the beam." She smiled with a mouthful of burger. Jack said, "I knew it had something to do with a broad." He chuckled and took a bite of his burger.

About ten minutes later the burgers were gone and Trudy sat back with her hands on her stomach, she said, "Jack, that was some burger, I think I'm broad in the beam." Jack laughed and Melody came over with the bill. It came to $36.55. Jack pulled $50 out of his wallet and told Melody to keep the change. She smiled and said, "Please come again." Jack smiled back and said, "Maybe we will Melody, maybe we will."

Jack and Trudy got back into the Mustang and headed over to Wooster Street in the Bowery. They crossed over Brooklyn Bridge and drove through the maze of New York City traffic lights. About twenty minutes later they arrived at Wooster Street, and he found the bar that Harry had told him that Mike Mercury hung out at. It was a seedy section of Wooster Street. A series of three-story brick buildings with 1st-floor storefronts and apartments on the upper floors. The bar was

in a building that had light-colored wood panels on the front of the building, and green frames around large glass windows and a double door. The building looked to be very well maintained. There was no sign on the building, but Jack was sure it was the bar. It was directly next to a tattoo parlor. Jack drove past the building and parked about eight car lengths beyond the bar. He looked at his cellphone and the app told him that Mike Mercury was in the building. He took a deep breath and turned to Trudy and said, "Now, Trudy, I'm going into the bar, if I'm not out in 10 minutes, call Harry Soul at the precinct and ask for some backup." Trudy was shaking her head, she said, "I don't like this, Jack." He smiled and said, "Don't worry, Trudy. I got this." Trudy had heard this line several times before. It didn't always create confidence, and it was not always an accurate statement.

Jack got out of the car and walked towards the bar, a couple of street toughs passed him on his left and gave him the stink eye. To the people in the neighborhood, Jack looked like he was a cop or an IRS agent. Either way, it was obvious that he didn't belong here. He was wearing black pants, a white shirt and a red tie, and a black jacket. He was also wearing his favorite *Flechet Fedora* hat. He entered the bar and scanned his surroundings as if he was a cyborg. It was just a simple bar about thirty feet long, and about nine or ten tables scattered throughout. And there was also a small room in the back with a pool table. Jack noticed a couple of old guys drinking at the bar, they both looked suspiciously at Jack with one eye as he walked by. The bartender stood and watched as Jack headed towards the poolroom in the back. Jack pictured himself as *Dirty Harry*, about to make someone's day. To the bartender and the men at the bar, it appeared that Jack was headed for a showdown. As he reached the poolroom, he noticed two men standing at opposite sides of the table. They both had on white muscle shirts and jeans. One of the guy's shirts was dirty with what looked like grease and oil and a little dried blood. Jack called him Grease Boy. The other had light brown hair all hanging down over his eyes like a sheepdog. Jack called him Shaggy. As he approached the table, Grease Boy drifted behind Jack, so Jack was facing Shaggy. He said, "Hello boys, care for a little friendly game of pool?" Shaggy scowled at Jack and said, "You're in the wrong neighborhood buddy, why don't you just turn around and leave while you still can." Jack smiled, he said, "Boy's I'm just looking to hook up with an old friend. Do either of you two jokers know where I can find Mike Mercury? We have some business to take care of." Shaggy looked at Grease Boy and gave him a nod and a wink. There was a mirror behind Shaggy, and Jack could see Grease Boy winding up with his pool cue like he was holding a baseball bat. Jack could see that Grease Boy was about to clock him in the back of the head with the pool cue. Jack's cat-like reflexes kicked in. As Grease Boy was swinging the pool cue at Jack's head, in one move, Jack ducked down, and grabbed the cue ball from the pool table. The pool cue passed over Jack's head and struck Shaggy directly in the forehead. It made a hollow crack sound. Shaggy went down like a sack of old dirt. Jack stood up with the cue ball in his hand. He swung his hand around and hit Grease Boy in the head with the cue ball, and Grease Boy went down like a second sack of old dirt. Jack dropped the cue ball back onto the pool table. There was a little spot of blood on the top of the cue ball. He stepped over Grease Boy and started walking towards the exit. He stopped and turned back towards Grease Boy and Shaggy and said, "Tell Mike Mercury that Jack Trane is looking for him." They were both rolling around on the floor holding their heads. Jack turned away and casually walked out of the bar as the two old guys and the bartender just watched him make his way to the exit. No one made a move. As he walked back towards his car, he figured that Mike Mercury must have just left the bar before he arrived, so he couldn't have gotten very far, but since he knew where Mike lived and Mike knew where he lived, he was pretty sure that they would be seeing each other again soon. In fact, he was counting on it.

It was after 4:00 PM so Jack figured that it would be best to call it a day and drop Trudy off at home and get a fresh start on the case tomorrow. He had plans with Debra Thorn this evening anyway. They were going have a bite to eat down at *Big Jim's* and take in a movie. He really just wanted to spend some time away from this case. At least that was his plan.

CHAPTER 13

After Jack dropped Trudy off at her apartment, he called Debra down at her precinct through the blue tooth on his dashboard. He was still enjoying all the fancy features in his new car. She answered, "Hello, detective Thorn." Jack smiled, he said, "Hey babe, I was just in the neighborhood and thought I might pick you up a little early." Debra laughed, "Jack, pick me up with what? Your car was blown up. I'm not getting on the back of a bicycle." Then she laughed again. Jack raised one eyebrow and smiled. He said, "Yeah, well about that, I think I got that covered. I'll pick you up at about 5:30 PM in front of the precinct." Debra smiled, "Jack, you're just full of surprises, aren't you?" Jack laughed, he said, "I'd argue if I could, babe."

Jack went back to his apartment and freshened up a bit. At least he took off his white button-down shirt and put on another white button-down shirt. Instead of taking a shower, he just sprinkled on a little aftershave. He used his favorite, *Taylor of Old Bond Street*, an English classic with a masculine light scent. Then he brushed his teeth, and he was good to go. He left the apartment, put the matchstick below the bottom hinge in the door, and walked down the stairs and out the door to the street. He got into his car and stretched his neck so he could see himself in the rearview mirror. There were a few more lines in his face than yesterday, but he had also survived three attempts on his life in the past 24 hours. He sat back and looked at the dashboard. Many of the gauges and instruments still looked foreign to him, but he really enjoyed the new car smell. One of new features that he particularly liked is the fact that he didn't need to start the engine with a key. All he needed to do was push a button. Jack pushed the button and the engine roared to life. He cracked the window open and put on the radio. The song that came on was an old Guess Who song, *"American Woman.* That song wasn't going to work for him, so he changed the station, and an old Grand Funk song came on "*Some Kind of Wonderful."* He turned up the volume, put the car in gear and drove off into traffic.

Jack drove through the city with one eye on the road and one eye in the rearview mirror. He knew that it was only a matter of time before Mike Mercury caught up with him to try to finish the job that he had already failed to do three times now; once at his apartment, once in the subway, and once in blowing up his car. He knew that Mike drove a black car and he was pretty sure that it was a late model Dodge Challenger. When there is a price on your head and a target on your back, you tend to be a little more cautious, but not Jack. He was hoping with eager anticipation for Mike Mercury to appear either in front of him or in back of him. He was anxious to try out his new Mustang in a high-speed pursuit. But that would have to wait, he pulled up in front of the precinct, shut off the engine, and waited for Debra Thorn to come out. He wondered if she was going to recognize his new car, even though it was a green Mustang just like his old one.

Debra was always punctual, that's one of the things that Jack liked about her, even though Jack was rarely punctual. No doubt it fits into the theory that "opposites attract." At precisely 5:30 PM Debra came out the front door of the precinct and stood at the bottom of the stairs looking up and down the street for Jack. She didn't know that he had purchased a new Mustang which was the exact color of his recently destroyed 1968 classic Mustang. But within about 10 seconds, her detective instincts kicked in and she recognized Jack in the front seat of the green Mustang parked on the opposite side of the street from the precinct. She walked over with a casual stroll, and she approached the *Mustang* she bent over and looked at Jack with a skeptical look and said into his open window, "Jack, tell me you didn't buy another Mustang." Jack laughed and said, "Come on Debra, get in and if you behave yourself, I might even let you drive it." Debra laughed, "I just hope you can afford dinner after buying this car." Jack smiled, he said, "No problem, babe, the insurance from my other Mustang covered this one with a few bucks left over. Debra was smiling and shaking her head. She said, "That's what I like about you Jack, you always seem to make the best out of a bad situation." Jack smiled and looked at Debra. Even after a long day at the precinct, she looked like a movie star as seen through a soft filter. Her reddish-blond hair framed her face in a way that her green eyes invited a stare. Jack found himself staring at Debra whenever they were together. Debra looked at Jack and said, "Jack, what are you looking at? Do I have some food in my teeth or something?" Jack laughed, he said, "Sorry, babe, you just have that effect on me. You're strong, you're beautiful. You got it all. I just like looking at you." Debra was crossing her eyes and making her lips go to one side. Jack laughed and said, "See, I still can't look away." Debra shook her head and said, "You're crazy Jack." Jack was nodding his head up and down and he said, "That's my super-power Debra, I'm a little bit crazy." She laughed. Jack pulled into traffic and said, "Debra, are you up for a little action tonight? Debra looked puzzled. Jack said, "I'm pretty sure that I catch Mike Mercury tonight. The man responsible for blowing up my car." Debra was shaking her head and in a low voice, she said, "To tell you the truth, Jack, I was just looking forward to a nice meal and a movie. You know, just to relax." Jack smiled and said, "No problem, Debra. I think we can do both." Debra raised one eyebrow and looked in Jack's direction with a disapproving look. Jack continued driving in the direction of *Big Jim's Sports Bar*. He was pretty sure that at some point in the evening, Mike Mercury would make an appearance and Jack already had a plan in place.

Jack pulled into the parking lot for *Big Jim's* and parked his car. They both got out of the car and Jack put his arm around Debra, and they walked into the restaurant. As they walked past the bar, Jack waved to his friend Teddy K, and they sat down at a table. Teddy brought two ice-cold *Guinness* over for Jack and Debra and then asked, "What can I get for my favorite police officer and her pain in the butt PI friend?" Jack smiled and said, "Thanks for the compliment, Teddy, I'm feeling like a deluxe burger with extra fries tonight." Debra smiled and said, "Make it two, Teddy." Teddy gave them a wink and went back towards the bar.

Debra and Jack made small talk about the day's business and time passed quickly. Before long Teddy K returned with their burgers. He placed the burgers and fries on the table in front of Jack and Debra and then he whispered into Jack's ear, "That thin guy with the dark hair was in here looking for you earlier. And he's back. Just to let you know, he's sitting at the table over in the corner." Teddy moved his head towards the corner. Then Teddy said, "I don't think he's seen you yet. Do you want me to create a distraction or get rid of him?" Jack smiled and said, "Thanks Teddy, no worries, I was hoping for this. I'll take it from here." Teddy K winked at Jack and walked back to the bar. Debra was watching as Teddy was whispering to Jack but couldn't hear what was said. She looked at Jack, raised her hands and said, "So Jack, what's going on? Are you going to let me in on your little conversation with Teddy K?" Jack raised his head up a little and looked towards the corner of the room. He could see Mike Mercury sitting at the table by himself. He said to Debra, "Mike Mercury, A.K.A. the thin man, is sitting at the table in the corner. He hasn't seen me yet, but I know that he's looking for me. I'm going to let him see me and then follow us out of the bar.

Then I'm going to lead him on a little chase and then you can apprehend him and take him in?" Debra looked at Jack with wide-open eyes. She said, "Apprehend him? Apprehend him for what? Do you have any evidence that he put the bomb in your car? You can't just go around arresting people because you suspect that they did something wrong, Jack." Jack shook his head, he said, "You don't understand Debra, I have a history with this guy. He came to my apartment with a loaded Glock. He tied me up and put me on the subway tracks to try to kill me, and then he blew up my car." Debra was looking at Jack with her right eyebrow raised. She said, "But Jack, to this point, you have no solid evidence that he was responsible for any of those things. I can't arrest anyone because of suspicion. You need to have some solid evidence." Jack said, "But Debra, he came to my apartment with a loaded gun." Debra said, "But that's not enough to arrest him, Jack." Jack nodded, he said, "Debra by the end of the evening, we'll have some solid evidence." They both picked up their burgers and took a bite. Jack poured some extra ketchup on his fries, and they enjoyed the best burgers in the city.

When Jack had finished, he stood up and waved to Teddy K. He purposely cleared his throat and yelled "Hey, Teddy, we'll take that check now." He wanted to make sure that Mike Mercury noticed him. As Jack was yelling across the bar to Teddy K, he could see out of the corner of his eye that Mike Mercury had indeed noticed him, and Mike stood up and inconspicuously walked out of the bar. It was obvious now that Mike Mercury would be waiting for him in the parking lot. No doubt Mike felt that he was in control of the situation and that's what Jack wanted him to think. This was all playing out exactly as Jack had planned.

Jack paid the bill and left Teddy K a $20 tip. This was generous even by Jack's standards. But Teddy had been passing information Jack's way for a long time, and Jack appreciated it, and Teddy K understood appreciation in the form of dollar bills. Jack and Debra got up from the table and started walking towards the exit. Jack reached over and put his hand on Debra's shoulder and they both stopped. He looked into Debra's eyes and said, "Mike Mercury is going to be waiting for us in the parking lot. I'm not sure what his next play is, but I'm pretty sure that he's not going to try to shoot me since I have his gun at my apartment. But just stay alert, I'm going to take him on a car chase that will make his head spin," Debra looked at him with squinted eyes and a curled lip, she said, "Please, Jack, we just ate. I really don't need my head to be spinning." Jack laughed, he said, "No, Mike Mercury's head will be spinning, not yours." Debra was shaking her head, she said, "I don't know Jack, car chases and hamburgers don't usually go too well." Jack smiled, he said, "Just keep your badge and your gun handy and forget about all the traffic rules we might be breaking." Debra raised one eyebrow and said, "You know, Jack, by the end of this night, I might be arresting you." Jack laughed, he said, "I'll bet you say that to all the boys." Debra made a face and they left *Big Jim's*, arm in arm.

The night air was crisp. Darkness had fallen over the city and the streetlights were now responsible for illuminating New York City. As the door to the restaurant closed behind them, Jack scanned the parking lot for the black Dodge Challenger that he suspected Mike Mercury was driving. In the back row of the parking lot, he could see the Challenger parked along the edge of the lot. This was a strategic position if you wanted to leave quickly or tail someone. Jack knew that Mike Mercury was planning on following him, no doubt he planned to kill Jack at some point during the night. But Jack had a plan of his own. He and Debra got into his Mustang. He looked at her with a determined look and said, "Tighten your seat belt, babe." And he started the car. The engine idled for about 20 seconds and Jack made his way to the parking lot exit. He stopped and waited until he was sure that Mike

Mercury was going to follow him. He watched as Mike pulled out of his parking space and start towards the exit. Jack put the gas pedal to the floor, his tires squealed, and a little blue smoke came up from the tires. Within four seconds, he was going sixty miles per hour. He looked in his rearview mirror and he could see the black Challenger coming out of the parking lot with tires screeching and blue smoke rising into the air. Debra just sat and watched as Jack's plan unfolded. She knew that it was best not to talk during a high-speed pursuit. She had been in plenty of high-speed chases during her time on the police force, just never in a brand-new Mustang Shelby GT-500. Jack turned onto the Avenue of The Americas. There were six lanes, three on each side, so Jack had plenty of room to accelerate and maneuver. He looked in his rearview mirror and he could see the black Challenger about 10 car lengths behind. Jack took a sharp left onto Vandam Street. It was a one-way street and there was work being done on the left side of the street. Orange cones blocked off the left side of the street and there were large construction vehicles all along the street. A woman wearing what appeared to be a white nightgown was crossing the street. Jack swerved to avoid her and took out three or four of the orange cones. The black Challenger followed but had lost some ground. The Challenger ran over the cones that Jack had tipped over. Jack quickly came up on Varick Street and he made a hard left. He avoided a car entering at his right, as he had just gone through a red traffic light. His tires squealed, but they held the road. Debra reached out and put her hands on the dashboard out of concern for her safety. Jack could see the sign pointing to the Holland Tunnel. He accelerated and almost immediately he was going eighty miles per hour. He loved the immediate response of the engine in his new Mustang. Right before he got to the entrance for the Holland Tunnel, Jack slammed on his brakes and made a hard right into Broom Street and spun his car around 180 degrees, so he was now facing Varick Street. Debra was still holding on to the dashboard and now she was looking at Jack in disbelief. Mike Mercury had assumed that Jack had entered the Tunnel. Jack sat and watched as the black Challenger drove past him and entered the Holland Tunnel. Now the chase was on.

The Tunnel was dimly lit with six-foot fluorescent light bulbs that were lining the ceiling on each side. The walls were white tile, but they looked gray inside the Tunnel. There were only two lanes inside the Tunnel. One direction was going East towards New York and one was going West towards New Jersey. They were in the West-bound Lane. As Jack entered the Tunnel, he could see the Challenger about six car lengths ahead. It was unusual, but the Tunnel had very light traffic and there was plenty of room to maneuver. Jack pulled up on the Challenger's rear bumper and he flashed his lights on and off a few times. Mike Mercury now noticed Jack behind him, and he sped up. The Challenger had a Hemi-engine and was just as capable of reaching high speeds as quickly as Jack's Mustang. Jack accelerated and stayed right on Mike Mercury's rear bumper. Suddenly the Challenger swerved to the left and Jack didn't react fast enough and hit a large patch of oil that had somehow dripped from the ceiling onto the road. Jack's car began fish-tailing. He tried to compensate but his Mustang spun 180 degrees and was now facing in the opposite direction. The car was still in motion, so Jack hit the gas pedal and turned the car back 180 degrees, so he was again in pursuit of the Challenger. Jack looked over at Debra. She was holding her stomach and the worry lines in her forehead showed in the dim Tunnel light. The high-speed chase continued throughout the Tunnel. As they were approaching the end of the Tunnel, the Challenger once again accelerated and passed a small pickup truck, but as he did, he clipped the back of the truck and the Challenger spun to the left and hit the guard rail as he came out of the Tunnel. They were now in New Jersey, the Garden State. Mike Mercury tried to compensate as he swerved away from the guard rail, but he ended up jumping the curb and came to rest on a neatly manicured patch of grass with the nose of his car just coming into contact with a small tree. The damage to the Challenger was just enough so that Mike Mercury could no longer drive the car. For now, he was out of commission. Jack slowed down as he came out of the Tunnel, and he waved and smiled at Mike as he passed by. Jack could see the rage on Mike's face as he drove past him with his Mustang. It wasn't exactly the outcome that Jack was looking for, but for now, it gave him a little satisfaction. He was sure that he would be seeing Mike Mercury again soon.

Jack turned to Debra with a wry smile and said, "Ok, now how about that movie? Debra was still holding her stomach, she looked at Jack as if she was in pain, she said, "What do you say we call it a night, Jack? I don't know how much more fun I can take tonight." Jack looked surprised, he said, "Are you sure, babe? I was looking forward to a little extra butter on my popcorn tonight." Debra shook her head, "Not tonight, Jack. But we'll have to do this again real soon." Jack smiled and said, "You read my mind, Debra, you read my mind." Jack's dating skills needed work.

CHAPTER 14

It was 8:00 AM and the alarm was buzzing, so Jack reached over and turned it off. He sat up in bed and rubbed his eyes. It never really never helped him to wake up but at least it got his blood circulating. As he sat on the edge of the bed, he could hear music coming through the wall from the next apartment. He was going to bang on the wall with a broom so they would turn down the music, but he recognized the song. It was *"The Wanderer"* by Dion. He always liked that song, so he let it play. He got out of bed and went into the bathroom. About 20 minutes later he came back out all showered and shaved and ready for what the day might bring. Today he was going to interview Kristen Monree and hopefully tie up this little conspiracy around Heinrich King's death and maybe make some sense of who might be involved in his murder. So far, Marie Robbin, Audrey Linn, Victoria Pichettes, and Siobhan Peison all claimed that they were out with friends on the night of "King Heini's" death. Jack was wondering if Kristen Monree would corroborate their story or perhaps implicate herself. He went over to his walk-in closet to pull out his clothes for the day and to his surprise, he could actually walk into his closet. The cleaning lady that he had hired must have shown up when he was out yesterday, and it looked like she had organized his clothes like never before. For the first time in recent memory, Jack was able to walk into his closet. He could actually see pants and jackets hanging on hangers. It kind of threw him for a loop. It had been a long time since he could actually choose the pants and jackets that he wore each day, it was always a matter of chance and it always seemed to work out just right. Now the pressure was on. Whatever clothes he picked out to wear today was a reflection of his own taste, good or bad. If he looked like a dufus, it was totally his own fault. He stood looking at the pants hanging on the hangers. There were blue ones, brown ones, gray ones, green ones. The choices were overwhelming since Jack usually just randomly picked his clothes for the day without really looking. After he weighed all the options, he decided that today would be a good day to wear khaki pants. He wasn't expecting any bleeding or accidents with oil, so they should stay clean all day. He grabbed a light brown jacket and a paisley brown tie and put them on his bed. He walked over to his armoire and took out one of his perfectly pressed white button-down shirts. He put it on, and then he added the pants and the tie. He looked at himself in the mirror and gave himself a nod of approval. He was now ready for his day. More specifically, he was ready for breakfast. He picked up his cellphone from his nightstand and put it into his right jacket pocket, then he picked up his wallet and put it into the left jacket pocket. He looked around to make sure he had everything, put on his hat, and he left his apartment. He remembered to put the matchstick just above the bottom hinge in the door.

As Jack came out of his apartment building, it occurred to him that Mike Mercury would be looking for him this morning and Mike knew that he usually had breakfast at the *Coffee Café*, so he decided that he would have to have breakfast somewhere else this morning. There was a place called *"Eggs and Bagels"* over on the West Side, so Jack thought it would be a good idea to have breakfast there this morning to avoid any confrontation with Mike Mercury. He wanted to be prepared for their next encounter, he wanted to be able to control the outcome. We don't always get what we want.

Jack didn't want to drive his new Mustang over to the West Side, so he hailed down a taxi. A mustard yellow *Crown Vic* with a taxi sign on the car roof pulled over and Jack got in. The driver turned around and asked "Where to, man? Uptown, downtown, midtown, it don't matter none, I'll be driving all day. You just tell me where you want to go and we'll just…" Jack broke in, "How about the *Eggs and Bagels* on the West Side?" Jack recognized the driver, it was Larray. He had taken rides with Larray before. Larray was the kind of driver that never stopped talking. He had been on the streets for 20 years; he had a good insight into the city and 20 years of stories and complaints to go with them. Larray liked to share all these with his fares. Larray turned back towards the steering wheel and focused on the road. He flipped on the meter and pulled out into traffic. Larry said, "Oh yeah, the *Eggs and Bagels*, man I haven't had breakfast there in years. But I'll tell you this, the last time I ate there I had the ham and eggs, and man that was probably…." Larray kept talking and just Jack just blocked him out. Jack was deep in thought thinking about his next encounter with Mike Mercury. Larray turned around and looked at Jack. He said, "Hey, wait a minute man, haven't I seen you before? I know you been in my cab. You got one of those faces that looks like you could hurt somebody." Larray laughed and kept driving and kept talking. "You know man, I've been driving for twenty years, and people in this city just…." Larray's voice became background noise for Jack. Mixed in with the sound of car horns blowing and sirens blaring there was a sense of comfort as Jack sat back and closed his eyes.

Fifteen minutes later the taxi pulled over in front of *Eggs and Bagels*. Larray was still talking, but he turned off the meter and looked at Jack in the back seat, and said, "That will be $17.75, my man." Jack pulled out $30 and handed it to Larray. He said, "Keep the change, my man." Larray had a big smile. He said, "My pleasure, man." He stuffed the $30 in his shirt pocket. Jack got out of the taxi and Larray pulled back into traffic. Jack walked into the *Eggs and Bagels* and looked around. It was very crowded, so he found a seat at the counter and sat down. Almost immediately a large woman with light brown hair and heavy red lipstick was standing in front of Jack with a coffee pot raised in her right hand. She had a small white name tag on her shirt that said "Monique". She said to Jack. "You want regular or decaf?" Jack smiled and said, "Well, I'd really like a Vanilla Latte if you have that." Monique looked at Jack with one eye squinted and said, "Starbucks is down the street, buddy. If you want coffee, that's what we have here." Jack turned over his coffee cup and Monique filled it up with a dark blend of Colombian brew. Monique said, "So what'll it be?" Jack said, do you have a menu?" She said, "We're Eggs and Bagels, that's the menu. You choose the Eggs, we cook them. You choose the Bagels, we toast them." She pointed to the wall and there was a variety of Bagels listed on a black chalkboard. Jack cleared his throat and said, "Give me two scrambled eggs and a raisin bagel." Monique yelled over her shoulder, "Two eggs, shake them. Bagel with spots." Monique walked away. Jack looked at his black coffee and breathed in the aroma. It smelled a little skunky. He noticed a small tray with sugar packets and a little tin container with cream. He added as much cream and sugar as he could to make the coffee palatable to his taste. He closed his eyes and took a sip. He put the cup down and added another packet of sugar.

Jack tried to get comfortable. There was a heavy-set man in work-pants and a plaid shirt to his left and another heavy-set man wearing sweatpants and a sweatshirt to his right. Jack couldn't move without touching elbows with one of them. He just sipped his coffee and grimaced. Monique came back and put a plate down in front of Jack. It had what looked like a pile of eggbeaters and a toasted bagel on the side. There was also a little cup of cream cheese on the plate as well. Monique said, "Eat up and just yell if you need something." She topped off Jack's coffee with more of the dark brew. Jack smiled and put a fork into the eggs and took a bite. The texture was like eggs but there was no taste.

He spread the cream cheese on the bagels and took a bite. It was very chewy and there was actually a nice cinnamon flavor. The restaurant was very noisy with the sound of plates being stacked, spoons and forks hitting the floor, the morning banter of the customers, and Monique yelling orders across the room. Jack missed the *Coffee Café* but he knew that until he had Mike Mercury out of the picture, it wouldn't be safe to go there. He finished his meal and Monique came over with the check. She said, "How was everything, honey." Jack could see that Monique had changed gears and now she was working him for the tip. Jack smiled and said, "Unbelievable, Monique. It was unbelievable." And he really meant it. Monique smiled and Jack put $20 down on the counter, the bill came to $10. He said, "Keep the change, Monique." She picked up the $20 with her thumb and index finger and said, "Please come again, honey." Jack smiled and thought to himself, "Not on a bet, honey." The restaurant left a bad taste in Jack's mouth. Or maybe that was just the coffee. He gave Monique a wink and left the restaurant. He walked outside and he raised his hand to hail a taxi.

A taxi pulled over and Jack got in. The driver was an older gentleman with silver hair and a well-manicured mustache, and he spoke with a very proper English accent. The name on his driver's tag read, "Ellsworth Bagby." The driver turned around and asked Jack, "Where might I deliver you today, my good man?" Jack smiled, he said, "Hey Ellsworth, I like your accent. I guess you didn't grow up in the Bronx." Ellsworth made a disgusted face. He said, "I should say not, my friend. For 30 years I was at the service of the Royal Family. On many occasions, I ferried the Queen herself." Jack was still smiling in the back seat. He said, "Sounds like a nice gig Ellsworth. How come you're driving taxis in New York instead of ferrying the Queen?" Ellsworth turned and looked out the front windshield, cleared his throat, and said, "Well let's just say there was an incident, and my services were no longer needed." Jack patted Ellsworth on the shoulder, he said, "Don't worry old boy, you can drive a taxi in New York no matter how many incidents you have." Jack laughed, but Ellsworth didn't." He gave Ellsworth the address for his parking garage and Ellsworth started the meter and pulled into traffic. Ellsworth was not a talker; like a proper Englishman he just drove the taxi and kept silent. Jack was good with that. About 15 minutes later Ellsworth pulled up in front of Jack's garage and turned off the meter. He turned around and looked at Jack and said, "That will be $15, old boy." Jack smiled, he gave Ellsworth $25 and said, "Get yourself a spot of tea, Ellsworth." Jack got out of the taxi and Ellsworth looked at him as if he had just been insulted. Perhaps he had been.

Jack took out his cell phone and dialed Trudy's number. The phone rang twice, and Trudy picked up. "Jack, it's only like 9:30 I don't usually hear from you until at least 10 o'clock. What's the matter? You couldn't sleep?" Jack was shaking his head, he said, "Trudy, where are you?" She said, "I'm in the office, Jack. Where do you think I am?" Jack was still shaking his head, he said, "I thought we agreed that you would take it easy and work from home today." Trudy was snapping her gum, she said, "No Jack, we didn't agree to that, you did. Besides, I'm fine, staying home makes me anxious." Jack was looking up at the sky, he said, "Ok Trudy, why don't you just give me Kristen Monree's address so I can go out there and interview her." Trudy raised her voice, "No way, Jack. You said I could come out in the field on this case! If you want Kristen Monree's address, you have to come and pick me up. We'll go out to her house together, just like the last two interviews." Jack knew he had been beaten. He said, "OK Trudy, I'll be in front of the office in about 15 minutes. I'll call you when I'm there." Trudy smiled, she said, "Now you're talking, Jack. Let's go fry us some Kristen Monree butt." Jack exhaled, "Relax Trudy, we just want to interviewer her, not cook her for dinner." Trudy giggled, "Sorry Jack, that was just my Private

Investigator mojo. You know what I mean." Jack said to himself, "I wish I did."

Jack walked into the parking garage and gave Fernando, the parking attendant, a wave, and he walked up the ramp and over to his car. He got into his car and sat for a minute. That new car smell can be intoxicating. He started the car and drove out of the garage towards his office. About twenty minutes later Jack pulled up in front of the office and Trudy was waiting for him out front. Jack pulled the car over and she got in. Trudy was dressed in dark pants, and a red turtleneck shirt and a brown leather jacket. She had on matte pink lipstick and her blond hair rested on her shoulders. Jack looked at her and said, "Trudy you look like a blonde *Nikki Heat*." Trudy smiled and said, "Glad you noticed, Jack. Now put this address in your GPS, and let's get some answers." She gave Jack Kristen Monree's address. She lived at 4819 91st Place Queens, New York. Jack put the address into his GPS and said, "OK, Trudy, but we do this interview as a team. I'll take the lead and you can ask some follow-up questions if you want." Trudy snapped her gum, and in her low gravelly voice, she said, "Whatever you say, boss." Jack shook his head and drove off towards Kristen Monree's apartment.

About 20 minutes later they pulled up in front of Kristen Monree's residence. She lived in a three-story brick apartment building with a couple of small trees on the sidewalk and a small yard out front. It was a well-kept neighborhood and Kristen lived on the second floor. They both got out of the car and walked in synchronized steps up to the front door of the building. Trudy reached out and rang the bell. The door buzzer went off immediately and the door unlocked. Jack grabbed the doorknob and pulled the door open. They started climbing the stairs to the second floor and Jack looked up and saw Kristen Monree standing at the top of the stairs waiting for them. She was dressed in a light pink skirt and a white pullover shirt. Her hair was pulled back into a ponytail and her soft features were accentuated by her tasteful makeup. Her blue eyes had an innocent yet piercing effect and they were framed by long lustrous eyelashes. She looked down at Jack and Trudy and said, "I've been expecting you." Jack looked at Trudy with a surprised expression and then looked back at Kristen and said, "Well, here we are." They walked up the stairs and Kristen led them down the hall and into her apartment. Once they were all inside, she closed the door behind them. There was a moment of awkward silence, so Jack pulled out the card that Harry Soul had given him, and he handed it to Kristen Monree. She looked at the front and back of the card a couple of times with no expression and handed the card back to Jack. The apartment was small. It looked to be a combination kitchen and living room and there was a bedroom down a narrow hallway. Two of the walls had windows, so the room was very bright. It was tastefully decorated yet simple. There was a couch against one of the walls in the living room. It was a turquoise couch, the kind you find at *Ikea*. There was also a chair to match opposite the couch. Kristen invited them into her living room to sit down on her couch. Jack sat at one end of the couch and Trudy sat on at the other end. Kristen sat on a chair that was directly opposite. She said, "Can I get you both something to drink? I have some wonderful green herbal tea. It does wonders for your nerves." Jack looked at Trudy, raised his right eyebrow and said, "No, Thank you, Kristen. Our nerves are pretty good. We just have a few questions that would like to ask you." Kristen looked down at the floor and said, "I just want to clear the air, this has gone on long enough." Jack smiled, he said, "We couldn't agree more, Kristen. But just how would you like to clear the air?" Kristen looked up at the ceiling and a small tear dripped down the side of her face. She said, "It's like I said to that other detective Slotz…" Jack broke in, "You mean Watts?" Kristen corrected herself, "Oh, yes, it was detective Watts. I told him that Jackie

King offered me $10,000 to say that I was out with some friends the night of Heinrich King's murder." Jack broke in again. He said, "You told him that?" Kristen was nodding her head up and down. She said, "I didn't take the money, Mr. Trane, but I thought about it."

Jack tried to gain her confidence. He said, "Relax, Kristen, we're just here to help. If you didn't…" Before Jack could continue, Trudy broke in with her Dragnet voice, "So where were you on the night that Heinrich King was murdered?"

Jack looked at Trudy with his eyes wide open. He was a little irritated that Trudy had just interrupted his line of questioning. But Kristen answered in a low voice, "I was here, alone. But I didn't kill Heinrich King! And I didn't take the money!" Jack broke in, "Calm down, Kristen, we don't think you killed Heini King. But you may have some information that will help us to solve this case." Jack handed Kristen a tissue from his pocket, and she dried her eyes. Jack said, "Kristen, did you notice anything about Heinrich King before you left the office on that Friday night he was killed?" Kristen thought for a moment, then she said, "Yes, he was irritable. More irritable than he normally was. He was nervous. I remember that he dropped his cellphone on the floor, and I could hear him yelling and screaming but no one was there. And then he asked me to leave and go home early. He never did that before." Jack was taking all this in. He asked her, "Did you tell all this to Detective Watts?" Kristen was nodding her head yes. She said, "Yes, but after I told him that Jackie King offered me $10,000, he didn't seem too interested in anything else I had to say." Jack was nodding his head. Under his breath, he said, "That incompetent fool. He couldn't recognize a cow if it was mooing in his face." Kristen folded her arms, and raised her eyebrows and said, "I think Jackie King had something to do with the murder." Trudy was nodding her head, in her Dragnet voice, she said, "Can you back that up with any evidence, Miss

Monree?" Kristen looked sheepish and said, "Well no, but it does seem a little suspicious that she offered me $10,000 to say I was with some friends that night." Jack nodded his head, "Yes, Kristen, you might just be right." Trudy was about to ask another question, but Jack said, "Thank you, Kristen, I think you have helped us a great deal with this case. If we need anything else, we'll be sure to be in touch." Jack stood up from the couch and Trudy hesitantly followed. Kristen stood up and led them to the door. Trudy shook Kristen's hand and said, "Thank you Miss Monree, you've been very helpful." Jack thanked Kristen and they left the apartment.

When they got back to the car, Trudy looked at Jack with a surprised look and said, "Jack, I think she was going to crack. I had a couple of more questions that I wanted to ask. Why did we leave?" Jack smiled, he said, "Trudy, there is no need for Kristen to crack. She wasn't involved in the murder, but as for Jackie King and those other four women, that's another story." Trudy blew a bubble and snapped her gum. She said, "OK Jack, so what's our next move?" Jack smiled and said, "I'm glad you asked." Trudy was looking at Jack with one eyebrow raised. He said, "I want to get Audrey Linn, Victoria Pichettes, Siobhan Peison, and Marie Robbin all in the room at the same time and I think I can flush out the killer." Trudy looked at Jack with a skeptical look on her face, she said, "How are you going to do that, Jack? How are you going to get them all together in one room?" Jack was smiling, "That's where you come in, Trudy. I'm going to drop you off at the office and you're going to call them invite them all to show up at the precinct tomorrow." Trudy looked at Jack with squinted eyes and said, "Why would they come, Jack?" Jack smiled and said, "You just tell them is the courtesy of the NYPD. I'll set it up with Harry." Trudy smiled, "Yeah, I like that, Jack. Do I get one of those cards that Harry Soul gave to you? The one that says we're working with the NYPD?"

Jack laughed, "That card is about as good as a teaspoon after a snowstorm. Just use your Dragnet voice, that will be much more effective." Trudy smiled and gave Jack an exploding fist bump. Jack drove into traffic and about 20 minutes later dropped Trudy off at the office. As Trudy was leaving the car Jack yelled out, "Remember, Trudy, set up the meeting for tomorrow afternoon and let me know when it's all set." Trudy gave Jack a thumbs up and walked into the office.

Jack's cell phone rang, and he picked up. It was Mike Mercury. Mike said, "Hey, Trane man, I think that it's time that we meet face to face." Jack was gritting his teeth, he said, "Name the place and time, thin man. I'll be there." Mike's voice was slow and deliberate, he said, "On the corner of Terrace Drive and 5th Ave, park your car at the entrance to Central Park. Get out of your car and sit on the bench and wait for me. I'll be there." Jack's car was already on the way to Terrace Drive. He was a little uneasy about the meeting set up, he wanted to be in control, but at least it was in a public place. Jack said, "I'll be there in ten minutes, punk. Don't stand me up." They both hung up the phones. Ten minutes later Jack parked his car on Terrace Drive, he got out of the car and sat on the bench. It was a bright sunny day. Jack sat back on the bench and crossed his legs. Then everything went dark.

CHAPTER 15

Jack opened his eyes and tried to focus. There was a throbbing pain in the back of his head. He blinked a few times and things started to come into view. He could see that he was in a very large open room and there were racks on each side of the room. On one side of the room, the shelves were filled with different kinds of merchandise. It looked like there were boxes with cameras, laptops, diapers, cigarettes, candy bars, and much more, all stacked three shelves high. On the other side of the room, there were car tires, hand tools, sporting goods, and a variety of construction equipment. He realized that he was in a warehouse. He also realized that he was sitting on the floor tied to a support beam with his hands behind his back. The last thing he remembered is that he was sitting on the bench outside Central Park waiting for Mike Mercury. Obviously, Mike was waiting for him too, and now he needed to come up with a quick plan quickly to get out of the warehouse before Mike Mercury showed up. That was going to be a little difficult since he was tied up to a support beam. Jack could hear the buzzing of the fluorescent lights overhead, other than that, it was completely quiet. Jack assumed that for the time being he was alone. He tried to move his hands, but his wrists were bound tightly with what appeared to be industrial zip ties. He would need something sharp like a knife to cut through them. He had two knife blades in the heels of his shoes but there was no way to get them into his hands. He figured that he would just wait until the thin man showed up and then he would use his superior intellect to outsmart Mike Mercury. He didn't have to wait very long.

Jack heard a door open and then slam shut. Then he heard foot-steps. It sounded like several people were coming his way. At the far end of the warehouse, he could see three figures walking together in his direction. As they got closer, he was able to recognize all three. On the left was Shaggy from the pool room and he had a bandage around his head. On the right was Grease Boy from the pool room and he too had a bandage on his head. No doubt the result of their little altercation with Jack. And in the middle was Mike Mercury, the thin man. As they approached, Jack could hear Shaggy and Grease Boy arguing about what they were going to do with Jack, they were looking for some payback after what Jack did to them in the pool room. Mike Mercury told them both to shut up and let him handle this. When they got about ten feet away from where Jack was sitting, Jack smiled at them and said, "Hey, don't I know you guys from the pool room? Sorry, we never got to finish our little game." Shaggy gritted his teeth, and said, "Don't worry funny man, we're going to finish you now." Grease Boy was smiling and punching his fist into his other hand. Mike Mercury pushed them both away and said, "Ok, Trane, before I let my boys here, loose on you, do you have anything to say for yourself?" Jack thought for a moment and said, "It looks like your boys have already been in a little fight. Don't you think they've had enough?" Jack laughed. Shaggy walked up to Jack and punched him in the ribs. Jack held his breath and tightened his muscles and absorbed most of the punch. Shaggy was not much of a tough guy. Jack smiled and said, "Is that all you got, junior?" Shaggy reached back to punch Jack again and Mike held his arm back. Mike said, "All in good time boys, all in good time." Jack exhaled and relaxed his stomach muscles. Just then Mike Mercury swung his fist and hit Jack square on the jaw. Jack's head pivoted to the right, and he saw a flash of light. There was a little blood from the inside of his lip trickling down his face. Jack spit some blood onto the floor, he said, "I hope your janitor doesn't mind."

Jack needed to distract them until he could come up with a plan to escape. But Mike Mercury had a plan of his own. Mike squinted at Jack and said, "All right, enough games. Let's get down to business." Jack knew that Mike had already tried to kill him three times. He was pretty sure that this was the business Mike was talking about. Mike scowled at Jack and said, "How much do you know about this case, Trane, and who else knows?" Jack could see that before Mike could kill him, he needed to know how much Jack knew about the case and if anyone else knew anything that could implicate him. Obviously, Mike was trying to clean up all the loose ends. Jack once again found himself as a loose end. But this was good. Jack was going to use this to his advantage. He was developing a plan in his head that was hopefully going to get him out of this mess. Jack started to make small talk. He said, "Mike, what are you running here, some kind of supply depot for the underground? I'll bet all the merchandise on these shelves just fell off the back of a truck, right?" Mike was not amused, he said, "Shut up, Trane. I'll ask the questions here. Now tell me what you know." Jack smiled and said, "Well, I know your two associates over there probably never made it past the 9th grade. I know that you're probably going to regret that you kidnapped me. And I know that before this is over, you're the one that's going to be sitting on the floor." Shaggy and Grease Boy were moving closer as if to intimidate Jack. Mike looked down at Jack and said, "Oh, so you're a tough guy?" Mike looked at Shaggy and Grease Boy and said, "Work him over, boys."

For the next two minutes, Jack absorbed punches to his stomach, his ribs, and both sides of his face. When Shaggy and Grease Boy stopped, there was a little blood dripping from Jack's nose, there was a cut under his left eye and his ribs were throbbing. Shaggy and Grease

Boy stepped back and in a calm voice, Mike said, "Are you ready to talk now, Trane?" Jack looked up at Mike and he closed his eyes to fake passing out. Mike looked at Shaggy and Grease Boy and said, "Let's leave him here for a little while and when he wakes up, maybe he'll be ready to talk. The three of them walked away in the direction that they had come from. Jack heard the door open and close, and once again he was alone in the warehouse. Jack knew that Shaggy and Grease Boy didn't have a complete brain between them, but the real weak link was Mike Mercury. Mike thought of himself as the boss. He was self-centered and he liked nice things. Jack remembered how Mike particularly liked his garnet pinkie ring, which he no longer had. Jack was going to use this to his advantage. Jack was going to tell Mike that he had his garnet pinkie ring, and if he wanted it back, Jack would lead him to it. Of course, Jack was going to lead him right back to his apartment, where he had Mike's Glock in his desk drawer. It was a long shot, but it was the only plan Jack could come up with. In the end, he was hoping to turn Mike Mercury over to Debra Thorn to be arrested. He might not have enough yet for a murder charge, but he could definitely get him for grand larceny and distribution of stolen property for all the merchandise in this warehouse. He sat back and waited for Mike Mercury and his two flunkies to return.

About thirty minutes passed and Jack heard the door open and close again. He could see Shaggy, Grease Boy, and Mike Mercury walking towards him slowly. They seemed to be having a heated conversation, but once again Mike told them both to just "shut up" and follow orders. They walked up to Jack and stood over him. Jack looked up and said, "Well, if it isn't the Three Stooges. You guys just returning from your Mensa meeting?" Grease Boy and Shaggy looked at each other and Grease Boy said, "What's a Mensa?" Mike looked down at Jack and said, "Are you ready to talk yet?" Then Shaggy chimed in, "Or do you want some more of what we just gave you?" Jack smiled and said, "I'll tell you what I want. I want to get out of here." Mike smiled and said, "Yeah, well, I don't think that's going to happen." Mike took Jack's cell phone from his jacket, and he walked over to Jack and dropped the cell phone on the floor and crushed it with the heel of his shoe. Jack had a disgusted look on his face and said, "First my car, now my cell phone. You know Mike you're starting to irritate me a little." Jack stretched out his legs on the floor as if he was quite relaxed and said, "Mike, I think you want something too. And I might just be the one to give you what you want." Mike made a puzzled face and said, "The only thing I want from you is information." Jack said, "Really, Mike? I remember that you used to wear a really cool pinkie ring with a garnet stone in the middle. I'll bet that you would like that back." Mike gritted his teeth and said, "What do you know about that ring, Trane? My mother gave me that ring before she went to the big house. Yeah, I want it back. What are you saying? You have the ring?" To Mike, that ring was more important than covering over Heinrich King's murder or the information he wanted from Jack. Jack knew now that he had Mike just where he wanted him. Jack said, "I don't have the ring, Mike. But I know where it is. And I'll take you there. All you need to do is take off these zip ties from my wrists, and I'll get you the ring. We'll call it even." Mike still had his teeth gritted, he said, "OK, Trane. Here is how it's going to go down. I'm going to cut those zip ties off and I'm going to put a set of handcuffs on you. And you are going to drive me to wherever my ring is. And you better not be lying to me. Because if you are I'll take you apart, piece by piece." Mike pulled a handgun out of his pocket; it was a 38 Special. He said, "One wrong move, Trane, and you get it with this." Shaggy and Grease Boy were in the background nodding their heads.

Mike cut the zip ties off of Jack's wrists. Jack stood up and stretched a little bit. He said, "I've been looking over your operation here Mike, you must be paying off on *Don Corleone* himself if you're fencing all this stuff with no hassles." Mike pointed the gun at Jack and said, "Shut up, Trane. Get moving, you just focus on getting me my ring." Mike looked at Shaggy and Grease Boy and said, "You guys stay here and mind the store. I'll be back when I get everything I need out of Trane." Jack could hear the conversation, but Mike didn't seem to care. Mike kicked Jack in the back of his legs and said, "Get moving, we don't have all night." Jack didn't know if it was day or night. He had lost all track of time. But From what Mike had just said, Jack now knew that it was night and had probably just lost only a few hours. As they were leaving, Jack turned back towards Grease Boy and Shaggy and said, "Now you boys stay out of trouble until we get back." Jack laughed and Grease Boy and Shaggy gave Jack a rude gesture. Jack and Mike walked out the exit doors and onto the street. Up until now, Jack had no idea where they were, but now he could plainly see that he was on Wooster Street in the Bowery, not far from the pool room where he met Shaggy and Grease Boy. Mike pointed to a car. It was the black Challenger with a dent in the front hood. Jack walked towards the passenger seat, but Mike said, "You're not riding, Trane, you're driving." He motioned for Jack to come over to the driver's side. When Jack opened the door and got in, Mike threw the handcuff keys at Jack and said, "Open the cuffs and put one cuff on the steering wheel and the other on your wrist." Jack complied and handed the keys back to Mike. Mike got in the car on the passenger side. He pointed the gun at Jack and said, "Drive." The car had a pushbutton starter, so Jack pushed the button, and the car came to life. Jack could feel the power behind the Hemi engine. The Challenger had a *Scat-pack* and about five hundred horsepower. Jack looked at Mike and said, "I'm surprised that you didn't give my Mustang a little more of a run for my money with this car." Mike wasn't amused, he said, "Just shut up and drive!" Jack put the car in gear and drove into traffic in the direction of Uptown. He was headed to his office.

As Jack was driving through the city, with one hand handcuffed to the steering wheel, he was trying to think of ways to get under Mike's skin. He said to Mike, "You know, leaving me tied up on the subway tracks, that was pretty sloppy." Mike pointed the gun at Jack and said, "Shut up!" Jack continued, "But blowing up my Mustang, now, that was personal. Did you know that you almost killed my assistant with that stupid plan?" He got Mike's attention. Mike said, "Your assistant? What's your assistant's name?" Jack laughed and said, "Wouldn't you like to know." Then Jack got serious and said, "It's a good thing nothing happened to my assistant because I would already have stuffed you down a storm drain and closed the lid." Mike was smiling at Jack, he said, "Oh, I forgot, you're a tough guy." Jack smiled back and said, "Tough enough to handle you and your two flunkies back at the warehouse." Mike gritted his teeth and pointed the gun at Jack again and said, "Hey, dipstick, you're the one handcuffed to the steering wheel, and I got the gun." Jack was nodding his head, he said, "For now, dimwit, for now." There was silence in the car for about two minutes and then Jack said, "That was a pretty stupid plan you had of stashing Heinrich King's body in the dumpster." Mike snapped back, "That was Jackie…." Mike stopped midstream. He realized that he had just implicated Jackie King in this crime. Mike squinted his eyes and gritted his teeth and pointed the gun at Jack again and said, "Just drive, Trane. And I don't want to hear any more talk out of you. Do you understand?" Jack looked at Mike and gave him a wink. Twenty minutes later Jack parked the car in front of his office, and said, "Here we are."

Mike looked around and said, "Hey this is your apartment." Jack raised one eyebrow and said, "No kidding, Einstein." Mike threw the keys to the handcuffs at Jack and said, "Undo the cuff from the steering wheel and put it on your other wrist. And no funny stuff or I'll let you have it right here." Mike pointed the gun at Jack's head. Jack smiled and said, "Funny stuff? Come on, Mike, I don't do funny stuff, we're just here to get your ring." Jack threw the keys back to Mike and he put them in his jacket pocket. They both got out of the car and walked into the apartment building and up the stairs to Jack's apartment. There was a spare key above the door molding, so Jack reached up with his two hands cuffed and retrieved the key. He opened the door, and they went in. They stood just inside the closed door and Mike said, "All right, now where is the ring? I ain't got all day." Jack's plan was about to unfold. Jack said, "Keep your shirt on thin man, I'll get your ring. It's in the bottom drawer of my desk." Jack walked towards his desk and Mike stood just inside the door watching Jack's every move. Jack opened his desk drawer, and deep in the drawer he could see the pinky ring and right next to it, the Glock that Jack had taken from Mike, the last time he was here. Jack picked up the pinkie ring and held it up for Mike to see. He said, "You want your ring, Mike? Here it is." He lobbed the ring towards Mike. It seemed to stay up in the air for an eternity. It was almost as if things were happening in slow motion. Mike's focus became glued to the ring. As the ring floated through the air, Mike held out his hand to grab it. At the same time, Jack reached back down into his desk drawer and pulled out the Glock. Mike hadn't noticed him since he was so focused on the ring. Jack aimed the gun at Mike and his thoughts flashed back to his Mustang blowing up and Trudy in the hospital bed, and he aimed directly for the heart. Then at the last second, he repositioned his aim and pulled off two shots. One shot hit Mike in the hand, and he dropped his gun. The other hit him in the foot and he fell to the floor. Mike never caught the ring, it bounced on the floor and rested next to his bleeding foot. Jack walked over and stood over Mike and said, "You see, Mike, I told you that by the end of this, you would be the one on the floor." Then he hit Mike in the head with the Glock and Mike passed out. He reached into Mike's jacket pocket and took out the keys to the handcuffs and unlocked the cuffs and put one cuff on Mike's good foot and the other cuff on a cast iron radiator.

Mike came to, and did his best to get away, but he since he was handcuffed to the radiator, he couldn't move. Jack said, "So Mikey, are you ready to admit to the murder of Heinrich King? You don't want to go down for this all alone. It's pretty obvious that Jackie King is behind this whole operation. Why don't you make it easy on yourself and just come clean?" Mike was in excruciating pain because of the bullet that passed through his hand and foot. He said, "Why don't you just take a flying leap off the top of this building?" Jack had a serious look on his face. He said, "Come on, Mike, it's over. You're going to prison." Mike gave out a little laugh. He said, "Don't fool yourself, Trane, this isn't over. Now this has gotten very personal. I'm going to finish this job, even if I wasn't working for Jacki….." Mike didn't finish the sentence. But Jack had heard enough to know that he had just implicated Jackie King again. He said to Mike, "Sit tight Mike. Pretty soon you'll be resting with your fellow convicts in a prison cell." Mike yelled back at Jack, "I need some medical attention here. I'm bleeding and I need a doctor." Jack laughed, he said, "All I see is a couple of little pinholes, man-up, Mike. Don't be such a crybaby." Jack walked away and picked up the phone on his desk. He dialed the number for Debra Thorn. The phone rang three times and Debra picked up. She said, "Hello, Jack. I see that you're calling from your landline. Did you want to take me for another joyride in your Mustang?" Jack was smiling, he said, "Debra, I got something for you. That guy we were chasing is on the floor in my apartment. He's been shot two times and he handcuffed to the radiator." Debra answered quickly, "Jack, are you crazy? You can't just go around shooting people and chaining them up to a radiator." Jack was laughing, he said, "Debra, this time, I have him cold. He kidnapped me and worked me over with his two associates. It was self-defense, he had a 38 Special. He's also running an illegal warehouse full of merchandise that he's been fencing all over the city. There're millions of dollars in stolen merchandise in the warehouse that they kept me captive in. It would be a good collar for you. And in the meantime, it would get him off of my back while I pin the murder on him." There were a few moments of awkward silence, then Debra said, "Are you doing all this to make up for the other night, Jack?" Jack smiled and said, "Would that do it?" Debra said, "Well, it's a start."

Within ten minutes Debra was at Jack's apartment with several uniformed police officers. They took Mike Mercury into custody. Mike sneered at Jack at they took him away in handcuffs. He said, "I'll get you for this Trane! This isn't over? I'll find a way." Mike spit at Jack. As Mike was being dragged to the door, Jack said, "Dream on, thin man. Where you're going the only thing you're going to find, is the way back to your cell." Debra was taking this all in, then she noticed the cuts and bruises on Jack's face. She said, "Jack, you look terrible. What happened?" Jack smiled, he said, "I was hoping that a few cuts and scrapes just added to my rugged good looks." Debra smiled and laughed a little, she said, "I see what you mean Jack, another couple of cuts and you'll look just like Clint Eastwood." Jack laughed and winked at Debra. Then Debra said, Jack, what about the warehouse you mentioned on the phone?" Jack told Debra the location of the warehouse on Wooster Street. Debra made a call back to her precinct and an army of squad cars swooped down on the warehouse and took Shaggy and Grease Boy into custody. When the other officers had left the room, Debra kissed Jack and said, "Thanks Jack, you really know to treat a woman." Jack kissed her back. He said, "I'd argue if I could, babe."

CHAPTER 16

The alarm went off and Jack reached over and pressed the button for the buzzer to stop. He had been out late last night with Debra, but it was worth it. Debra's *Chanel Coco Mademoiselle* perfume was still in the air, and it left Jack kind of feeling like just gotten off of a roller coaster. Besides that, knowing that Mike Mercury and his two idiot flunkies were now behind bars put Jack in a good mood to start the day. He knew that he would be able to work the Broadway case now without any interference or obstruction by any outside parties. At least that's what he was thinking. The sun seemed a little bit brighter today, and the air seemed a little bit cleaner. He hopped out of bed and strolled into the bathroom for his morning shower and shave. As he looked at himself in the mirror, he could see the cuts and bruises from being worked over by Shaggy and Grease Boy, and maybe it was his imagination, but it appeared that a few of the other lines in his face and around his eyes had smoothed out. He smiled at himself in the mirror. Things had really started to turn around for Jack and he was sure that he would have this case solved in no time.

After a quick shower and a shave, he came out of the bathroom and walked over to the walk-in closet. He stood there looking at all the pants and jackets and ties, all perfectly hung up on hangers. Jack still wasn't comfortable with this; he had gotten used to the random approach. There were just too many choices, so he backed out of the closet and closed his eyes and reached in and felt around and pulled out of pair of blue dockers. He threw them across the room onto the bed. He reached back into the closet with his eyes closed and pulled out a jacket. It was a royal blue jacket. He reached back in and grabbed a tie. It was a paisley blue tie. Once again Jack had hit the trifecta. Jack had never been a slave to fashion. Picking his clothes by chance every morning was his best bet to leave the apartment looking like himself, it always seemed to work out for him. He walked over to his armoire and pulled out a perfectly pressed white button-down shirt and put it on. He put on his pants, then he tied his tie around his neck. As he pulled the tie to tighten the knot, he noticed something shining on the floor next to the door. He walked over and bent down to see what it was, and he realized that it was Mike Mercury's garnet pinkie ring that he had flung across the room yesterday. Mike never caught it. Jack picked it up and put it on his right pinkie finger. He held his hand out and admired the red shine. He liked the way it looked. He figured that Mike Mercury wouldn't be needing it where he was going, anyway. For the time being Jack owned the garnet pinkie ring. He thought to himself, "I'll keep it safe while Mike is making number plates." He laughed a little bit to himself.

Jack had purchased a spare cellphone a few months ago for a backup, he thought that it might come in handy someday. Today was the day. He took the cellphone out of the drawer in his nightstand and turned it on. It came to life and downloaded all the data from his previous phone through the cloud. He put his cellphone in his pocket and grabbed his keys He put the matchstick in the door jamb, and he left his apartment.

As he walked out the door to the street, he pulled his cellphone out of his pocket and checked the time. It was almost 9 o'clock. He didn't know if Trudy would be in the office yet, but he knew that detective Harry Soul would be at the precinct. He dialed Harry's private cellphone number and Harry picked up, he said, "Hello Jack, I'm glad to see that you're still alive. I heard what happened yesterday with Mike Mercury." Then there was a pause and Harry said, "Jack, maybe it's time that you just give up on this case. I don't know if it's worth all these complications." Jack broke in quickly and said, "Harry, are you kidding? I almost have this case solved. And besides, I handed you Mike Mercury, on a silver platter. He's going to do time for grand larceny, trafficking, racketeering, and probably murder if I can find the evidence that ties him in. In fact, that's why I called. I need to ask you a favor." Harry breathed deep and said, "Ok, here we go. Every time you need a favor, my neck is the one that's on the line." Jack pleaded his case. He said, "Don't worry, Harry, this is no big deal. I just want to use the interrogation room down at the precinct to sweat some suspects." Harry's eyes opened wide, he said, "The interrogation room! Jack, are you crazy? I just can't let anyone use the precinct like it was their own personal playground!" Jack spoke slowly, "Now, wait a minute, Harry. We made a deal. I'm a consultant with the NYPD. You even gave me this lame card that nobody takes very seriously. I think as a consultant, that I should be able to use the precinct facilities to pursue this case." Harry was thinking, He said, "I don't know Jack…" There was a pause and Jack broke in, he said, "I'm having Trudy set up the meeting right now. I'll have her call you with the details." Harry's face perked up. Now he had a smile on his face. He said, "Trudy is going to call?" Jack breathed deep and said, "Relax Harry, I know you think that somehow you can get a date with Trudy, but I don't think that's going to happen." Harry wasn't listening, he was just thinking of hearing Trudy's voice calling his name. Harry said, "OK, Jack. This sounds like a good idea. I'll set it up. I'll wait for Trudy's call." Harry sat there at his desk with a smile and a schoolboy look on his face. Jack shook his head and said, "Thanks Harry, we'll be in touch." They both hung up their cellphones and Jack made his way down the street towards the Coffee Café.

Jack stopped in at the newsstand and picked up the morning paper from the rack and dropped $2 on the counter. He gave a wave to Nicky who was stocking shelves with potato chips and Nicky grumbled something under his breath. Jack smiled and continued on his way to the Coffee Café. It was a bright sunny morning and Jack felt a sense of relief since Mike Mercury was out of his hair. He had a feeling of optimism that when he got Victoria Pichettes, Marie Robbin, Siobhan Peison, and Audrey Linn in the same room together, he was going to break this case wide open. So far, he felt that he had exposed a conspiracy that had hidden this crime as well as the real guilty party. But once he got these 4 women in the room together, it would only be a matter of time before they started turning on each other like a group of hyenas and he'd get the evidence he needed on Jackie King.

Jack walked into the Coffee Café, and he saw Betty standing by the counter. She had on her usual white uniform with the light blue piping around the collar and sleeves and she always left her top two buttons open. She worked on tips. He yelled out, "What's shaking today, Betty?" She looked at Jack with a surprised look and said, "Well, if it isn't Jack Trane. Where have you been Jack? I thought that you didn't like me anymore." Jack laughed, "Come on Betty, how could anyone not like you? You got it all, including pancakes." Betty looked at Jack with a smile and one eyebrow raised, she said, "That's right, Jack, I got it all, but the pancakes are extra." Jack laughed, he said, "That's why I come in everyday Betty, for the extra." Betty laughed, "Well when you didn't come in yesterday, I thought that you might have found a better place to go." Jack smiled, "Come on Betty, what could be better than having breakfast with the best-looking waitress on the planet?" Betty smiled and blushed a little and hit Jack with her washcloth. Jack said, "Yesterday, I had to take care of a few situations." Betty looked at the bruises and cuts on Jack's face and said, "It looks like a few situations took care of you." She hit Jack on the arm with her washcloth again. Jack said, "Well, you should see the other guys." They both laughed. Betty said, "What can I get for you, Jack?' Jack thought for a moment and started to speak, but Betty showed Jack her pad. It read, blueberry pancakes, small orange juice, and a large Vanilla Latte. She said, "How's that, Jack?" He smiled and said, "You're amazing, Betty. If I didn't know better, I'd think you could read my mind." She laughed and said, "Maybe I can, Jack. Maybe I can." She walked back to the counter and placed Jack's order.

Jack opened up the newspaper to see if Mike Mercury's arrest made the headlines. But there was nothing there. Small-time operators like Mike Mercury were no more than a blip on the radar compared with the volume of hardened criminals in the big city. By the time Jack got to page 2, Betty had returned with his Vanilla Latte. She placed it in front of Jack and said, "I put a little extra vanilla in it for you this morning." She smiled, hit Jack with her washcloth, and walked back towards the counter. Jack was glad to be back at the Coffee Café. He had really missed this early morning banter with Betty.

Jack took out his cellphone and dialed Trudy at the office. She picked up and said, "Hey, Jack, I tried to call you last night, but you didn't pick up. What, were you on a hot date or something?" Jack smiled, he said "Yeah, Trudy, something like that. Have you scheduled the meeting for today with Victoria Pichettes, Siobhan Peison, Audrey Linn, and Marie Robbin?" Trudy was snapping her gum, she said, "Yeah, Jack. It's all set up for today at 1:00 PM. I told them to meet us at the precinct." Jack smiled, he said, "That's great, Trudy. Now there is just one more thing." Trudy raised her right eyebrow and said, "What's that, Jack?" Jack spoke slowly, he said, "You need to call Harry Soul, down at the precinct and set up the time and the room." Trudy coughed and spit out her gum onto the desk. She said, "No way, Jack! I'm not calling that jerk. He gives me the creeps." Jack was shaking his head, he said, "Come on, Trudy, this is just business. Just give him a call, tell him what we need, and hang up. You're good at hanging up." Trudy put another piece of gum in her mouth, she said, "I swear, Jack, if he asks me for another date, I'll slam the phone down so hard, there will be pieces of the phone in your office." Jack laughed, he said, "You know, Trudy, I believe you would. I really do." Trudy made a disgusted face, she said, "All right, Jack, I'll do it. But you owe me for this, big-time." Jack was nodding his head, he said in his low gravelly voice, "Whatever you say, Boss." Jack returned to his regular voice and said, "I'll meet you at the precinct at 1 o'clock." They both hung up their phones.

Betty came back with the pancakes and put them down in front of Jack. She said, "Enjoy, Jack. Those are Maine blueberries, I picked them myself, especially for you." Jack smiled, he said, "One of these days you'll have to show me where you pick these Maine blueberries. I have a sneaking suspicion that you pick them up from the fruit stand down the street." Betty hit Jack with her washcloth and said, "Jack, are you spying on me?" Jack smiled and said, "I've definitely got my eye on you, Betty." They both laughed and Betty walked back to the counter. He poured the maple syrup over his pancakes and took a bite. It was just right, a little crunchy on the outside and soft on the inside with a blueberry in every bite. He devoured the pancakes in about 5 minutes, slugged down the glass of orange juice, then he sat sipping his Vanilla Latte. About three minutes later Betty came back to the table and asked, "So, how was it, Jack?" Jack sat back and took a deep breath, he said, "The best, Betty, the best!" Betty smiled and said, "I was talking about the pancakes, Jack." They laughed and she dropped his bill on the table. The bill came to $15. Jack put $30 on the table and gave Betty a wave and walked out of the restaurant onto the street.

He walked towards his parking garage. He felt good this morning that Mike Mercury would not be pursuing him, but he never let his guard down. He continually scanned both sides of the street to make sure that no one was following him. His paranoia had saved his life on many occasions. He reached the parking garage and gave Fernando, the attendant, a wave and walked up to the second level and got into his Mustang. He started the car and sat for a minute just listening to the engine idle. The rhythmic sound of the eight cylinders gave him a sense of calm. He put the car in gear and drove out of the parking garage into the street. It was only 10 o'clock and Jack's meeting wasn't until 1:00 PM. He needed to kill some time. He thought it might be a good idea to take a ride out to Jackie King's apartment and see if there was any unusual activity. He drove in the direction of West 57th Street. When he arrived at her apartment building, he noticed that Jackie King's Mercedes was parked in her spot, but directly behind her car was a blue Dodge Charger. It wasn't parked in a parking space; it was just parked towards the back of her car. Jack figured that someone must be inside talking with Jackie King. He parked his car and just sat and watched for about half an hour, but nothing was happening. He wanted to wait to see who would come out of her apartment and get into the Charger, but he didn't' have time. That would have to wait. He needed to be at the precinct to meet with the four ladies at 1 o'clock. He started his Mustang and drove in the direction of the 23rd precinct.

By the time Jack got to the precinct, it was about noon. He parked his car and went into the building. He walked up to the sergeant at the front desk and handed him the card that Harry Soul had given him. The desk sergeant looked at the card and laughed out loud. He said, "Where did you get this? Is Harry handing out these joke cards again?" Jack took the card back, he said, "Hey, this is no joke card! The department hired me as a consultant to solve some cold cases. I'm working on the

Broadway Murder case." The sergeant looked up at Jack and said "Oh, the Broadway Murder, huh? That's one that got away." Jack smiled, he said, "Not for long, Serge. I'll have this thing wrapped up in a couple of days." The Sergeant laughed, he said, "Whatever you say, gumshoe." Real New York cops had very little respect for private investigators, they considered them one step above the felonious riff raff of the city. He pushed the button under his desk and the door to the precinct opened. Jack went through the door and entered the police building. There seemed to be very little activity. Policemen in blue uniforms were standing around talking to one another. Detectives were sitting behind their desks, some with their feet on their desks and there was a stale smell of dirt, perspiration, and dust in the air. Jack made his way across the room towards Harry's office. As he passed by Danny Watt's desk, Danny stood up and stared Jack down. Jack gave him a wink as he passed his desk. He got to Harry's office and went in and sat down. Harry looked up from his desk and said in a sarcastic voice, "Make yourself at home, Jack." Jack sat back in the chair, and he said, "You know, Harry, I don't think everyone in the precinct appreciates me being here." Harry laughed, he said, "Jack, no one in the precinct appreciates you being here. My head is on the block for bringing you in. How is the Broadway murder case going?" Jack smiled, "Relax, Harry, this case will be in your solved file within a couple of days." Harry was shaking his head. Jack looked around, he said, "What's it take to get a cup of coffee around here?" Harry pointed across the room to a small, dingy cafeteria. He said, "Help yourself, Jack."

Jack got up and walked into the small cafeteria. The floor was tiled with dirty gray tiles. The walls were painted a light green and some spots were peeling, and there were no windows. The light overhead was a fluorescent light that blinked on and off every 10th of a second, it was like a strobe light. There was a vending machine with what looked to be really old ham and cheese sandwiches and various snack foods and an old Cory coffee maker on a shelf beside the vending machine. Jack took a disposable coffee cup from the shelf and filled it with the brown liquid from the coffee carafe. It looked like coffee, but it smelled like someone had added some old sweaty sneakers to the mix. There was some powdered creamer on the shelf and as he went to grab for it, another hand came from behind him and grabbed it first. Jack turned around and saw Danny Watts standing behind him holding the creamer. Danny looked at Jack with his teeth clenched and said, "What are you doing here, Trane?" Jack smiled, "Nice to see you, too, Danny. I'm about to solve the Broadway murder that you couldn't solve. What do you think about that?" Danny got in Jack's face, he said, "I already told you once, you should leave police business to police. You could get hurt getting into things that you have no business getting into." Danny threw the creamer back down on the shelf and started to walk away. Jack said, "I'll try to remember that Danny, all the way to the bank with the $5,000 I get for solving your case." Jack laughed and put some of the creamer into his coffee. Jack took a sip of the coffee and squinted as he swallowed. He poured the rest of the coffee down the drain.

Jack noticed that Trudy had just entered the precinct and was walking towards the interrogation room. She was wearing a short black skirt with a black patent leather belt. She had on a low-cut white top and a black double-breasted blazer with two large gold buttons on each side. She was also wearing some black stiletto pumps with 3 ½ inch heels. With her blond hair bouncing on her shoulders, she really stood out as she walked past all the detectives in the room. Harry Soul took note as Trudy's *Versace Bright Crystal* perfume filled the air. As Trudy passed by Harry's office, he immediately stood up from his desk and followed Trudy towards the interrogation room like a mosquito being drawn to a light zapper. Jack rushed over to provide some interference for Trudy. He intercepted Harry and said, "Well, Harry, is that a new tie you're wearing today? I must say it makes you look about 10 years younger." The tie was an old stripe tie with visible gravy spots on the front of the tie. Harry wasn't listening to Jack, he said, "Excuse me, Jack, I'm kind of busy right now." Harry pushed Jack aside and made his way to Trudy. As she was about to open the door to the interrogation room, Harry said, "Trudy, I just wanted to say that you're looking amazing today." Trudy rolled her eyes, she said, "Thanks, Harry, whatever." Jack stepped into the conversation, "We'd like to sit around and chat, Harry, but we've got work to do. See you later." As Jack and Trudy were closing the door behind them, Harry was on the other side of the door, he said, "So Trudy, maybe later we can go out for a…." The door closed and Harry never got finish the sentence. Trudy looked at Jack and said, "Jack, I think I should get $3000 from this case after all that I've been through. Getting blown up was better than that scene with your friend Harry!" Jack put his hand on Trudy's shoulder, he said, "Relax, Trudy. Remember, it was your idea to come out into the field on this case. Sometimes you just have to suck it up." Trudy made a disgusted face, she said, "I wish that Harry would get sucked up in a giant vacuum cleaner and leave me alone." Jack smiled, he said, "Maybe with your $2500 you can buy a giant vacuum cleaner and take care of the job yourself." Trudy raised her right eyebrow and said, "Very funny, Jack." He smiled and said, "You know, Trudy, if you didn't come down here all decked-out, maybe Harry wouldn't even notice you." Trudy shot back, "I could come down here in a pair of sweatpants and a hockey jersey and he'd still be all over me." Jack nodded his head, "Yeah, you might be right Trudy, you might be right." They both sat down and waited for the four ladies to arrive.

CHAPTER 17

Jack and Trudy sat waiting in the interrogation room. Trudy was filing her nails and Jack was drumming his fingers on the table. Trudy looked at Jack with one eyebrow raised and said, "Must you do that, Jack?" He smiled back at Trudy and said, "Yes, I must." Trudy rolled her eyes. One by one the four ladies walked through the precinct doors. The first to arrive was Victoria Pichettes. She was wearing a bright red skirt, a low-cut yellow pullover shirt, and a red blazer. She had on a pair of yellow high heel shoes. Her dark hair had just been cut short, and she looked like she had just come from a beauty parlor. She looked like she was made up for the lead role in a Broadway musical. She walked like she was on a red carpet. Right behind her was Audrey Linn. Audrey was wearing a simple pair of blue jeans, a plain white shirt with buttons down the front, and a khaki blazer. On her feet, she was wearing some brown flat shoes. Her hair was combed to the side, and she was wearing flat red lipstick. Audrey was not trying to impress anyone. She was just a working girl struggling to make ends meet. As she walked towards the interrogation room, she checked out all the detectives sitting behind their desks, and she wondered if any of them would be interrogating her. Her nerves were frayed but she didn't let it show. Right behind Audrey was Siobhan Peison. Siobhan was wearing a hot pink, lapel neck, double-breasted blazer, and pants suit, with a soft white shirt. This was probably an outfit that she had designed herself. She was wearing brown leather loafers, they looked to be alligator skin. Her dark black hair was pulled back into a ponytail and her makeup looked like it was professionally done. Her glossy ruby red lipstick completed the package. Siobhan looked like she was ready for business. She ignored the detectives as she walked by. Finally, Marie Robbin entered the precinct. She was a little older than the other three women, but she carried herself with confidence. She had been around the block a couple of times, and she knew the score. She was wearing a beige knee-length skirt with a blue striped pullover shirt. She had on a pair of blue high heels and her brown hair was neatly combed to the point where every hair was in place. She gave the detectives the snake eye as she passed by.

As the four women strolled through the precinct towards the interrogation room, the detectives all looked up as the parade of beauties passed by their desks. Danny Watts took particular note. He stood up and watched as they passed his desk. He tried to make eye contact with each woman as she went by, seemingly trying to stare down each woman with an intimidating look. None of the women seemed to be too impressed. One by one, the women filed into the interrogation room. Jack invited them to sit down on the opposite side of the table that faces the two-way mirror behind him. He knew that Harry would be standing behind the mirror not to observe the interrogation, but to observe Trudy. Once all the women were seated Jack asked them, "Well, ladies, would anyone like a coffee or a donut?" Siobhan spoke up, "Look, I don't have all day. Let's just get this over with! What do you want to know?" Jack smiled, he said, "I like that. Right to the point. No fooling around." Marie spoke up, "Well, I'd like a cup of coffee." Audrey chimed in, "Yeah, I'd like a cup of coffee too." Jack turned to Victoria, "How about you, Victoria?" Victoria made a disgusted face, and with her French accent, she said, "I don't want any swill coffee from a police station! Let's just get on with this." Jack smiled, "All in good time ladies, all in good time." Siobhan was breathing heavily and shaking her head. Jack turned to Trudy and said, "Trudy can you get a couple of coffees for Marie and Audrey? In the meantime, we'll just chat." Trudy squinted at Jack with mean eyes. She knew that Harry Soul would be

166

waiting for her just outside the door and he would follow her into her cafeteria. She looked at Jack with her teeth clenched and said, "Maybe you should get the coffee, Jack. I think I sprained my ankle when your car blew up the other day." Jack smiled sheepishly and left the room to get the coffee.

When Jack left, the room got very quiet. The women weren't saying anything to each other. They just kept giving each other meaningful stares. Trudy was filing her nails and looking at the clock. The silence was broken when Jack re-entered the room with the coffee. He put the cups down in front of Marie and Audrey. He said, "OK, I think now we can all get down to business, right Siobhan?" Siobhan looked shocked. She said, "Why are you talking to me? Aren't we all here for the same reason?" Jack smiled, he said, "And what reason is that, Miss Peison?" Siobhan squirmed in her chair, she said, "I have absolutely no idea of what you're talking about. I'm here because your secretary over there dragged me down here." Trudy objected, "Hey lady, I'm not a secretary, I'm an associate." Siobhan chuckled, "Oh, excuse me." Then she said in a slow deliberate voice, "ASSOCIATE." Trudy made a face with her lip raised and her eyes squinted at Siobhan. Audrey took a sip of her coffee and coughed. She said, "What is this? It tastes like someone boiled some old socks in here." Marie Robbin took a sip of her coffee and spit it out. The spray went up in the air to the right of Trudy. Trudy bent over as not to get sprayed. Marie said, "What are you trying to do? Poison us?" Jack smiled, he said, "Ladies, I never said that the coffee was any good. Don't blame me. This is what your New York City taxes are paying for." Victoria spoke up loudly with her French accent, she said, "All right! I've had enough of this. Tell us why we're all here, or I'm walking out that door right now!" Then she stood up. Siobhan chimed in, "Yeah, that goes for me too!" All the ladies spoke up and began harping on Jack to tell them why they were there. Jack stood up from his chair and said, "OK, ladies, now let's all settle down. You're all here because I believe that you are all somehow connected to the murder of Heinrich King." The room got very silent. You could hear Trudy snapping her gum. Audrey spoke up, she said, "You don't think any of us murdered Heinrich King, do you?" Jack sat back down in his chair, he said, "That's what I'm trying to find out Audrey, that's what I'm trying to find out."

As the four ladies all sat back down and squirmed in their chairs Trudy stood up and held out a file that she had in her hands. The file was full of blank papers, but the ladies didn't know that. Trudy said, "Look, ladies, there have been some serious irregularities in all your bank accounts. We'd like to know how you explain that?" Jack had assumed that they had all received the sum of $10,000 after Heinrich King's murder, but he had no proof. The fact that Kristen Monree had been offered that amount was a pretty good indicator that the others would have been offered the same deal. Jack was hoping that they would all come clean. Siobhan spoke up, she said, "Irregularities? What irregularities?" Trudy replied, "We did a little checking into your bank accounts, and it appears that each of you received a sum of $10,000 in your bank accounts about a week after Heinrich King was found dead in a dumpster. That seems like more than a little coincidence. Wouldn't you say?" Jack chimed in, he said, "Maybe you'd all like to explain where that $10,000 came from." The four ladies were quiet. No one was saying anything. One thing was for sure. The ladies didn't deny receiving the $10,000. This pretty much confirmed that they were all part of some kind of conspiracy either to commit the murder or to cover it up. Trudy said in her Dragnet voice, "So who would like to go first?" The painful silence lasted for another minute, but it seemed like ten minutes. Marie Robbin finally spoke up, she said, "Look, all of us were together on the night of Heinrich King's murder, between the hours of 7:00 PM to 1:00 AM. None of us could have killed Heinrich King." Jack nodded his head, in a loud voice he said, "Yeah that same old story you told me before. All of you were out together between 7:00 to 1:00 AM. That's a good story, very convenient, very consistent, but I'm not buying it. What do you think, I was born yesterday? This is the big leagues, ladies; I want the truth and I want it now!" Jack's vociferous outburst did not get the reaction Jack was looking for from the four ladies. Audrey Linn looked up at the ceiling, Siobhan stared at Jack and squinted, Victoria Pichettes was examining her nails, and Marie Robbin was looking down at the floor. Jack had another plan that he knew couldn't fail. He said, "OK, let's play a little game, ladies. Trudy, I want you to give each one of the ladies a piece of paper. Trudy put a piece of paper in front of each of the ladies. Then Jack said, "OK, now one by one I want each of you to bring your blank piece of paper over here, in front of me, and then write on it that place where all four of you met the night that Heinrich King was found murdered." Victoria Pichettes stood up and in her French accent said, "I resent this treatment. We've all been interrogated by that other detective Witts when King Heini was murdered. I think I want a lawyer." Jack laughed, "Yeah, you can get a lawyer if you want, but you're not under arrest yet, and I'm not a cop. Let's just say that I'm giving you a chance to get out in front of this thing before the hammer comes down. It would be in all your best interests if you come clean now and tell me the truth." Marie held up her blank piece of paper and said, "OK, so maybe we forgot where we met six months ago. What does that prove?" Trudy spoke up in her *Dragnet* voice, she said, "That proves that you don't have an alibi for the murder. Wise up ladies, you're one step away from the slammer." The room got very quiet.

After about a minute passed, Audrey spoke up, she said, "I was home, by myself that night." Siobhan spoke up, "Shut up you little halfwit, you're going to get us all in trouble." Jack looked at Siobhan and said, "You're already in trouble." Siobhan said, "That's ridiculous, Audrey doesn't know what she's talking about. Who can remember where they were six months ago?" Victoria spoke up and her voice was breaking up as if she was about to cry. She said, "I really needed the money, but I didn't kill anyone." Marie chimed in, "I would have liked to kill him, but I didn't. I figured the $10,000 was like a severance package." Jack looked at Siobhan, he said, "It looks like you're all by yourself now Siobhan. Do you care to come clean?" Siobhan made a disgusted face, she said, "All right, I was home alone that night too, but I didn't kill anybody." Jack smiled and sat back in his chair, he said, "OK, ladies, now we're getting somewhere." Audrey put her head in her hands, Victoria was looking down at her fingernails, Marie had a tear coming down her face and Siobhan was still looking at Jack with her eyes squinted. Trudy handed Marie a tissue to wipe her eyes. Jack said, "Here's the thing ladies. There is a big difference between a conspiracy to cover up a murder and committing a murder. Now the fact is, I don't believe that any of you were involved in the murder of Heinrich King, but you did all accept some kind of payment in the amount of $10,000 a week after Heinrich King was found dead. How do you explain that?" Victoria spoke up, she said, "I got a phone call. It was Jackie King. She said all I had to do was to say I was with these other three ladies the night Heinrich King was found murdered and there would be $10,000 in my bank account. I didn't do anything wrong. I just took the $10,000 because I needed the money." Audrey spoke up, she said, "That's exactly what happened with me too. I didn't think we were getting involved in anything illegal. I just needed the money." Jack was nodding his head, he said, "I suppose that's what happened with you other ladies too?" Siobhan and Marie both nodded their heads. The room fell silent again.

Jack stood up and looked at the four ladies, he said, "All right, ladies, I think that there might be some extenuating circumstances here. It appears that Jackie King wanted it to look like you four conspired to kill Heinrich King. That's why she gave you all the $10,000. She wanted you all to agree that you were out together that night. That made you all look guilty, and it took the focus off of her. She set you up, ladies." Siobhan breathed deep and said, "I can't believe that I fell for that. I needed the money, and I just looked the other way." Victoria was nodding her head, she said, "Yeah, acting roles have been hard to come by. I needed the money too." Marie agreed, she said, "Heinrich had just fired me. I was broke, and I needed the money too." Jack folded his arms, he said, "You see, ladies, Jackie King knew all that too. She knew that you all needed money and with the $10 million settlement she got from Heinrich King's insurance policy, she could easily afford to pay you all off and set you up as patsies." Audrey looked very concerned, she said, "We're not going to jail, are we?" Jack smiled at the four ladies and said, "Ladies, if you cooperate, I think that there is a good chance that the D.A. will go light on you and let you off with community service or something like that." Marie Robbin spoke up she said, "What do you want to know? I'll tell you everything."

For the next two hours, Jack and Trudy questioned the four ladies, and they came away with a much clearer picture of who was really involved in the Broadway murder. All fingers now pointed to Jackie King. But Jackie King wasn't really strong enough to strangle Heinrich King and throw him in a dumpster. That's where Mike Mercury came in. None of the ladies could make the connection, but it just seemed like Jackie King must have hired Mike Mercury to do the job. After all, she was in line to get a $10 million insurance settlement. There was a lot of money to go around. Jack knew that the best thing to do was to follow the money trail and see where it led them. He was sure that it would lead them right back to Jackie King. As the ladies were about to leave the interrogation room, Siobhan asked, "What now, Mr. Trane? Are we going to be arrested or something?" Jack smiled, he said, "Ladies, for now, everything that you just told me is between us. We're not going to share this with the department, the D.A., or anyone else. If this leads us to solve this case, well, I think we can all just look the other way and forget about everything, if that's OK with you." Victoria smiled a broad smile, and said, "Oh, Mr. Trane, thank you, that would really be kind." Jack smiled and said, "But, ladies, if anything else comes up, if Jackie King tries to contact you again, I want to know immediately." The four ladies agreed, and Trudy handed them each a business card with Jack's contact information. In her *Dragnet* voice, Trudy said, "Thank you, ladies, we'll be in touch." The four ladies got up from their chairs got up and left the interrogation room and walked out of the precinct.

Jack and Trudy got up and left the interrogation room too and standing right outside the door was Harry Soul. He had a crooked smile on his face and a goofy look. He said to Trudy, "So, Trudy, I was thinking that maybe later, you and I could grab a bite to eat and head uptown, and…" Trudy didn't let Harry finish the sentence. She said, "Look, Harry, you're a nice guy and everything, but I don't see it. Besides, I'm kind of seeing someone right now." She was trying to let Harry down easy, but Harry wasn't hearing it. He said, "Oh, right, well maybe I'll call you sometime." Trudy looked at Harry with cold steel eyes and said, "Harry, no calls, no letters, no nothing. Got it?" Harry stood there with his mouth open. He was crushed, but he finally got the point. Harry had a better chance of winning the lottery than he did with Trudy. The thing was, Harry liked playing the lottery.

As they walked towards the exit, Danny Watts approached Jack and pulled him aside. He got in Jack's face and said with clenched teeth, "Look, Trane, I'm telling you for the last time, stay away from the Broadway Murder case. A guy could get hurt poking around in things he has no business in. Capisce?" Jack smiled, he said, "Danny, I didn't know you spoke Italian." Danny held up his fist to Jack's face. Jack said, "Now, Danny, you know I don't want to make you look bad, but I'm going to solve this case that you so badly screwed up, and I'm going to walk away with $5,000. And there's nothing you can do about it. Capisce?" Jack walked away as Danny stood there giving Jack the evil eye as he made his way to the exit with Trudy. They left the precinct and got into Jack's Mustang. It was about 3:30 in the afternoon and Jack wasn't through for the day. He said to Trudy, "I got one more interrogation I want to make today. I thought that we'd take a ride out to Jackie King's apartment and see if we can shake her up a little. Are you up for it?" Trudy smiled and in a low gravelly voice she said, "Whatever you say, boss." He started the car and put it in gear and headed in the direction of 600 West 57th Street. He knew that he had to follow the money trail to connect Jackie with the murder and the trail started with Jackie herself. He was hopeful that she would turn on one of her accomplices in order to save herself. Jack had a better chance of winning the lottery. Jack never played the lottery.

CHAPTER 18

As Jack drove across the city Trudy turned on the radio. It was a blues station, and an old John Lee Hooker "*Boom, Boom.*" song was playing. Jack was bobbing his head, he said to Trudy, "Don't you just love those old blues tunes." Trudy looked at Jack and said, "Yeah, they really get my mojo working." Jack laughed as he continued to bob his head to the music. As Jack took a right onto 3rd Avenue, he looked in his rear-view mirror, and for a second, he thought that he spotted a blue Charger about six car lengths behind him. He came to a traffic light at East 46th Street and looked again, but he couldn't see any blue Charger in sight. He figured that was just a coincidence, there must be hundreds of blue Chargers in New York City. What are the chances he was being followed by the same blue Charger that was in front of Jackie King's apartment earlier today? That's the thing, you just never know. Jack stepped on the gas and accelerated through the traffic lights on 3rd Avenue all the way up to East 57th Street. He took a left turn and went up East 57th Street. There was no blue Charger in sight. He took a left on Park Avenue, then a right onto East 55th Street. He took a right onto Madison Avenue then a left back onto East 57th Street. Jack checked his rearview mirror and there was still no blue Charger in sight. He continued onto East 57th Street and eventually it turned into West 57th Street. He pulled up on the side of the road next to 600 West 57th Street and parked the car. Jack asked Trudy, "Would you mind taking a few notes when we get in there, I'm hoping that Jackie says something that we can use against her later." Trudy looked at Jack with one eye squinted and in a low gravelly voice said, "Whatever you say, boss." Jack smiled, he said,

"Keep it up, Trudy, and I'm going to give Harry Soul your personal cell-phone number." Trudy made a disgusted face and said, "You better not, Jack, because if you did, I'd have to hurt you, really bad." Jack laughed, he said, "I believe you, Trudy, I really do."

They both got out of the car and walked up the stairs of the apartment building and walked in the entrance. The security guard was sitting in the middle of the room, it was Joe Bourdon, the same security guard Jack had run into the last time he was here. Jack walked up to Joe and said, "We'd like to see Jackie King, could you please ring her for us?" Joe looked up at Jack and said, you look familiar, Haven't I seen you before?" Jack nodded his head and said, "Jack Trane, with the NYPD." Trudy looked at Jack and under her breath, she said, "The NYPD?" Jack looked at Trudy out of the corner of his eye and said, "I do have this consultant's card, you know." Trudy laughed. Joe made a call to Jackie King, then hung up the phone. He pointed to the elevator and said, "Go on up, she's expecting you." Jack thought to himself, "We didn't call her, why would she be expecting us?" They took the elevator up to the 50th floor where Jackie King had her luxury apartment. They got out of the elevator and walked up to her door and Jack rang the bell. Almost immediately the door opened, and Jackie King appeared. Her long shiny black hair rested on her shoulders. The last time Jack was here, the way she looked reminded him of Cleopatra. She still had the same look along with her ruby red lipstick. She was also wearing a long low-cut silver and blue dress with a long slit running down the left leg. In her low sultry voice she said, "Why, Mr. Trane, so nice to see you again, darling. And it looks like you've brought along your little workmate." Trudy spoke up, she said, "That's, associate, Ms. King." Jackie King laughed, she said, "Whatever, darling, won't you both come in?" Jack had been here before; he knew the layout of the apartment. They walked into the living room and Jack and Trudy sat down on the gray couch in the middle of the room." In her low sultry voice, Jackie said, "Can I get either of you anything to drink?" Then she paused and said, "Oh, That's right, no drinking on the job." She laughed again and walked over to the wine cooler in the corner of the room. She pulled out a bottle of *Pinot Noir* and poured herself a large glass. Then she walked back over and sat on the gray chair opposite the couch. She said, "Now what is it I can do for you, darling?" She sat back and sipped her wine while crossing her legs and allowing her leg to show through the slit in her dress.

Trudy looked at Jack, then in her *Dragnet* voice she said, "Ms. King, we have reason to believe that you have taken steps to cover up the murder of your late husband Heinrich King." Jack wasn't expecting Trudy to be so blunt. He coughed when he heard what Trudy had said. Jackie smiled and said, "I'm sorry, dear, I don't think that I got your name." Trudy rolled her eyes and said, "It's Trudy." Jackie took another sip of wine and said, "Trudy, yes, that's a nice name. It kind of sounds like it comes from a comic strip." Trudy's face was getting red, so Jack stepped in, he said, "Now Jackie, we've uncovered some evidence that suggests that you made deposits of $10,000 into the bank accounts of four different women and you also attempted to give the same amount to another woman. How do you explain that?" Jackie smiled a long smile at Jack and said, "Mr. Trane, I'm a very generous woman. I always try to help the hapless, wretched, pitiful people. I guess that's just the way I am." Trudy spoke up, she had her eyes squinted as she looked at Jackie. She said, "All right, let's cut to the chase. You paid off these four women to say they were all out together the night your late husband Heinrich King was killed. We think that you did this to take the focus off of yourself. In my book that's called conspiracy." Jackie laughed, she said, "Darling, I don't know what you're talking about. I saw four women that had been brutally abused by my late husband

and I thought that I would try to make amends. I thought that a small monetary gesture might ease some of their pain." She took another long sip of wine. Jack chimed in, he said, "Jackie, all four of these women have come clean. They told us that you gave them the money and you also told them to lie to detective Watts, so it would look like they were all out together that evening. I got to tell you, Jackie, this looks bad for you. Obstruction, conspiracy, and who knows what else." Jackie laughed, "Who knows what else indeed. You have no proof of anything. Jackie's demeanor changed. She had gone from aloof to dead serious. She said, "In fact, you have it all wrong." Jack sat back and said, "Oh, really, then why don't you just clear it up for me, darling." Jackie took another sip of her wine and her demeanor changed back to aloof. She said, "Very well, darling, this is how it really happened. Those four women came to me and told me that if I didn't give them all $10,000, they would all testify against me that I killed my late husband. They all hated him, they wanted him dead. I believed that they were responsible for killing him and they needed a patsy. So, I was scared and gave them the money. Then just last week they approached me again and asked for another $10,000 or they would go to the police with their story. Well, Mr. Trane, I had enough. I knew that I was innocent, so I refused to give them any more money. They were furious, they threatened me again. Victoria Pichettes said she was going to cut off my ears. I was very frightened, but I pulled myself together and told them to leave my apartment and I never wanted to see them again. You see, Mr. Trane, I realized that $10 Million can buy lawyers, and darling, lawyers can solve a lot of problems."

When Jackie had finished her story, Jack sat forward and said, "Well, that's a very interesting story, Jackie, I particularly like that part about Victoria cutting off your ears, but I'm not buying any of it. What kind of a sucker do you think I am? I'm pretty sure that you killed your late husband Heinrich King, or more specifically, you had someone kill Heinrich King, and now I'm going to prove it." Jackie took another sip of her wine, she said, "Mr. Trane, darling, you're such a passionate person, I like that." Jack had an ace in the hole, he smiled at Jackie and said, "You know, Jackie, Mike Mercury is behind bars. It's only a matter of time before he accepts a plea deal and starts singing like a canary." Jackie got a very serious look on her face, she said, "Mike Mercury? I don't know any Mike Mercury. Furthermore, I resent being accused of killing my late husband! You should be looking at those four women who extorted money from me and tried to blackmail me. I'm the victim here." Jack smiled, he said, "Jackie, I don't think you've been a victim of anything your whole life." Jackie slugged down the rest of her wine and put the glass on the floor. She said, "Is that all, Mr. Trane? Because I really have things to do." Jack smiled and said, "That's all for now, Jackie. But don't get too comfortable, the next time you see me, it will probably be to fit you with a pair of handcuffs." Jack and Trudy got up and walked towards the door. Trudy turned around and in her *Dragnet* voice said, "We'll be in touch, Ms. King. Please don't leave town." Jack and Trudy left the apartment and closed the door behind them. Jackie picked up the wine glass from the floor and threw it at the door. Jack and Trudy could hear the wine glass shatter into pieces behind the door. Jack looked at Trudy and she laughed. They entered the elevator and went back down to the ground floor. They gave Joe Bourdon a wave and they left the building.

It was about 5:00 PM and Jack figured that he had done enough for one day. He was ready for a couple of cold ones and some well-deserved fish and chips down at *Big Jim's Sports Bar*. They got into Jack's Mustang and Jack turned to Trudy and said, "What do you think, Trudy? Is Jackie King sweating yet?" Trudy looked at Jack with one eyebrow raised and said, "She's probably putting on her *Secret Anti-perspirant* right now." They both laughed and Jack started the car and headed towards Trudy's apartment. As he drove through the city Jack was thinking about his next move. He didn't say anything, he just silently drove to Trudy's apartment. When they arrived, Jack turned to Trudy and said, "Trudy, you know that friend that you have down at the bank?" Trudy looked at Jack expressionless, she said, "Yes." Jack said, "I'd like you to get him to check into Jackie King's bank records for us." Trudy looked at Jack with eyes wide-open, she said, "Jack, you just can't take a look at people's bank records, you need a warrant to do that." Jack had one eyebrow raised and said, "Come on, Trudy, we're not even cops." Then Jack laughed and Trudy shook her head, she said, "Ok, Jack, I'll ask him, but you know this is going to cost you." Jack crossed his arms and said, "How much?" Trudy opened the car door and put one leg out onto the sidewalk and said, "I'll let you know." She got out of the car and went into her apartment. Jack drove off in the direction of *Big Jim's*.

All the way over to *Big Jim's*, Jack continually checked his rear-view mirror looking for the blue Charger. He didn't see any blue Chargers in sight. He pulled into the parking lot for *Big Jim's*, and he scanned the lot for blue Chargers and there were none. He parked his Mustang and went into *Big Jim's*. The lighting was a little low, just the way Jack liked it. It gave his eyes a little rest from the strain of the day. He sat at the bar and saw his friend Teddy at the other end of the bar near the cash register. Jack yelled out, "Teddy K!" An ice-cold *Guinness* came sliding down the bar and stopped right in front of Jack. Jack yelled out, "You're the best, Teddy!" Teddy walked over with his bar-rag over his shoulder and stopped in front of Jack. He said, "So, what's shaking, Jack? Looks like you have few more cuts and bruises on your face than the last time you were in here." Teddy laughed. Jack smiled and said, "You know what the Bible say's Teddy, *there is more happiness in giving than receiving,* I think that goes double when it comes to giving a beat down. Teddy laughed and said, "You've been on the wrong side of that proverb for a long time now." Jack nodded his head. Jack said, "I think I'd be happy if I could get an order of those fish and chips." Teddy smiled and said, "Good choice, Jack, the fish is fresh, just caught today." Jack smiled and said, "I hope you didn't catch it in the East River." Harry laughed, he said, "No way, Jack. We got these fish out of the Harlem River. Nothing but the best." They both laughed and Teddy walked back towards the register.

Jack sipped his *Guinness* as he watched a New York Yankees game on the large TV above the bar. He felt a poke in his back, and he turned around to see who was poking him. It was Danny Watts. Jack made a disgusted face and said, "Danny Watts, what are you doing here? Are you trying to ruin a good meal?" Danny was about six inches from Jack's face, he had his teeth clenched and said, "I'm going to ruin more than a good meal unless you back off this case, Trane. You know this is going to make me look bad if you solve the Broadway murder case. Now I'm asking you nicely, let this case go and just move on to another one. As I said before, a person could get hurt poking around in places that he doesn't belong." Jack took another sip of his beer, then he looked at Danny with his eyes squinted, he said, "First of all Danny, I could squash you like a bag of gumdrops if I wanted to. And second, stay out of my way, jackass, or you'll find out what it feels like to get squashed." Danny was breathing heavily now. His fists were clenched, and his face was beet red. Jack was hoping that he took a swing at him, but Danny backed down. He just took two steps backward and pointed at Jack like he was holding a gun, then he left *Big Jim's.* Jack turned back towards the bar and sipped his *Guinness* and watched the Yankees game above the bar.

Teddy K. came back with Jack's fish and chips and put them down in front of Jack. Teddy said to Jack, "That big guy that you were talking to, was in here earlier. Was he giving you any trouble?" Jack laughed and said, "That guy is a cop, and his middle name is trouble." Teddy laughed and nodded his head and went back towards the cash register to ring up some customers. Jack smothered his fries in ketchup and took a bite. As usual, they were the best in the city. He yelled down to Teddy, "Teddy K!" and another *Guinness* came sliding down the bar. Jack gave Teddy a thumbs up. About fifteen minutes later, the fish and chips were gone, the *Guinness* glass was empty, and the Yankees were behind six to nothing. Jack had told off Danny Watts, enjoyed two *Guinness*, had the best fish and chips in the city and the Yankees were losing. Jack thought to himself, "It doesn't get any better than this. He put $40 down on the bar and gave Teddy K. a wave and he left *Big Jim's*.

Jack got into his Mustang and drove back to his parking garage. It was about 9:00 PM. He parked his car on the second level of the garage and walked the two blocks to his apartment. He went into his apartment building and up the stairs to the second floor. He walked over to his door and looked down. He could see that the matchstick was on the floor. Someone had been in his apartment or is still in there. He grabbed the door handle and turned the knob. The door was unlocked. He slowly pushed the door open, and he could see that the room was in total darkness. He slid into the room and closed the door behind him. He stood still and just listened to see if he could detect any sound, any indication that someone was in the apartment. It remained silent. He reached down to the heel of his right shoe and pulled out the knife blade, then he flipped on the light switch. The apartment came into view. Nobody was there, but someone had certainly been there. Everything had been thrown around the apartment. Drawers had been emptied, the couch cushions were on the floor, pictures were off the walls, his kitchen cabinets had been emptied on the counter and the trash had been emptied onto the floor. Jack shook his head in disgust. This was no coincidence that just a few hours after he questioned Jackie King, his apartment was ransacked. One thing was for sure, Mike Mercury was behind bars, but someone had now taken his place. Probably the person in the blue Charger. Jack was determined now to move fast. He didn't want to give Jackie King any more time to cover up her crime or eliminate any more witnesses. Depending on what Trudy found with Jackie King's bank records, Jack thought that it would be a good idea to take another run at her again tomorrow. He knew that Jackie King had certainly been rattled by his accusations. Now it was a race to see if she could stop Jack before he could tie her to the murder. Jack liked his odds. He cleaned up the apartment as best he could, took a shower, and went to bed. His odds were getting better all the time. The problem is that you never bet against the house.

CHAPTER 19

Jack woke up to the sound of loud buzzing at 8:00 AM. He reached over and turned off the alarm and fell back into bed. He laid there thinking about who might have broken into his apartment yesterday and he was pretty sure that whoever broke in was going to make another run at him soon. He rubbed his eyes and sat up on the edge of the bed. He took a deep breath and coughed a couple of times, then he stood up. As he stretched his arms, he heard the sound of joints cracking and popping. There was no pain, but the sound itself was a little unnerving. He knew that he was getting older, but he wasn't about to throw in the towel just yet. He ignored the sound and walked towards the bathroom. As he left the bedroom, he noticed something over by his door. It was a small white envelope that someone had slipped under the door. He walked over and picked it up. He opened the envelope and found a single white piece of paper inside. He unfolded the paper and read it. In bold black letters, it said, "**IF YOU WANT TO KNOW WHO KILLED HEINRICH KING...MEET ME BACKSTAGE AT THE MAJESTIC THEATRE AT 9:00 AM.**"

Jack was pretty sure that whoever wrote the note was the same person that broke into his apartment yesterday. He also knew that this was probably a set-up, but he also figured that he needed to get to the bottom of this if he was going to solve this case. He had an hour to get to the Majestic, so he jumped into the shower and shaved all within fifteen minutes. He pulled some brown pants, a yellow tie, and a brown jacket out of the walk-in closet and got dressed as quickly as he could.

He walked over to his desk and took Mike Mercury's Glock pistol out and put it in the back of his pants. He never usually carried a gun, but there had been too many attempts on his life recently, and he knew that he was going into a dangerous situation. He also put on his shoes, the ones with the knife blades in the heels. He grabbed his cellphone, and his keys, put on his *Flechet Fedora* hat, and left the apartment. He put the matchstick in the bottom of the door and made his way down the stairs and out onto the street. He looked at his watch, it was 8:35 AM, there was no way that he was going to be able to make it to his garage and drive his Mustang down to the Majestic, so he hailed a taxi. The taxi pulled over almost immediately and Jack got in. Jack said, "The Majestic and step on it!" The driver was a thirty-something Spanish man. Jack looked at his name tag and it read '*Jose Armente.*" The driver looked at Jack and said, "So you in a big hurry, man?" Jose was wearing a well-worn brown leather jacket and a matching brown leather hat and a pair of old blue jeans. Jack said, "Look, if you get me there in less than fifteen minutes, there's a $20 tip in it for you. Jose smiled, he said, "No problema, man. We'll be there in twelve minutes. For the next ten minutes, Jose ran red lights, cut off every car on the road, brushed up against a parked garbage truck, and pulled up in front of the Majestic at 8:47 AM. Jose turned around and looked at Jack and said, "That will be $15.75 plus the tip, man." Jack gave Jose $40 and said, "Keep the change, Jose, you're the man." Jose smiled and said, "Yeah that's right, I am the man." Jack got out of the taxi and Jose pulled the taxi back into traffic.

Jack walked up to the entrance for the Majestic Theatre and the door was open. He knew that something was amiss, the door was never open this early in the morning, so Jack had to assume that whoever invited him here was already inside. Jack opened the door and went in. It was eerie and dark inside and it was so quiet Jack could hear the heels of his shoes scraping on the carpet when he walked. He made his way backstage and now the clicking sound of his heels hitting the old hardwood floor echoed through the auditorium. There was no one in sight. He walked past the ropes that were connected to the curtain and stopped and listened again for any sounds that would alert him to any trouble. The space backstage was very narrow, parts of the floor were marked off with yellow tape, stage props were laying around and it smelled like a cat might have died back there at some point. Jack heard some rustling up above. He looked up and he could see one of the large stage lights coming down from the upper platform directly towards him. He dove to the right and the light missed him but smashed into pieces right where he was standing. The light and the housing weighed about fifty pounds, if that would have hit Jack, it would have been lights out for him. He got up from the floor and dusted himself off. Now he knew that the person who was trying to kill him was up in the catwalk that traversed the whole building. There was a rickety set of stairs that led to the catwalk. Jack quietly made his way to the stairway and carefully walked up the stairs to the catwalk. There were actually a series of catwalks visible when he reached the top of the stairs. Some covered the sides of the auditorium and others went straight across to the other side. Jack scanned from one side of the catwalks to the other, trying to detect any movement. Suddenly he saw a bright flash coming from his left and shards of wood seem to explode on the top of the railing where he was standing. A bullet had just missed him. He ducked down to hide himself from the shooter. There were a couple of small lights that were shining in the backstage area, but it was still pretty dark up on the catwalk. Jack peered above the entrance to the catwalk, and he could see a dark figure about forty feet away. He couldn't make out any facial features, just that it was someone with a gun. There was no way that Jack could enter the catwalk without being seen by the person with the gun. He had to find another way to draw him out. Jack yelled out,

"Put your gun down, now, or somebody's going to get hurt!" Two more shots rang out and hit the floor above where Jack was standing on the ladder. Wood chips flew in the air and landed on the top of Jack's hat. Jack yelled out again, "OK, this is your last chance. Put down the gun." Another shot rang out and hit the railing above the catwalk. Obviously, the person with the gun was here on a mission to eliminate Jack. There was no doubt that Jack had the shooter's attention and he wanted to keep it that way. He took off his hat and put it down just where the stairs meet the catwalk, so the person with the gun would focus his attention there. Jack slowly made his way back down the ladder to the ground floor. He knew that there was more than one entrance to the catwalk, he just had to find it. He could use the darkness to his advantage. He made his way from backstage to the main auditorium. In the orchestra pit, there was a door that led to a sub-stage area. From here there were several access points where he could get to the catwalk. There were six vertical ladders on the wall that led to different points on the catwalk. He knew that the person with the gun was on the left side of the stage so he started to go up the ladder that would lead him to that point. Jack had a gun in the back of his pants, but he didn't want to use it. In fact, he wanted to take the person with the gun alive so he could connect him to Jackie King. He reached down to the heel of his right shoe and pulled out the knife blade. He figured that this would do enough damage to stop the shooter. One by one, he ascended the steps on the ladder until he could see the catwalk. As he slowly raised his head above the catwalk floor, he could see the dark figure of a man standing about ten feet to his left. Jack knew that if the shooter heard him, at this range, he would be an easy target. He needed to create a diversion. He took the knife blade and threw it to the place where his hat was on the other side of the catwalk. The person with the gun started shooting at the hat and hit it with at least two rounds. In the meantime, Jack pulled the other knife out of his left shoe and threw it at the shooter. The knife blade found its target. It hit the shooter in the back of his right leg, and he screamed a blood-curdling scream and dropped to the ground. The shooter still had his gun in his hand so, Jack stayed where he was, waiting for an opportunity to pounce.

Just then the lights went on below in the backstage area and the auditorium and there were sounds of voices. It appeared that the crew had arrived to start preparations for the evening show. Jack heard someone call out, "Hey, is someone up there? What's going on up there?" Jack started going down the ladder and yelled back, "There is a man with a gun on the catwalk, call the police." The man with the gun got to his feet and ran to the other side of the catwalk and went down the stairs to the backstage area. Jack continued going down the ladder and ended up in the sub-basement. He came out the same way he went in, through the orchestra pit doors. He ran around to the backstage area but the man with the gun had already run out of the building. There was no need to chase after him, he was long gone.

Jack walked back up the stairs to the catwalk and picked up his hat. It had two holes in the front crown of the hat. Jack shook his head; this was his favorite hat. He put it on. He picked up the knife blade that he had thrown for a distraction and put it back in the right heel of his shoe. Then he walked over to where the man with the gun was stand-ing and saw his other knife blade on the floor and there was a circle of blood around the knife. The man with the gun had been injured and no doubt now would be limping. Jack was hoping that would be a clue in identifying him the next time he ran into him. He picked up the knife blade and put it back into the left heel of his shoe. He walked down the stairs to the backstage area and just rested with his back against the stage wall. The crew gathered around him in a semi-circle. One of the crew members came closer to Jack, he was tall, well built, wearing a green turtleneck and light blue jeans. He said, "What's going on? I thought that I heard gunshots. Who are you anyway?" Jack held his hand up, he said, "Wait a minute, I'm with the NYPD. Did anyone see the man who came down from the catwalk and ran out of here?" One of the young girls on the crew came forward. She had light brown hair tied back in a ponytail. She said, "I saw him. He was a white man, he looked like he was in his 30s. He had dark hair and he was wearing dark clothes." Jack smiled, he said, "Do you think that you would recognize him if you saw him again?" The girl nodded her head, "Yes, the lights were on, and he looked right at me." Jack nodded his head, he said, "What color eyes did he have? She thought for a moment, she said, "I think they were blue. Jack said, "That's good. What's your name?" She said, "Carol Best." Jack smiled, he said, "Carol, we might need you to identify this man when we bring him in. Do you think you can do that?" Carol nodded, she said, "Of course, I work with the makeup crew, I'm good with faces." Jack laughed, he asked her for her address and phone number and put it in his cellphone, then and he gave her one of his cards. He said, "We'll be in touch, Carol." She put the card in her purse and Jack gave her a wink. As Jack was walking out the door as the police were coming in. He could hear the officer ask, "Did someone report a shooting here?' Jack continued walking to the street where he hailed a taxi.

A taxi pulled over and Jack got in. The driver was an older man with a plaid scarf around his neck and a plaid hat to match. Over the driver's seat, he had a name tag, "Seamus O'Doul." Seamus looked back at Jack and with a very pronounced Irish accent, said, "How ya getting on? Where can I take you?" Jack smiled and gave him the address of his parking garage. Seamus turned back toward the road and turned on the meter, he said, "No problem lad, if you don't mind me saying so, you look a bit knackered, and those two holes in your hat make it look like you've been drinking a little too much black stuff if you know what I mean?" Jack smiled, he enjoyed the Irish accent and the slang. He wanted to answer Seamus in a way he would understand, so he said, "Sure look, what can ye do? I was chasing down some Yoke this morning, but he got away." Seamus smiled a big Irish smile and said, "Oh, are you a peeler?" In his Belfast slang, Seamus was asking Jack if he was a cop. Jack thought for a minute and figured out what Seamus was asking, he said, "I work with the NYPD." Seamus smiled, he said, "Fine group of lads." Jack truly enjoyed interacting with taxi drivers. Just about every ethnic group was represented in the city and there always seemed to be a rich cultural exchange. The diversity was something that Jack always loved about the city.

Jack pulled out his cellphone and dialed up Trudy's number. She was already at the office. She answered the phone in a sarcastic voice, "Hello Jack, you're right on time, after 10 o'clock. Don't you get tired of always being late?" Jack sat back in the seat, he said, "Good morning to you too, Trudy. Did you get in touch with your friend at the bank?" Trudy was snapping her gum, she said, "Yeah, Jack. He's going to get back to me with some kind of report that lists all of Jackie King's transactions for the last six months. I should have it by noon." Jack smiled, he said, "That's great, Trudy! Good job, there's a reason why I keep you around. You make things happen, Trudy." Trudy smiled and raised one eyebrow and said, "Well Jack, don't thank me too fast. I told you this was going to cost you. You're also going to be paying for him and me to go to dinner at the Rainbow room this weekend. That includes our bar tab." Jack breathed in a deep breath and said, "If this report is what I think it is, that's money well spent." Trudy smiled, she said, "Glad you feel that way, Jack. I still have bruises from the car explosion I'm trying to get over. A few drinks at the Rainbow room should do the trick." Jack laughed, he said, "I'm sure they will, Trudy, I'm sure they will." They both laughed. Jack said, "I'm going to get a little bite to eat at the Coffee Café. I'll be in around noon." Trudy snapped back, she said, "Jack, you haven't had breakfast yet? It's after 10 o'clock!" Jack was shaking his head, he said, "It's a long story, Trudy. I'll be in around noon." They both hung up their cellphones.

The taxi pulled up to the curb outside Jack's parking garage. Seamus shut off the meter and turned around and said to Jack, "I was earwigging on you. Sounds like you have a full day ahead of you." Jack smiled, he said. "I guess I'll just Bang On through." Seamus smiled, he said, "That's the spirit, lad. Now that will be $15.75 for the taxi ride." Jack gave him $30, he said, "Thanks for the pull, Seamus." Seamus smiled a big Irish smile at Jack and said, "Thank you lad, may your heart be light and happy, may your smile be big and wide, and may your pockets always have a coin or two inside." Jack chuckled and tipped his hat and got out of the taxi. Seamus pulled off into traffic. Instead of going into the parking garage, Jack walked down the street to the Coffee Café. He walked in and saw Betty standing by the counter, he said, "Betty, how's my girl today?" Betty had a pencil and a pad in her hand, she said, "Is my watch broken? Jack, it's after 10 o'clock. Are you in here for lunch or breakfast?" Jack made a puzzled face, he said, "Very funny, Betty. I had some extenuating circumstances." Jack sat down at a table. Betty came over and said, "It looks like two of your extenuating circumstances went right through your hat." Jack laughed, he said, "That's why I come in here Betty, you always know how to make me smile." Betty hit Jack with her washcloth, she said, "I'll bet you say that to all the girls, Jack." Jack raised his right eyebrow and said, "No just the pretty ones." Betty smiled and blushed a little. She said, "So what can I get for you, Jack." Jack smiled, he said, "What's the special today?" Betty recited the special like a grammar school poem, "Two eggs, two pieces of toast, bacon, sausage, and home fries." Jack was nodding his head, he said, "Sounds good to me, Betty." Betty smiled, she said, I'll be right back with your Vanilla Latte and small orange juice." Jack smiled, he said, "You're the best, Betty." She said, "You mean as a waitress?" Jack smiled and said, "As my waitress." Betty hit Jack with her washcloth again and went back to place his order.

About five minutes later Betty came back with Jack's order. It was a full plate of eggs, bacon, sausage, home fries, and toast. Jack's eyes got big when he saw the plate, he said, "If I finish all this, you're going to have to wheel me out of here." Betty laughed, she said, "Don't worry, Jack, you won't be the first one I've wheeled out of here." They both laughed and Betty went back to the counter. For the next fifteen minutes, Jack enjoyed the eggs, bacon, sausage, home fries, and toast until the plate was as clean as a whistle. He sipped the rest of his Latte and slugged down his orange juice and just sat back and savored the meal. Betty came over and said, "How was everything?" Jack said, "Amazing, Betty, just amazing." Betty smiled, she said, "I was talking about the meal, Jack." Jack smiled, he said, "Yeah, that was pretty good too." They both laughed and Betty put Jack's check down on the table. The bill came to $15.35. Jack pulled $30 out of his wallet and put it down on the table. He got up and waved to Betty as he left the restaurant. Betty yelled at Jack, "Don't be a stranger, Jack." He gave her a wink as he walked out the door. Jack walked up the street towards the parking garage. He figured that this was the day that he would finally close the Broadway murder case. Or would he?

CHAPTER 20

Jack arrived at the office just before noon. He had stopped on the way to pick up some tacos for Trudy. He walked into the office and dropped two tacos on Trudy's desk. Trudy looked up at Jack with big eyes and said, "For me? Gracias, Jack, you know I love tacos." Jack smiled, he said, "I just like to keep my best girl happy." Trudy raised one eyebrow and had a little attitude, she said, "Jack, every girl you know is your best girl." Jack laughed, he said, "That's true, Trudy, I don't discriminate." They both chuckled. Trudy looked at Jack's hat and said, "Jack, did you know that your hat has two holes in it?" Jack raised one eyebrow and said, "There was a little incident at the Theatre." Trudy snapped her gum, she said, "Jack you have an incident like every day." Jack laughed, he said, "So, Trudy, did you get the report for Jackie King's bank transactions?? Trudy had a mouthful of tacos, she said, "hmff, hmff, hmff…" Jack waited until she swallowed. Then she said, "Yes, Jack, I put it on your desk." Jack was excited. He clapped his hands like he had just won a bet, he said, "Well, let's have a look at it. I think this is going to finally tie up all the loose ends on this case." Trudy stuffed another bite of the taco into her mouth and walked over to Jack's desk with him. Jack was walking noticeably different from his normal stride. Trudy noticed and said, "Jack, why are you walking like Frankenstein? You look like you have a load in your pants or something." Jack laughed, he said, "Yeah, I got something in my pants. It's the gun that I took away from Mike Mercury." Trudy had a worried look, she said, "But Jack, you never carry a gun!" Jack said, "I know, but since there have been so many attempts on my life on this case, I thought this might be a good time to start." Trudy slowly nodded her head.

On Jack's desk, there was a simple 8 x 10 envelope, but Jack knew that the contents of the envelope would not be simple at all. He picked up his bronze letter opener and slid it through the top of the envelope. The anticipation was killing him. He pulled out the contents and laid them on his desk like he was a professor grading papers. He sat down in his chair and Trudy was right behind him looking over his shoulder. He took the top page of report in his hands and started scanning all the transactions that had taken place over the past six months on Jackie King's bank account. One thing became obvious after the very first entry. Jackie King was either very careless or very lazy. Every entry was made out for a check instead of an untraceable amount of cash. This meant that every entry could be traced back to the person who received the money. Had she withdrawn cash, the money trail would have been much more difficult to trace. But as they looked over the report, it became very clear who had been involved in Jackie King's criminal behavior. With his index finger, he went down the list. One day after Heinrich King was reported to have been murdered, Mike Mercury received $50,000. Two weeks after the death of Heinrich King there were four $10,000 entries. Victoria Pichettes, Audrey Linn, Siobhan Peison, and Marie Robbin all received $10,000. The next entry took Jack by surprise. There was a $50,000 entry for Danny Watts. Things were starting to come into sharp focus. About the same time that Danny Watts received $50,000 there was also another $50,000 entry for someone by the name of Eric Able. Trudy spoke over Jack's shoulder with taco breath, she said, "Jack, who is Eric Able?" Jack said "That's what I'd like to know, Trudy. But don't worry, we're going to find out." There was also another $50,000 entry for Danny Watts that was made just this week. Every entry told a story, and every story was tied to Jackie King. Jack and Trudy sat there processing all the information.

The piece that didn't fit so far, was Eric Able. Who was Eric Able and how was he involved in Heinrich King's murder? Jack was glad Trudy was working the case with him. Jack was all thumbs when it came to the computer and Trudy was and ace. He said to Trudy, "Can you do a Google search on Eric Able? I think he might be a key to this case." Trudy flipped her hair back and strolled over to her desk. She took a bite of her second taco, then she typed a few lines into her computer, and then in a matter-of-fact voice, she said to Jack, "Eric Able was a medical examiner for the city of New York." Jack said, "What do you mean, he was the medical examiner?" Trudy took another bite of the taco she said, "It looks like he died in a car accident about three weeks after Heinrich King's murder." Jack was nodding his head, he said, "This is all starting to make sense. I've got to get a look at the report he filed for Heinrich King's death." Trudy said, "Jack you have a copy of that report in the Broadway murder file." Jack said, "No, I want to see the original report." He jumped up from his desk, put the report under his arm, and ran towards the door. On the way past Trudy's desk, he said, "I'll be back, I need to go down to the precinct to get Harry to access to the medical examiner's report." Trudy looked at Jack with no expression and took the last bite of her taco. Jack said, "Trudy, there is just one more thing that I need you to do." Trudy looked up, she said, "Really, Jack, don't' tell me that you want me to call Harry Soul, because I'm not doing it!" He bent down and put his elbow on Trudy's desk, and said, "No, Trudy, I want you to get in touch with Jackie King's insurance company and get a copy of the policy that Heinrich King had before he died." Trudy raised one eyebrow, she said, "Ok, Jack, I can do that. How quickly do you need it?" Jack smiled, he said, "How about yesterday?" She said, "Sure Jack, should I turn nickels into quarters while I'm at it?"

Jack smiled, he said, "Come on Trudy, you're the best. You can make this happen." Trudy was shaking her head, she said, "The things I'll do for $2,500." Jack tapped the desk with his knuckles, he said, "Oh, one more thing." Jack hesitated to ask Trudy this one last thing because it involved coming into contact with Harry Soul again. Jack bit his lower lip and said, "Trudy, I'm going to give you a call later this afternoon, and I'll need you to bring that insurance policy down to the precinct." Trudy made a disgusted face, she said, "Tell me, I don't' have to bring it into Harry Soul's office." Jack smiled, he said, "Come on Trudy, what you wouldn't do for $2,500." Trudy still had a disgusted face, she said, "I think the price just went up. And by the way, I'll expect my share of the $5,000 for solving this case before we leave the precinct." In a low gravelly voice, Jack said, "Whatever you say, boss." He left the office, ran down the stairs and out to the street.

He jumped into his Mustang, pulled out his cellphone, and called Harry Soul down at the precinct. The phone rang three times and Harry picked up, he said, "Good morning, Jack. Do you need to use the interrogation room again? Is Trudy coming in?" Jack rolled his eyes, he said, "Relax, Harry, no we don't need to use the interrogation room." Jack could hear Harry exhale, he said, "Look, Harry, I need to see the medical examiner's report for the Heinrich King murder." Harry was a little surprised, he said, "Jack you have a copy of the report in the file that I gave you." Jack said, "I know, Harry, but I need to see the original report. I think there might be some discrepancies on that report that will tie this whole case together." Harry was hesitant, he said, "All right, Jack, come on in. I'll have it in my office in about ten minutes." Jack smiled, "Thanks, Harry. See you in about ten minutes." Jack thought for a minute and he said, "Harry, by the way, what kind of car does Danny Watts drive?" Harry said, "A blue Charger. Why do you ask?" Jack pursed his lips, he said, "Nothing, I was just curious. See you in a few minutes." It was all adding up. The blue Charger that had been following Jack for the past few days had been Danny Watts. Ever since Mike Mercury had been locked up, Danny had been following him. Jack wasn't exactly sure how Danny fit into all of this, but nothing would make Jack happier than bringing Danny Watts into the precinct in handcuffs. Jack looked out the car window and pictured that scene in his mind. He sat back in his Mustang and breathed in the new car smell. It was a revitalizing scent and it made Jack feel like he was king of the road. He started the Mustang and let the low roar of the engine idle for a minute, then he put the car in gear and headed towards the 23rd precinct.

About fifteen minutes later, Jack pulled up into the precinct parking lot, got out of his car with his case file under his arm, and entered the precinct building. Officer McRae was working the front desk; he recognized Jack and buzzed the door open to the precinct and Jack went in. As he strode past all the detectives at their desks, he noticed that Danny Watts was not at his desk. He had a pretty good idea of where he might be. Jack went into Harry's office. Harry was sitting behind his desk with his fingers drumming on the desktop, and the medical examiner's report was sitting right in the middle of the desk. Harry looked at Jack and said, "Now, what's going on? You call me like your pants are on fire and you tell me that you need to see the original medical examiner's report. Jack, it should be exactly the same as the report that you have in your file." Jack looked serious at Harry, he said, "That's right. Harry, it should be exactly the same as my report. But something tells me that it won't be." Jack picked up the report from Harry's desk and compared it with the one he had in his file. His eyes got bigger and bigger as he read each line in the report. Harry noticed Jack's reaction, he said, "Jack, what is it? What do you see?" Jack threw the report back down on Harry's desk, he said, "Harry, I've to go arrest

Jackie King, but not for the murder of her late husband Heinrich King. For something else." Harry was scratching his head, he said, "Jack, what are you talking about? The Broadway murder needs a….." Jack interrupted Harry and he didn't finish his sentence. Jack said, "This whole case has just come together, and it's not what you think it is. I just need to tie up a few loose ends, and I'll be back to explain everything." Harry said, "Wait a minute, Jack, tell me right now. What's going on? And why did you want to know what kind of car Danny Watts is driving?" Jack smiled, he said, "All in good time, Harry. All in good time." Jack got up and quickly walked out of Harry's office. Harry stood and yelled at Jack, "Hey, wait a minute, Jack! Come back here and tell me what's going on!" Jack made like he didn't hear anything that Harry was saying. He just kept walking right out of the precinct and into his Mustang outside.

Jack started his Mustang and just let the engine idle for a minute while he contemplated his next move. His thoughts were racing through his head like his Mustang races through the streets of New York. The first thing that he had to do was to have Jackie King arrested and brought into the precinct to be formally charged. He needed to be accompanied by an actual police officer. He dialed Debra Thorn's phone and she picked up. "Hello, Jack, I was just thinking of you, funny you should call." Jack smiled, he said, "I'm always thinking of you babe." Debra smiled, she said, "Sounds like a line, you've used before, Jack." He laughed for a moment and then he got down to business. He said, "Debra, I've come to the point in my case where I want to bring in Jackie King to be charged. I'd like you to arrest her and bring her in for me." Debra sounded surprised, she said, "Jack you can't just go around arresting people, you have to have some kind of probable cause for me to bring anyone in." Jack smiled, he said, "I got more than probable cause, Debra. I got solid evidence against her. Debra sounded skeptical, she said, "You have enough to charge her with murder?" Jack said, "No, Debra, not murder. I got her on fraud, conspiracy to commit murder, accessory after the fact, obstruction of justice, all this is just for starters." Debra sounded confused, she said, "You have evidence to back all that up, Jack?" Jack smiled and said, "Tight as a drum, Debra, tight as a drum." Debra said, "OK, Jack, what's the plan?" Jack said, meet me at Jackie's apartment at 600 West 57th Street in about twenty minutes and you can put the cuffs on her and take her in." Debra said, "OK, Jack, I'll be there in twenty minutes."

Twenty minutes later both Jack and Debra pulled up outside of Jackie King's apartment. Jack got out of his car and went over to meet Debra at her car. He noticed that about four car lengths away from Debra's car, there was a blue Charger parked on the road. No one was in the Charger. Jack had a sneaking suspicion that the blue Charger belonged to Danny Watts and that Danny was up in the apartment with Jackie King. He said to Debra, "I think that you ought to call in for some back-up. I think there is another person up there and he might give us some trouble." Debra said, "Another person? What makes you think that?" Jack pointed to the blue Charger, he said, "Because I believe that blue Charger belongs to Danny Watts, and that Danny is involved in this case up to his eyeballs, and that he's upstairs with Jackie King." Debra wasn't alarmed. She was nodding her head, she said, "Jack, this was originally Danny's case. No big deal, maybe he's just tying up some loose ends." Jack squinted his eyes and said, "Danny is trying to tie up some loose ends all right, but it's not the way you think." Debra looked puzzled. Jack said, "Danny Watts is a suspect, in this case, Debra. He's in it so deep he's choking. Danny is a dirty cop, and we're going to take him down along with Jackie King." Debra was shaking her head, she said, "Jack, are you sure about this? I worked with Danny in the larceny division. He was an all-around jerk and everything, but a dirty cop? I don't know." Jack looked at Debra with a serious look and said, "Trust me on this one, Debra. Danny is dirty. I've got all the evidence." Debra said, "OK, Jack. I'll trust you on this one." And she called into the precinct for some uniformed policemen to arrive for some back-up.

Debra got out of the car. She was wearing black pants and a black cotton shirt and a light brown leather jacket. Her strawberry-blond hair seemed to glow in the sunlight. Jack admired the view. He said, "You are looking extra hot today, Debra." Debra made a face at Jack and said, "Come on, Jack, focus." Jack snapped back to the case at hand. He said, "OK Debra, be ready for anything. Danny doesn't know that I'm on to him. I think we have the element of surprise. But he can be dangerous, there is a lot of money at stake here." Debra looked at Jack with one eyebrow raised and a skeptical look and said, "OK, Jack, I'll follow your lead." They walked into the building and the security guard, Joe Bourdon, started to ask, "Can I help…" But Debra pulled out her badge and he didn't finish his sentence. In a very slow and serious voice, Jack said, "Open the elevator door, we're going to the 50th floor, and I don't want anyone to know that we're coming. Did you get that, Joe?" Joe looked at Jack, then at Debra, then back at Jack again and said, "Yeah, I got that." The elevator door opened, and Debra and Jack got in." Jack pushed the button for the 50th floor and the elevator rose quickly. Debra looked at Jack and said, "Jack, I hope you know what you're doing, arresting a cop could get pretty ugly." Jack smiled, he said, "No problem, babe. Have I ever steered you wrong before?" Debra smiled, she said, "How about the last time I was in your car?" Jack smiled, he said, "Oh, yeah, I forgot about that. But don't worry, I got this." Debra made some big eyes and they walked out of the elevator to the front door of Jackie King's apartment. Jack looked at Debra and he rang the bell. A couple of minutes passed, and no one came to the door. Jack rang the bell again. The door opened Jackie King appeared. She looked a little nervous. Her shiny black hair rested on her shoulders and her red lipstick still dominated her features. She said, "Mr. Trane, darling, you're back so soon. And you brought another little helper with you." Debra pulled out her badge. She said, "Can we come in, mam, we'd like to ask you a few more questions?" Jack could hear movement inside the apartment like someone was closing a door. Jackie looked back towards the inside of her apartment and then she looked back at Jack and said, "Very well then, darling, come in. But please make it quick, I have some place to go."

As they were walking into the apartment Jack said, "Yes, Jackie, you do have some place to go. You're going down to the precinct to be charged with a crime." Jackie looked shocked, she said, "But I didn't murder my late husband you fool! You've got it all wrong!" Debra took out her handcuffs and dangled them in front of Jackie King. Debra said, turn around Jackie." Jackie turned around and Debra put on the handcuffs. Jackie protested, she said, "I didn't kill my late husband!" Jack said we know you didn't kill your husband, Jackie. You're being arrested for something else; fraud, conspiracy to commit murder, and a slew of other charges." She yelled across the room to where the door was closed. She said, "Danny come out of there and tell the detective that I'm innocent!" The door opened and Danny came out. He was disheveled and limping. His $1,200 suit looked more like something that came from a discount store. His hair wasn't combed, and he was spitting as he spoke. He turned to Jackie King and said, "Shut up you stupid idiot!" Danny had his gun drawn and he was limping across the room in a lateral direction, keeping everyone in view. Danny looked at Jack with squinted eyes and said, "You just couldn't leave it alone, could you Trane? Now there is going to have to be two more unsolved murders." Danny started to raise his gun. Debra began to speak slowly to Danny. She said, "Now, Danny, you don't want to do this. Killing a cop is the death penalty in this state, you know that. Why don't you just put the gun down and we can talk about this." While Debra was distracting Danny, Jack was about to make his move. He could see that Danny was starting to sweat and he was becoming desperate. Danny had his eyes trained on Debra, but Jack was escaping his view. Jack slowly put his hand in the back of his pants and grabbed the Glock. In one quick fluid motion, he drew the gun and fired a shot at Danny. A bright flash came out of the barrel of Jack's gun. It seemed like things were now happening in slow motion. The bullet struck Danny's right hand and he screamed and dropped his gun onto the floor. Jack quickly kicked the gun to the corner and Debra pounced on Danny and pinned him to the floor. Just then the uniformed police officers arrived. Debra yelled, "A little help over here!" Both officers came to Debra's aid. They handcuffed Danny and stood him up. Jack walked up close to Danny and looked at him square in the eyes, he smiled and said, "Still buying your suits at Walmart, Danny?" Danny gritted his teeth, his face got red, and he tried with all his might to get loose from the handcuffs, but he couldn't. Then a relaxed look seemed to come over Danny and he said to Jack, "You got nothing on me, Trane! When we get back to the station, you're the one that's going to be in handcuffs, you'll see." Jack laughed, he said, "Danny, I got so much dirt on you, you stink. Nobody likes a dirty cop, Danny. You're a punk and a dirty cop." The officers took Danny away even though he was doing his best to resist. Then Debra and Jack took Jackie King down the elevator and put her into the back seat in Debra's unmarked police cruiser. Jack got in the front seat with Debra, and they drove back to the 23rd precinct.

When they got to the precinct, Jack stayed in the car, but Debra took Jackie King into the building for processing. She put Jackie in a holding cell and then sat down at a desk to fill out the proper paperwork. Jack called Trudy and told her to meet him in Harry Soul's office as quickly as she could with the insurance report. Then Jack got out of the car and went into the building. Officer McRae recognized Jack and buzzed him in. Jack went directly to Harry Soul's office. Harry looked up at Jack as he entered the office, Jack said, "Harry, I have some good news and I have some bad news." Harry looked confused, he said, "What are you talking about, Jack?" Jack smiled, he said, "Let me give you the bad news first. Danny Watts has been arrested in connection with the Broadway murder and is in a holding cell awaiting formal charges." Harry jumped up from his desk, he said, "Jack, why would you have Danny Watts arrested? I knew you guys didn't get along but isn't this a little extreme?" Harry, I'm going to explain the whole thing in a minute, just be a little patient." Harry chimed in, "So what's the good news?" Jack smiled a big smile, "I solved the case, Harry." Harry looked surprised and sat back down in his chair. Jack sat in a chair in front of Harry's desk. He said, "There is just one more thing. We need to wait for Trudy to get here with the last piece of evidence that will without a doubt close this case, once and for all." Harry perked up, he said, "Trudy is coming down to the precinct?" Harry started straightening his tie and smelling his breath in the palm of his hand. Jack looked at Harry with a pathetic look, he said, "Harry, get real, you have no chance with Trudy." Harry looked determined, he said, "Never say never Jack, never." Jack rolled his eyes.

Debra came back from processing Jackie King's paperwork and sat down in Harry's office. She said, "OK, Jack, I think that it's time to fill us all in on the Broadway Murder case. If you ask me there still seems to be a lot of pieces missing." Jack smiled, he looked at Debra with a sparkle in his eye, He nodded his head and said, "Trudy is on her way with the final piece of evidence. She should be here any minute. Harry straightened his tie. For the next ten minutes, Jack and Debra made small talk while Harry stared at the ceiling daydreaming about Trudy.

Finally, Trudy came through the door to Harry's office. Harry stood up and said, "Well, hello, Trudy. So nice to see you again." Trudy rolled her eyes and said, "Yeah, whatever, Harry." Harry sat back down a little dejected. Trudy handed the envelope with the insurance report to Jack, and she sat down in the chair that was furthest away from Harry's desk. Jack opened the envelope and scanned Heinrich King's insurance policy for about ten seconds. His eyes got big and said, "That's it! I know who did what, where, when, and how!" Harry, Debra, and Trudy all stared at Jack with blank expressions on their faces. Harry finally spoke up, he said, "Well, Jack, fill us in." Jack walked over and closed the door to Harry's office, and he remained standing while everyone else remained seated. He started to pace back and forth on the side of Harry's desk. He slid the insurance report inside the Broadway Murder case file and kept the file folder under his arm as he paced. At this point, Jack had a big smile on his face. He knew that he had just solved the Broadway murder case and now he was going to explain it to Harry, Debra, and Trudy.

Jack started speaking. "Let me tell you all a little story. There once was a man named Heinrich King. He was the most powerful man on Broadway. But as it turned out, he had more enemies than he had friends. His own wife couldn't stand the sight of him. But what people didn't know, including his wife, is that he was under tremendous pressure on many different fronts. He had financial problems, many of the shows that he was producing were bleeding red ink. He had legal issues, he was about to be sued by the countless women that he had abused over the years, they were suing him for millions. And he also had a bunch of unpaid gambling debts that the mob was about to collect, one way or the other. The walls were closing in on Heinrich King and he had nowhere to run. He had made his own bed and now he was going to have to sleep in it. One Friday night last November Heinrich King didn't come home after work. Jackie King was tired of waiting for him, so she went to his office only to find him hanging from the ceiling in the corner of his office. He had decided to end his wretched existence by hanging himself from the pipes above the radiator in his office. Now when Jackie King found her husband hanging from the ceiling like a fish on a fishing line, she wasn't exactly upset that her husband was dead but there was the matter of his insurance policy. Heinrich King had an insurance policy that would give his wife $10 million in the event of his untimely death. The only stipulation is that the death couldn't be from suicide. He saved his last despicable act to hurt his current wife. His suicide would nullify the policy, making it impossible for Jackie King to cash in on the $10 million payout. However, Jackie is a very resourceful woman, she immediately put a plan in place to make the suicide look like a murder. She hired Mike Mercury for the tune of $50,000 to make Heinrich King's suicide look like a murder. Mike took Heinrich Kings dead body, banged it in the back of the head, to make it look like there was a struggle, and put the body in the dumpster behind the Majestic Theatre. With all of Heinrich King's enemies, Jackie knew that there would be no shortage of suspects. Jackie's next move was to make sure that the case was unsolved, so she paid off Danny Watts to the tune of $50,000 to make sure that every-thing pointed to an unsolved murder and that eventually this case would be thrown into a cold case folder. Danny did his part. He made sure that every person of interest had a rock-solid alibi. Her plan paid off and within six months, the Broadway Murder became a cold case. One more loose end that had to be tied up was the Medical Examiner, Eric Able. Eric would have known that Heinrich King died of hang-ing by his examination of the corpse. And his original report, the one you just gave me, stated the cause of death was indeed suicide." Jack looked at Harry and said, "That's why I needed to see the original ME report." Harry quietly nodded his head. Jack continued, "Jackie King paid off Eric Able to the tune of $50,000 to create a fake report to say the cause of death was murder, by strangulation. The fake report was in the Broadway file that Danny was working. Danny never used the original ME report. Jackie couldn't guarantee that Eric would keep quiet, so she had Mike Mercury take care of Eric Able. That's why he was killed in what appeared to be a car crash. Eric Able was murdered. He was murdered at the orders of Jackie King. That eliminated Eric as a loose end. Jackie also paid off four different women, who all had a legitimate grudge against Heinrich King. She paid them all $10,000 to say that they were out together the night of the supposed murder, just to create the illusion of a conspiracy. Then Jackie collected $10 million from the insurance company, and it looked like she was home free." Jack looked at the group and said, "Are you all with me, so far." The room was quiet. They all nodded their heads. Harry said, "Continue, Jack."

Jack continued pacing as he talked, he said, "Now, I enter the picture agreeing to take on the Broadway Murder cold case as a paid consultant. This was the last thing that Jackie was expecting. When she learned that I had started to stir things up on this case again, she knew that she had to get rid of me, if she wanted to keep the $10 million and stay out of jail. She had already hired Mike Mercury to rub out Eric Able, now she wanted him to get rid of me. I will say this, He gave it his best shot. He tried to shoot me, he abducted me, tied me to the subway tracks, and tried to blow me up. But in the end, Mike Mercury was no match for me. He and his two flunky associates are all behind bars with a slew of charges, waiting for their day in court. When Jackie saw that Mike had failed, she went to plan B. She paid Danny Watts another $50,000 to finish the job. Danny attempted to rub me out but failed miserably. Danny is a clown and he's a dirty cop. He's also in a holding cell, waiting for a union rep, a good lawyer, and a whole lot of luck." Jack sat back down in his chair, he said, "The reason no one could solve the Broadway Murder case is that there was no murder. It was a suicide. The real crime here was the conspiracy to cover up the suicide in order collect the $10 million, and all the collateral damage that resulted." Jack let out a deep breath, reached out his arm, and dropped the file on the middle of Harry's desk. He said, "So there you have it, Harry. Case closed."

Harry clapped his hands, he said, "Jack, I don't say this often, but I'm impressed." Jack sat back in his chair with his arms folded. He said, "All in a day's work, Harry. But I'll take that $5,000, now. In fact, why don't you just make out the whole check to Trudy Fields." He took the consultant's card that Harry had given him, out of his pocket and threw it on Harry's desk, and said, "And you can have this lame card back too." The room was silent for a few seconds, then Harry laughed and picked up the phone and requested that the $5000 check be made out to Trudy and that she could pick it up on the way out. Trudy was smiling, she said, "Jack, you're giving me the whole $5,000! You're the best, Jack." Jack looked at Trudy and said, "You deserve it, Trudy. I couldn't have solved this case without you." Trudy gave Jack a wink. Debra looked at Jack with an affectionate look and said, "You never cease to amaze me, Jack." Jack smiled, he said, "That's all part of my plan, Debra, that's all part of my plan." They all got up and walked out of Harry's office. Jack was feeling good that he had just solved a case and put at least five bad guys, behind bars.

As they were walking out of the precinct, Jack was expounding on his success. He said to Debra, "Did you know that the lights never go out on Broadway, Broadway is where stars are born, Broadway is my kind of…." Debra broke in, she said, "Shut up, Jack." She took his hand as they walked together into the parking lot. They got into

Debra's car, and she drove towards West 57th Street, so Jack could pick up his Mustang.

Jack had solved the Broadway Murder. He had put Jackie King along with Mike Mercury, Grease Boy, and Shaggy behind bars. As a special bonus, Jack's nemesis, Danny Watts would also be serving time for his role in obstructing justice. All of this brought Jack a great sense of satisfaction. However, after 25 years as a private investigator, Jack had received his share of bumps, bruises, cuts, and scrapes and this case had delivered plenty. His back ached, he had stitches on his forehead and his legs were still healing from his car explosion. He wasn't getting any younger. He started to reflect for a moment on whether or not it might be time to start thinking about hanging up his private eye shoes. He looked over at Debra and noticed the sunlight reflecting off her reddish-blond hair, he thought to himself, "No, this is exactly where I want to be."